An Education in Murder

A Bailey Homeschool Mystery

Patty Joy

To Sarah
my favorite niece
Best wishes
Patty Joy

This book is a work of fiction. Names, characters, businesses, organizations, places, events and incidents either are the products of the author's imagination or are used fictionally. Any semblance to actual persons, living or dead, events or locales is entirely coincidental.

Published by Quillavendel Press, Moline, IL

ISBN-13: 978-1-7329857-0-4

Dedications

To write is to dream, and to dream is to create.

As I have cared and supported my family's endeavors over the years, they have encouraged my creative dreams.

To my family, without you this book would not exist. To my husband, for starting us down this road. To my children, for the hills and valleys we have traveled, together.

To Caleb, Amy and Marilyn, who helped me fine tune the story.

And to the original Patty, always loved, never forgotten.

Chapter One

THE FADED STREET LAMP ILLUMINATED the utter mess in perfect muddy detail.

I could almost hear the imaginary reprimand, "Rainbow Bailey, I safely delivered your family home after another trip into farm country. The least you could do is give me a bath."

For over twelve years she has met the challenge of transporting my family never once stranding us on the side of the road. Bessie, our mid-sized Astro van, deserved loving attention with a good cleaning inside and out. Traveling with five children on a four-day weekend created plenty of clutter

My father taught me young the art of the car wash. Young, and always full of energy and creativity, I used my set of paintbrushes set on a new canvas: the dirty cars and trucks in my Uncle's hardware store parking lot. Using a stool and water in a pail, I painted "wash me" on the filthiest vehicles in the lot.

As I finished the "A" on the seventh car, my father swapped my paint brush with a sponge and poured car soap into my bucket. The first car was fun, the second not so much. By the time I had finished washing all seven cars, I was in tears. He finished the last spray down, thanked the customer for their patience, and bought me a soda.

Choosing his words wisely, he only said, "Love, Respect, and handling money. The only three things you need to get along in this world. Today was a good lesson in the first two."

I have instilled those lessons into my own five children. Their mess meant their cleanup. This time, however, I barely had time to unload the children and dirty laundry at the house before I drove away. I was already late for my kick-boxing class.

Being late forced me to park in the only spot available, next to the dumpster. The next hour I kicked out every kink, and punched every problem until I had stretched every stressed muscle in my body. It was my attempt at staying sane now that my oldest were teenagers. I wrapped up the night with two hours of cleaning the gym as part of my free membership. The long day was ending and I just wanted to head home to my husband and a good night's sleep.

Bessie's voice in my head was right, and I knew it. Washing the outside would have to wait until daylight and an easy to reach hose, but the inside was another matter. I was already filthy from the morning farm work, workout, and parked just a few steps from a dumpster. What was one more mess to clean up for a good cause?

After tossing the gym's trash bag into the dumpster, I slid open the side door, and dug out the treasures my inquisitively busy children had left behind. Eating out was a rare treat for our large family, but Grandpa's list of projects lasted longer than expected, requiring dinner on the road. Separating the half-filled soda cups, sandwich wrappers, and the stupid restaurant toys, from the beloved Barbies and Lego creations, was never an easy task. My youngest two still enjoyed the little restaurant trinkets, while their older brothers enjoyed dissecting them to uncover their secrets. This trip had generated a fresh crop of the plastic trinkets.

In between melted crayons and spilled gummy worms destined for the trash bin, I found the twins' geometric graphing calculator. That cost me a pretty penny at the beginning of the school year. I held on the calculator with one hand while reaching into the last corner under the seat. Yuck! Dear Lord, I prayed, please let the little round fuzzy things be nothing worse than old Cheerios.

"That should do it." I muttered, dropping my last handfuls of trash into the dumpster.

Clunk, Clunk.

Oh, bummer! Looking down at my empty hands, that distinctive hard plastic on metal ding had to be the calculator. Originally costing almost two hundred dollars, leaving it behind was not an option. Digging into dark smelly trash containers late at night ranks right up there with cleaning up my kid's vomit at three in the morning, but I couldn't risk the garbage truck coming early tomorrow.

My inherited five-foot, zero-inch frame did not even allow me a view inside the industrial-sized dumpster without some form of elevation. Grabbing my keys, I unlocked the gym's back door, and grabbed a chair from the back hallway. I could see inside, but only lumpy dark shadows greeted me. The dumpster's high sides blocked the closest street light from illuminating the half-filled bin. Nothing could block the smell, though, as I recognized the rotten banana peels from the smoothies sold in the gym's shop. Bummer, dumpster diving looked like a distinct possibility if I couldn't reach the top layer.

I needed more light. My ever-prepared husband, Martin, kept a flashlight stocked in the emergency kit. With that in hand, I stepped up to look again. The beam of light easily cut through the darkness as I looked for the shiny silver calculator to reveal itself. Glancing past foil wrappings, an old clipboard, my eyes roamed until, just below and maybe just in reach, the calculator reflected the light. I stretched my fingers, and rose upon my toes. I could feel it with two, now three fingers. Just one more inch.

"Aaahhh", I yelped, somersaulting into the dumpster, my back landed on the lumpy bags that shifted and slid under my weight.

My plan for a relaxing Mom's night out was ruined, I thought as I reclined on the icky gooey mess now oozing out of the broken trash bags. These bags, obviously not made by Hefty, shredded into pieces, releasing their foul smells, as I scooped up the prize calculator. Priority number one was finding a way out before I sunk deeper into the muck.

The beam of light zigzagged as I looked for something steady to hold my weight. The dancing light reflected off a basic tennis shoe that had one amazing quality: it was still holding a socked foot and panted leg. Who would throw away a store mannequin, with clothes? And here? Jensen's department store had mannequins, but that was on the other side of the town.

As a home-schooling mom, I could always find some use for the mannequin once it was cleaned up. Maybe I could salvage this horrible adventure with a new-to-us treasure after all?

Following the flashlight up the shoe and the leg, I looked for any other pieces that were available.

My search didn’t last that long, at least I don't think it did. I really don't remember anything between seeing the leg and waking up with my cousin, Police Sergeant Corbin Cross, leaning over me.

"Boo, are you okay? Here, let me help you sit up." Corbin had inherited the height in the family. Couching down, his strong arms gathered my small frame into his shoulder. "Easy now. The ambulance will be here soon."

Squinting into his brown eyes, I asked, "What ambulance, Corbin? Can you turn off those stupid flashing lights? They are giving me a headache."

Corbin laughed wryly, "I think the headache is from the bump on the side of your head. I was hoping you could tell me why I found you lying here, smelling like a garbage truck just spit you out?"

I looked over at the dumpster and it all came back. The calculator, the fall, the smells, the shoe, and most of all, the leg. I vaguely recalled a crumpled body topped off with a hairy face, a mad scramble up and over the side of the dumpster, diving in the van for my phone on the front seat and dialing. To whom, and what I said, my mind was still a blank.

All that flashed in my brain as my stomach flipped like I was on top of a tall roller coaster heading down. When we were kids, Corbin had been the one who talked me onto the Screaming Eagle at Six Flags, and was blessed with a second look at that day's lunch. So, when I looked up in Corbin's eyes, shakily pointed a finger at the dumpster and whispered "dead Harvey," he knew right away to spin me away from him. Just in the nick of time, too. This time, as my earlier chicken nuggets dinner reappeared for all the world to see, it didn't land on my cousin. No, no, no. I, Rainbow Bailey, had the distinct pleasure of throwing up all over Corbin's new boss, Chief of Police Jonathan Flint, who had just walked up on my other side.

Chapter Two

WHAT WAS THE ETIQUETTE for meeting the new Chief of Police after you have thrown up all over his spit-shined shoes and expertly pleated pants? I didn't know, but that was the least of my worries.

Corbin released me in favor of surveying the crime scene. Using his industrial strength flashlight plus his six-foot frame, he peered into the dumpster.

"She's right, Chief. There is a body partially covered by a plastic trash bag." Corbin bent further over the edge, confirming what I already knew. "The body is cold and there are no vital signs."

That grabbed the Chief's attention from his filthy shoes, as the whooping sirens announced the arrival of the ambulance. Issuing orders, the new Chief directed Corbin to assist the paramedics in my quick removal from the immediate area, least I contaminate it more.

After the gurney was wheeled to the other side of the ambulance, Todd Standford, a veteran paramedic of ten years took the lead. "Okay, Mrs. Bailey, tell me what happened. What hurts?"

Chris Maurey, who graduated paramedic school just six months ago, pumped the blood pressure cuff as I began my story.

"I fell into the dumpster."

Todd smiled, "Dumpster diving a new hobby? Let me give you a hint: feet first."

I shook my head, then winced in pain from the movement. "I wasn't. I know that. I mean I didn't mean to. Oh, bummer."

"Whoa, slow down. Take a deep breath. Let me look at your eyes." Todd said, blinding me with his flashlight. "Are you dizzy?"

Breathing deeply, I began again. "No, not dizzy. It was just an accident. I was reaching for something I dropped. I remember scrambling out, and then waking up under the stars with Corbin leaning over me. Can you kill the lights? They are giving me a headache the size of Mount Everest."

Chris reported, "Blood pressure normal range. I will stop the flashes for you, Mrs. Bailey."

"Bless you, Chris."

The Chief walked into view, heading to speak with the newest arrival, Doc Caleb McCarthy, the county coroner.

Seeing the Chief, I whispered to Todd, "Then I threw up all over Chief Flint's shoes."

I knew the minute I spoke, it was the wrong thing to say.

Todd frowned. "Let's get you to the hospital."

"Nope," I said, turning to Todd. "Nada. Not going to happen."

"Mrs. Bailey, vomiting is an indicator a serious concussion. You need to get checked out at the hospital."

Having three rambunctious boys and two energetic girls at home, I was all too familiar with clunked heads and their danger symptoms.

"No," I repeated. "I know my rights. I am not leaving here in that ambulance!"

My very few memories of my mother come from a sterile-white hospital room. She lost her battle with breast cancer when I was four years old. I did not want to relive those memories, nor did I want similar memories to haunt my children.

"Is my favorite combative patient giving you trouble, Todd?" Doc McCarthy had been our family physician until he retired last year from the daily commitments of office appointments. He still wanted to stay connected, so he became the county coroner, and he still helped at the hospital as needed. "Chris, nice to see you on the job."

"Thank you, sir," Chris replied.

Todd demanded, "Doc, she needs to go to the hospital. She has at least three signs of a major concussion: head injury, bad headache, and vomiting."

"Once! It was once, and my stomach feels fine now." I rebutted.

"But your headache is still going strong. I can tell." Todd stated. Though not a doctor, he was good at his job. Identifying and reporting symptoms was a major job component for a first responder. "Plus, you fainted, and your eyes are just a bit dilated, though it is hard to tell in this light."

"Alright, kids, that is enough," Doc McCarthy scolded. Doc turned to Todd, "You know Rainbow has the right to refuse care."

I started to smirk until Doc added, "Plus, she is as stubborn as a mule on this topic."

"Hey, be nice to the injured party. I've had a rough night." I pouted.

"I only speak the truth," Doc said with a weary smile. "Now let me take a good look at you before I escort the body to the morgue."

Thinking of Harvey sobered me up, as did Doc's poking and prodding of my head. "Ouch!"

"I concur with Todd," Doc announced. "Mild concussion possible. However, I know the Bailey family has dealt with this before, so Rainbow can rest at home." Doc turned to me. "But, young lady, if you get dizzy or vomit again, I expect a phone call. From. The. Hospital. Nurse."

"Yes, sir." Mock saluting, I tried to get up, but Doc pushed me back down.

"You might as well rest here for now. Chief Flint said he still wanted to talk to you."

I wanted to glare back, but knew that wasn't Doc's fault. He was just the messenger. Leaning back on the gurney, I tried to relax.

Chris handed over some clean rags and water bottle to let me clean up a bit, while Todd held out a water bottle for drinking purposes only.

I hate bottled water. It tasted like liquid plastic that congealed into a lump in my stomach. Still, I sipped the water every minute or so to keep Todd happy. His frustration at my refusal was written all over his face: deep down inside, he was plotting a way to drag me to the hospital. To my advantage, Todd believed in the doctor's credo of "do no harm". Of that, I was glad. He would respect my choice for now. But if my health gave any indication of going downhill, he would rush me to the hospital in a heartbeat.

The cool wet cloth washed off the dirt, but didn't put a dent in the throbbing pulse. To push my mind off my headache, I went back to the first question. Was I supposed to apologize to the Chief tonight, while he was busy? Or wait until tomorrow? Of course, I would pay for the cleaning, or replacement any item, if necessary.

More questions rolled in the stormy brain clouds. Did he know I was Corbin's cousin? Would the Chief hold it against Corbin? The Chief would find out sooner or later. Charlottesville, a small town of under ten thousand, had a well-developed grapevine, much to the dismay of many young citizens over the years.

Being new in town, the Chief was currently at the center of grapevine conversations. I tried to stay out of the loop on purpose, having been burned on a few occasions myself. Everyone deserved privacy and second chances.

The town newspaper didn't share my ideas. General information on the candidates was printed on the front page before the final City Council vote, revealing the new Chief was a decorated detective hailing from a St. Louis precinct. Second page grapevine column spoke of his widower, childless status. All were true. Thomas Brubaker, the editor, insisted on reliable documented sources. But the second page ruminations were none of our business. Why the big city detective applied for this small-town Chief's job was anyone's guess. He was voted the best qualified applicant for the job based on his professional credentials and that was all that should matter when posting a job.

Chief Flint certainly had everyone working hard tonight. All three police cars, plus a few of the ambulance lights, lit up the scene. I did my best to block it out as the alternating flashes did nothing for the headache pounding at my temple, but refused to close my eyes. I did not want to give Todd a reason to load the gurney and make a run for the hospital. My evening plans included my comfy bed, my husband of sixteen years and my children. Tomorrow I would awaken to realize this was all just a bad nightmare.

Martin! The kids! They had to be crazed with worry.

"Todd," I called out. I would have asked Chris but he was nowhere to be found. "What time is it? Where is my phone? It is high time I called Martin."

"No, it is time for you to answer some questions," answered Chief Flint from behind me.

At the sudden sound of his voice so close, I half fell backwards off the gurney. His quick grab of my arm prevented a nasty fall.

"That is, if your stomach is feeling better," he added.

"I'm really sorry about your clothes and shoes. I swear I didn't know you were there. I will pay for the cleaning. And after a quick phone call home, I will happily answer any questions you have. If I could just have my phone, please." I pleaded, jabbering like a school girl, a sure sign I was beyond exhausted.

"Your phone is still inside the crime scene. After I get a statement, Officer Hawkins will take you to the police station for a signature and you can call home for a ride."

Wait, what? Just who did he think he was, keeping me sitting here waiting, and not letting me call home? I just reported the crime, I didn't commit the crime! I was innocent. And I had rights.

I told him as much, "My phone had nothing to do with the crime scene. I fell into the crime scene, if you recall. I had to scramble OUT of the crime scene to reach my phone and report the crime like a diligent community member should." He had really pushed my half Irish-half German blood buttons, "I am sweaty, dirty and stinky with who knows whatever was put in the dumpster with the, the, the..."

I paused with tears in my eyes. I could not say the word.

"Corpse?" Chief Flint supplied through tight lips.

"Yes. That." I had lost control, but I was too tired to care. "Where was I? Oh, yes, I ache all over..."

"Mrs. Bailey," Chris appeared at my side. I ignored him.

I was on a roll now, "And I have a headache a mile wide. I have been extremely patient, considering..."

"Mrs. Bailey," Chris pleaded, tapping on my arm.

"But no one gets between me and my family. My husband and children have a right to know that I will be a little late, but I am perfectly fine!" I bellowed, forcing the Chief to take a step back. I jumped off the gurney with every intention of stomping across the yellow tape, now surrounding my van, to get to my phone.

Sadly, my legs didn't seem to share my mother bear zeal and promptly dropped me to the ground.

"Mrs. Bailey!" Chris barked, as he handed over a gas station soda cup. Gas & Go was a quick walk down the alley. "Here, drink this."

Nirvana bubbled through the straw. It was as cool and refreshing as mountain spring water is for hikers, only this was much better than water. This soda was my vice, my drug of choice. I sat on the ground, happy to ignore the men around me debating.

Todd cautioned, "I don't know if that is a good idea with a possible concussion."

"What is that?" Chief Flint asked.

Chris explained, "Just her favorite, a Coca-Cola from the gas station, sir. I checked with Corbin first."

"Is Sergeant Cross a doctor now?" snapped the Chief.

"Uh, no, sir." Chris responded. "Sergeant Cross is Mrs. Baileys' cousin. Actually, more like a brother because she grew up with his family."

"Mm mm," I slurped the last drops. "Speaking of, where is Corbin?"

Chris put his hand on my shoulder. "He escorted the body to the hospital, but he called home for you. He told Martin you were fine and that he would bring you home as soon as he could. Now, may I help you up, Mrs. Bailey?"

I smiled, and held out my hand. "I can't believe I drank the whole thing, but I do feel better. Thank you, Chris."

The longer I live, the more I realize everyone had a vice of some sort. It is not always a bad thing; just something that made you smile on a frowning day. While some people drink alcohol, smoked cigarettes, relished a chocolate bar, or did yoga to relax, I enjoyed a fountain soda to settle down and brighten the day.

"No, Mrs. Bailey, thank you." Chris said, assisting my climb back onto the gurney. "I owe you a lot for helping me study for my exams last year. Any time you need anything, just ask."

Once situated, I decided to live up to my cheery name.

"Chief Flint, could we start over again?" I asked, offering to shake hands. "I am Rainbow Bailey, and I am now ready to answer some questions.

Chapter Three

CHIEF FLINT DECLINED to shake my hand. I didn't blame him, since I was filthy, smelly, and a bit hyper. I also didn't bother apologizing for the tantrum. After all, I had fallen on a dead body, in a dumpster of all places, a little break down in decorum could be understood. With my renewed energy, I vowed to do my best to answer every question. Thanks to the caffeine overload, my headache lowered to a dull roar, but it wasn't gone. Not by a long shot.

He began, "When did you arrive at Power Fitness tonight?"

"About 7:05pm. I know because I was late for stretching in my kick-boxing class, which starts at 7pm."

"Where were you before class?"

"My children and I were at my father's farm for a long weekend. We left on Friday and returned after dinner today," I reported. "It is a two-hour drive home, but we stopped at my Aunt's house for a quick visit. It became later than I planned, so half way home we picked up a fast food dinner. The receipt is probably in the dumpster now."

"Can you name the other members of the class in attendance tonight?"

Could I name them? In my sleep. Having lived most my life in our small town, I knew everyone by name.

"Most of the regulars attended." I counted on my fingers, "Judy Thiessen, Nancy Parker, JC Bancock, Samantha Stone, Tammy Connor and Jill Jensen. And, of course, Janice Peterson, the instructor."

"Was anyone else in the building?"

"Some nights there are. I don't know about tonight, as I didn't look around but ran straight to class."

"When does class end?" he asked.

"Around 8pm." I replied.

"When did each person leave?"

"Well, I don't know for sure. Usually I take a shower after class, along with everyone else."

"What made tonight different?"

"Well, I usually come in at 5 o'clock to do my chores before class, but tonight I did them after."

"What chores were those?"

"I switched laundry, folded towels and ran the vacuum." I explained, "I barter my time here a few hours a week to pay for my membership dues."

"Did anything seem unusual at this time? Did you hear anything different?"

"No." I answered, wincing as I shook my head. "I didn't notice anything."

"How do you know everyone had left?"

"I checked the locker room before locking up. Best friends, Judy and Nancy, are usually the last ones out. Tonight was no exception."

"What about the men's locker room?" he inquired.

"I called in there, like I always do, but no one answered. I didn't go in to look around."

"Why not check?"

"Not my job to kick people out. Some members pay extra for keys to work out after hours. There could have been someone in the men's room who just planned to lock up behind himself. If they didn't answer, then they didn't need anything."

The Chief noted that before continuing, "After everyone had left, what did you do?"

The caffeine and sugar buzz were no match for the continual flashing police lights. My headache throbbed as I recapped the story. "Well, I followed the ladies out, locked up and decided since I was parked next to the dumpster I might as well clean out my van. I dug out some trash, dropped it in the dumpster, and went back for more. On the last trip, I heard the calculator thump inside the dumpster. It is too expensive to just replace so I reached in with the aid of the chair and my flashlight. I almost had it, when yuck happened."

He sighed, "Define 'yuck'."

"I flipped head over heels into the dumpster. That's yuck!" I shuddered. "Once inside, the whiff of rotten banana peels curled my stomach. I wanted to get out fast, but I wasn't leaving without what I came for. I grabbed the calculator, glancing the light around searching for a place to put my feet to get out, when I saw what looked like a shoe on a mannequin's foot. It seemed out of place here, so far from the department stores, so I held my breath a little longer and took a second look for more pieces. Once I realized the mannequin was real, scrambling up and out was my only goal."

"List everything you saw inside the container," he asked.

I massaged my temples while I thought back. It took a lot of patience not to explode at his tedious questions. As a mother of five, I had plenty of practice counting to ten to stretch my patience. For the police chief, I quickly counted to twenty before continuing. This was the stuff I didn't really want to remember. In fact, I just wanted to forget the whole thing. Somewhere behind my wall of pain, I knew that everyone was worth remembering, even quiet crazy Harvey.

"I directed the flashlight up the leg about two feet, 'til I noticed some of the light being reflected back. It was a ring on a finger. Harvey's face wasn't more than a few inches from that. He had his eyes open, looking up at me."

"Did you touch him to see if he was alive?"

I shook my head, "Honestly, I didn't think much after seeing Harvey's face. His eyes vacantly starred off in space. His face was partially covered with shiny fabric or plastic bag. He had not made any sounds, while I had just fallen on top of him. If he was drunk or asleep, I would think he would have moved, or at least grunted. And Harvey isn't homeless, so there was no reason he should be sleeping in a dumpster. I just knew I had to get out of there. I barely remember scrambling up, out of the dumpster, to reach the phone. I have no idea who I even called. Just that I woke up to Corbin leaning over me, and, well, you know the rest."

"Chief Flint, sir," Corbin interrupted, returning from his errand.

"What is it, Sergeant Cross?"

"The photos and evidence bags are on the way back to the station," Corbin reported. "Officer Pinzinsky is set to stay with the crime scene for now, with Hawkins providing relief in four hours. Doctor McCarthy said the autopsy will be performed tomorrow at 8am."

"Thank you, Sergeant Cross," Chief Flint stated. When Corbin didn't leave, he added, "Is there anything else?"

"Yes, sir. Requesting permission to take Mrs. Bailey home if you are finished. She lives just up the hill. I will then return for you, sir."

The new chief took his time replying, "Yes, you may take your cousin home now." Corbin startled at the mention of the family relation, but just nodded at the Chief.

Turning to me, the Chief added, "I am finished for now. I will let you go home for the night, but I expect you at the police station first thing in the morning, Mrs. Bailey, to sign your statement."

Asleep on my feet, I yawned, "Yes, sir."

The Chief head back to the crime scene, but called over his shoulder, "After Officer Pinzinsky bags her clothes first."

That woke me up in a hurry. "What do you mean, 'bag my clothes'? You can't possibly think I am a suspect." I cried out.

The Chief turned back to say, "Until we check your alibi, Mrs. Bailey, you are the only person of interest in Harvey Henson's murder. And those clothes are part of evidence."

"And I suppose I can't grab any clothes out of my gym bag in the van?"

"Evidence!" He called back.

"What am I supposed to wear home?" I started after him.

Corbin grabbed my arm, swinging me around towards his cruiser. "Boo, it's going to be OK. I have some of my old clothes in the trunk for just these occasions."

Grabbing a gym bag, he walked me into the Power Fitness. Officer Pinzinsky followed.

"Corbin, you know those clothes are going to be way too big. And who is going to bring my van home?"

"The clothes will fit well enough for the short drive home. We can't release your van, Boo. Not yet. But as soon as Wilson's garage opens in the morning, I will get a van to you to use."

Poor Bessie wasn't going to get her bath yet. "It better not be the Purple People Eater. Who is going to pay for this rental? And what about my purse?"

Corbin sighed, "Enough with the questions, Boo. Let's just get you home tonight and deal with those details in the morning."

Chapter Four

CHANGING CLOTHES WAS A SLOW, painful process. Purple bruises popped up all over my body in that last hour and fireworks appeared in my vision every time my head moved. I wished for my pajamas as I sunk into Corbin's clothes. They were six sizes too big in length! I looked ridiculous, as I wrapped the sweatpants drawstring all the way around me twice before tying it, plus rolled the pant legs up to the knees. Corbin was in good shape, but his body frame was twice the size of mine. The shirt so loose it was falling off my shoulders.

Corbin handed over some size eleven sneakers that fit no better than Bozo the Clown's would, and helped me to the cruiser. The car door window felt refreshingly cool against my skin, numbing the thumping pain.

"Chief wanted me to tell you not to talk to anyone about what happened," Corbin pulled away from the scene. Slowly the red and blue police lights faded in the distance as he heads towards home. "Rainbow? Did you hear me?"

"Yes, yes, don't talk to anyone," I mumbled, dismissing his comments immediately. Thanks to our small-town grapevine, everyone will know tomorrow that I was klutzy enough to roll onto the dead body belonging to Harvey.

Poor sweet Harvey. He was a quiet, simple member of our community who lived at Hilltop House for the mentally disabled. He was also a faithful employee at the Workshop, a factory that employed people with physical and mental challenges. In his free time, he was often found wandering the streets, talking to himself, and smiling at everyone he passed.

"What happened to Harvey?" Voicing my curiosity, I asked, "Am I really a suspect?"

Corbin sighed, "Never under my watch. If I was chief..."

"You were too young. The City had to find someone else."

"By just a couple of years," he reminded me. "And I have the experience. And the Bachelor's in Criminal Justice. You could have helped me you know."

"This is the reason I didn't. No special treatment, and you know why," I said.

"Then to answer your question, Miss Independent, Yes, the person who reports finding a corpse that died under suspect circumstances is usually the first suspect."

"Are you quoting from a textbook? All I did was find him dead and report it. Isn't that what I was supposed to do?" I bemoaned. "I just got back in town, for heaven's sake."

Corbin reached over to rub my shoulder. "I know, Boo, and by tomorrow the Chief will verify that and everything will be fine. Then this will be easier for all of us."

"What do you mean easier for all of us?" I ask.

"I just wish you hadn't told the chief we were related," Corbin sighed.

"I didn't. You know I wouldn't. Chris mentioned it when he delivered the soda," I explained. "Thank you, by the way. I was starting to lose my mind right then."

"I knew you could use some sugar and caffeine to help deal with the shock. Bailing you out, again, like when we were kids." Corbin smirked at me, then frowned. "I just can't believe it. His first week here, his first ride with me even, and my cousin falls over a dead body."

Tears sprang to my eyes. "Hey, do you think I like what happened any better than you? It's not like I planned a roll in the trash as my favorite night time activity."

"Rainbow, please, that is not what I meant and you know it," he scolded.

"Besides, I remember bailing you out more often than not, little cousin," I sniffled. "So how did you find me anyway?"

He thought for a moment, "I guess I can tell you that. You called my cell phone and said just one word before the line went dead: "Help". I called home to hear you went to kickboxing. We were only about a mile away on rounds. I snapped on the lights and we zoomed over. I saw your van in the back of the parking lot, and you know the rest."

"Thank you, Corbin, for coming so fast."

He parked the car in my driveway and leaned closer, "Rainbow, you are family. You know I will come running anytime you need me."

Click! Corbin unbuckled my seat belt, as I enjoyed the view of my brick two story house that held the loves of my life. A short fifteen years ago, it was a single-story home with a large backyard on a short street. Nestled between two corner lots, it had a charm of its own. Charming old plumbing, charming old electric wires, and charming small bedrooms. As our family grew, we slowly updated the first floor, and eventually added a second floor to accommodate our larger family. The five-bedrooms, three baths were a chore to keep clean, but I loved it.

Corbin came around and opened the car door before the other most important man in my life could walk down the porch steps. Martin Bailey, my husband of eighteen years, barely reached my side before I fell into his arms and buried my head in his neck. Tears I held back all-night burst through the mental dam, while he held tight, letting my sorrow run its course.

"She didn't just fall into a dumpster, did she?" Martin questioned my cousin over my heaving shoulder.

I heard Corbin clear his throat, "The house looks pretty quiet. Are all my nieces and nephews asleep already?"

"Working up at the farm always tires them out. I sent them to bed early," Martin replied.

I was still hiding, snuggled with the man I love, but I could just picture his right eyebrow rise when Martin accused Corbin, "And you didn't answer my question."

Rocks under Corbin's feet rustled as he thought how to answer. "Well, it is not so much what she landed in, but on whom she landed."

Martin stiffened, "Come again?"

"I can't talk about an ongoing investigation, and neither should Rainbow," Corbin cautioned. "Like I said on the phone, she somehow tumbled head first into the dumpster behind Power Fitness. That part is true."

I heard Corbin's feet shuffle, "But I neglected to mention she landed on a dead body."

Incredulous, Martin asked, "You didn't think it important to mention that when you called? I should have come to get her. Boo, are you alright?"

Corbin answered for me, "I called the paramedics first thing. You know Todd and Chris. They tried to get her to go to the hospital, but you can guess how well that went. Doc McCarthy arrived and checked her out. Regular pain meds as needed, but wake her every few hours as a precaution."

"A concussion then?" Martin asked. "From a dead body?"

"Mild, if any. She complained of a headache from the bump on her head, but her eyes are good." Corbin added, "She threw up once when I found her, but I think it was from the surprise in the dumpster more than anything."

I was emotionally drained, yet so happy to be home, I couldn't help myself. "All over Chief Flint shoes!" I giggled.

Corbin frowned at that, but had the good graces not to comment. "Yeah, well, she was very cranky for a while, but perked right up after a soda. Chris told me she sucked all 32 ounces down in two minutes flat, so she probably won't be able to sleep for a while."

"Wanna bet?" I mumbled with my eyes half closed.

"Let me know if her condition changes in the night." Corbin called out as he climbed into his cruiser. "I will be up sorting through garbage all night. Hope you feel better, Boo. Get some sleep."

As Corbin pulled away, Martin pulled me into another bear hug. "I love you. So, tell me the truth, how you do really feel?"

I sighed, "Happy to be home, exhausted, and sore. My headache is not so bad anymore. And I don't want to be anywhere but here."

Martin kept his arm around me as we walked into the house. "Well, I will give you all the hugs and kisses you want," he sniffed. "After you take a shower."

He smiled when I rolled my eyes. "Too dirty for a bath to soak these aching bones, I suppose."

"Hot shower now, then to bed. Take a bath in the morning if your old bones request it."

We walked into the living room to confront another disaster of the homemade variety. Shoes, as usual, a tumbled mess by the door. Books littered the couch; a sure sign that a few of my bookworms were back at it this evening. Suitcases were piled by the basement door. New Lego creations, and a crochet yarn ball prominent on the coffee table.

"Are the munchkins really asleep?" I asked. "I don't want them to see me like this."

"The best I can promise is they are all in bed. One or two are probably reading by flashlight. I told them you would be late, but very tired." Martin lead me through the living room maze, down the hall, straight to our master bathroom. "Now shower. Then I want to hear all about it."

The hot water never felt so good on my skin, pounding into the sore muscles and bruises. I shampooed twice and scrubbed until my skin was raw. Once the hot water turned to warm, I knew it was time to head to bed. Even by our family's night owl standards, it was now past bedtime.

Though I was born and raised in "up with the sun" farm country, marrying Martin changed all that. Martin and I own and operate the Pit Stop Sub Shop.

He discovered his incredible cooking talent in while college, during late night study sessions with his dorm mates. He created fancy nutritious finger food snacks with whatever was on hand. It quickly became a game for the boys to stock their refrigerator with various items, but Martin took the challenge seriously. Not all his inventive creations were truly edible, but he learned from his mistakes. When he graduated with a business degree, he turned his cooking hobby into successful business.

Martin opened the shop before we were married. The wonderful tastes and smells he created, even out of leftovers, was unbelievable, while my cooking skills included opening a box or a can and adding heat. I wasn't inclined to spend time slaving over the stove when that was his passion, so he did the cooking and I focused on the laundry, dishes, and educating our children. Our family worked well that way.

Martin headed to work a little after ten in the morning and came home about eleven hours later, with leftovers from the shop. With a work day a little later than the average father, our family adjusted with breakfast at nine and dinner when he returned, lunch and snacks. The ability to set our own schedule just another reason we began home-schooling the children.

Martin yawned in bed. "Now start from the beginning. Why were you digging in the dumpster?"

Snuggled onto his chest, deep under the soft sheets, I explained it all, pointedly ignoring our Chief's directives: dirty van, calculator, falling on Harvey, fainting and the Chief's shoes, allowing the tale to tell itself.

Martin just listened, as I knew he would. He was the calm in my storm, my bartender of confidences, my anchor when life threatened to swallow me whole. Besides, he needed to hear it from me before he heard it on the morning news.

"So, you see, I didn't plan on all of this. It just happened." I ended my tale.

"Sounds like just another Rainbow adventure," Martin quipped. "Tomorrow you can sign your statement and forget about it. The rest is up to the police to do their job. For now, why don't we try to get some sleep." Martin turned off the light.

Chapter Five

MOST OF MY FRIENDS, if they have a cup of coffee at dinner, they stay up for half the night. That is not me. I simply closed my eyes last night, and the next thing I knew a strong light was shining in my eyes. The sun had been up for hours, if I was correct about the angle of the rays. I moaned and rolled over, only to come nose to nose with my youngest daughter, Emily.

"How are you feeling, Mommy?" she asked.

As her voice filtered through my ears, I realized I heard quite a few noises coming from the other parts of the house. Homeschooling five children was not a quiet endeavor. From the sounds I guessed someone was in the kitchen, probably Audrey who inherited her father's cooking interest, and two others were in the living room fighting over the microscope.

Pain surged through every bump and bruise as I raised my head to look at the clock. My head thumped back down. Instead, I asked, "What time is it, Sweetheart?"

Her smile beamed as the sun, "It is 11:30, exactly when Daddy told me to wake you up. You sure were sleeping a long time. Daddy said we shouldn't disturb you until now, so Hunter and Skylar have been organizing the school lessons this morning, though I don't like how they teach. They get crabby. I need you back."

"Whoa, slow down, Emily. I need a morning shower before I can catch up to your speed." Not to worry her, I tried to smile. "Why don't you tell Audrey and the boys I will be out in just a moment."

"Sure thing, Mommy. I will tell Uncle Corbin, too."

"He is here?" I sat up suddenly, making the room spin. I definitely need to move slowly today.

"No, but he said to call when you woke up. Speed dial number four! Now you don't need to worry about anything while you take a shower. Daddy said to take care of things because you needed rest." Emily ran off before I could reply to that, allowing me a few blessed moments to plan my day before they all decided to check on me.

Audrey arrived before I could crawl out of bed. "Oh, Em was right, you are awake. You look awful, but how are you feeling? Are you hungry? I can make you some breakfast, or lunch."

I redirected the question to my stomach. A loud grumble reveled the answer. "A small amount of anything would be good, but I think I will refresh with a shower first. I will be ready for food in ten minutes." I would prefer a much longer shower, but optimistic thoughts would be required to survive this day.

I usually showered at night, so I could roll out of bed and hit the floor running in the morning, but today called for the exception. My headache had subsided to a dull temporal pressure, but I needed more Excedrin. I had to be presentable when I apologized to the Chief and signed my statement. Too bad I slept so long. No time for that bath.

This shower was just a bit quicker than last night. Still, every muscle enjoyed another hot water rub down as I mentally reviewed my calendar for the day. Tuesday. Only two days until the Ladies Aid meeting at church leading the city-wide fund-raiser on Saturday. It would be great if Audrey could make some of her Pecan Supreme cookies to share. That meant I would need to go shopping for supplies today. Oh, why did I have to sleep so long? I think I missed the Homeschool co-op planning meeting this morning.

"Mom, Grandpa Koontz is on the phone," I heard Travis, my third son, call through the door.

Dad? He never called unless it was an emergency, and we just left him yesterday.

I dashed out of the shower, threw on my robe without bothering to dry off, and headed to the kitchen phone.

Ding-Dong. Travis handed over the phone and dashed off. I reached for a juice glass and asked, "Hi, Dad, is everything alright on the farm?

"Fine here, but did you get home okay last night? I had a phone message waiting for me after morning chores to call a Police Chief concerning you."

I reached into the refrigerator for some juice, while I figured how best to respond. Telling Martin all the details was one thing, but telling Dad would not be fair to him. He has always tried to be overprotective of me. He wasn't able to spend the time with me growing up that he would have liked. He makes up for it by worrying about me.

"Dad, I am fine. Just a little misunderstanding here," I said.

Skylar, or was he Hunter, the twins could fool even me for a few seconds, called out, "Mom," as he led the visitors into the house. "It's Uncle Corbin, and Chief of Police."

"Uncle?" I heard Chief Flint question, as he stepped from the foyer to the living room. "I thought you were cousins."

Our house has an open first-floor plan, with the living room blending into the dining room. A breakfast bar separated the open rooms from the kitchen. Hearing his husky voice just feet away, I started, standing up too fast, making the world spin a little. I reached for the counter to steady myself, knocking the drinking glass off the counter, and onto the floor with a big crash. At the sound both men turned in my direction.

There I was, wet hair, wrapped in a robe, and the bird clock on the wall started to hoot twelve o'clock noon. 'Just another Rainbow adventure' Martin would say, if he were here.

"Rainbow, are you alright?!" Dad yelled through the phone.

At the same time Corbin commanded, "Don't move, Boo."

Trying to put the best construction on yet another disorganized mess in my chaotic life, I smiled at the Chief, "Phone for you."

At the sound of breaking glass, the children rushed in. Corbin, being used to my family at its chaotic best, quickly established order. He sent Travis to guide the Chief to the school room phone extension, handed Audrey a broom to sweep after the twins finished picking up glass. I dashed into the bedroom to change into something a little more presentable. Emily soon followed with my favorite instant breakfast: chocolate-chip toaster-hot waffles.

I slid into my favorite stonewashed jeans, and opted for a button-down shirt instead of t-shirt to attempt a little class. I switched my slippers for tennis shoes and headed out to face the doom. Bummer. I forgot the headache medicine again.

Chief Flint was just getting off the phone. "Mrs. Bailey, I assured your father that you were alright. He also confirmed the time you left yesterday."

"Hey, Mom, you have an alibi." Emily slid up beside me. She looked to the Chief solemnly, "I just learned that word last week. Does that mean my mom was a suspect? Because I will tell you right now that is just plain silly. My mom wouldn't hurt our friend. She wouldn't hurt anybody."

I almost laughed out loud as the Chief's face turned a little pink. "Uh, yes. Um, no. That is..."

Taking little pity on the newest member of Charlottesville, I interrupted, "Chief Flint, let me introduce Emily, our youngest. She is seven and recently discovered the mystery section of the children's library."

I led the way into the living room continuing introductions along the way, "You have met Travis, who directed you to our school room. He just turned ten last week."

Tousling his brown curls before he dashed out of my reach, I continued, "Audrey, age twelve, inherited her father's cooking ability, and is probably responsible for the warm muffins and coffee available. Help yourself."

Corbin and Chief sat on the blue couch, while I claimed my favorite rocker recliner. The children settled down on various surfaces: the twins on the floor, Travis and Audrey on the dining room chairs and Emily on the arm of my recliner. Finishing introductions, I added, "And you met Skylar at the door", pointing to the boy in the blue shirt, as by then I was sure which was which. "This is Hunter in the green shirt. They are both fourteen and growing like weeds."

"Mom!" they both sighed in exasperation.

Once we were settled, I attempted to clear up some of the Chief's confusion. "Chief Flint, let me answer your question from earlier."

The Chief looked puzzled, but I just plowed ahead. "You were asking why the kids call Corbin their uncle. Corbin is really my first cousin. But my mother died when I was four. My Dad is a farmer with long work hours. His sister Irene, and her husband, offered to help raise me. Corbin was born a year later. Dad and my two older brothers would drive the two hours to see me as often as they could, but I mostly grew up in Charlottesville, with Corbin as my brother."

"However, I am sure that is not why you made the trip here." I added.

"Mrs. Bailey, you were supposed to come in this morning and sign your statement. I asked Mrs. Dillon from the office to call your house for the last two hours, but the line has been busy. You weren't chatting with your friends this whole time, were you?"

"Never!" I insisted.

Audrey spoke up, "I can explain that, Chief Flint. The phone started ringing as soon as the local early morning news hit the air waves."

"Five phone calls in five minutes," piped Travis.

Audrey continued, "Dad explained Mom had a long headache night and needed her sleep, so he just turned off the ringers and let the answering machine screen the phone calls. They have been fairly non-stop all morning."

"I only answered Grandpa's call because I recognized his phone number." Travis added.

Hunter cut in, "And the muffins on the counter are not from Audrey, Mom. They are from Mrs. Anderson."

"We also have five casseroles, two pies, and three bags of cookies in the downstairs refrigerator," Emily counted on her fingers.

Skylar explained, "We have been taking turns answering the door before they could ring the bell."

"Oh, my. Did you remember to make a list?" I asked, already dreading the Thank You notes I would have to write. Dear Abby, I am not.

Audrey listed, "Name, food item and type of container written as they arrived so we can give each one back to the rightful owner, just as Grandma Irene taught me."

"Excellent! I am so glad you remembered. I wonder why people are bringing us food," I mused. "We aren't related to Harvey."

"Sheri, er, Mrs. Dillon, heard at the police station that some are bringing food here, and others are taking it where Harvey lived at Harvest House." Corbin mentioned, receiving a stare from the Chief.

"Dad said it is because you had such a shock, they expect you to be in bed for days," explained Audrey. "It is like they don't even know you, Mom."

Finding an opening in the conversation, Chief Flint asked, "And what do you know about last night?"

"Just what Dad told us after it was on the morning radio, that Mom fell into the dumpster while reaching for our calculator and fell on Harvey who was dead," Hunter recited.

The twins usually finished each other's comments, so Skylar added, "Dad said Mom had a late night and needed to sleep in, so we were not to bother her unless it was an emergency, but we should wake Mom at 11:30 at the latest."

"I opened the window blinds and let the sun shine in," Emily smiled.

"Yeah, Mom just got up so we haven't heard her side of the story yet." Travis loved reading adventures, so I knew he anticipating hearing all the gory details.

Remembering Corbin's speech about not talking, I thought I better keep things moving. "Chief Flint already knows my story. And now I better get to the office to finish my side of the paperwork, so they can continue work on Harvey's case."

Corbin and the Chief arose as I stood up. "Just let me check in with Martin, so he knows I am up and moving, and I will be at the station soon. I promise. Did you bring my van? Oh, and my purse? I don't want to drive without my license."

Corbin glanced at the Chief, as he cleared his throat, "About the van. We are still processing it. Same for your purse. But I made a copy of your driver's license. Here are the keys to a loaner van from Wilson's Garage. He said you could use it for a few days."

I walked to the window and moaned, "Not the Purple People Eater! Couldn't they borrow one from his brother's shop in Portmore?"

The monster twelve-seater was so named for two reasons: the deep plum paint job and Mr. Wilson's favorite song. It came in handy for church youth groups to conferences and scout trips camping. If truth be told, it was probably the only vehicle in town with enough seat-belts in town to carry my family of seven.

Corbin put his hands up to stop the tirade. "You have driven it before, when your transmission blew."

This was all the new Chief's doing. If Corbin was still interim Chief then I would still have my van. If my children hadn't been right there, being the learning sponges that they are, I would have ripped him up one side and down the other about his treatment of me, a responsible citizen whose only crime was reporting a crime. But for the sake of teaching respect and patience to my children, I slowly counting to ten before responding, "Alright, if you think it will help you find Harvey's killer. But only for a few days."

I walked to the phone, leaving Chief Flint and Corbin to field more questions from the children, and was shocked to see the children were not kidding. The answering machine listed twenty-three messages. They would have to wait, Martin and the Chief would not.

I caught Martin during the lunch rush, "Have you been extra busy today?"

"You could say that. Same number of high schoolers, but a larger number of concerned citizens asking about you." Martin replied. "If you feel up to it, it would be good for you and the kids to be seen out and about like nothing happened."

"I agree. See you soon." I hung up and turned around, right into Chief Flint creating a wall right behind me. He towered over me, feet apart and arms crossed. "Well, Mrs. Bailey, will you be coming with us to the station now?"

Most people towered over me. His attempt at intimidation would not work. "And leave my children here, unsupervised? No. There are too many people stopping by." I leaned in closer to whisper, "What if the killer is one of them?"

He whispered back, "What if the killer is right in front of me?"

"I couldn't have done it. I have an alibi from my father. You said so yourself." I rolled my eyes.

He shrugged, "You are not off the hook yet. Parents lie all the time for their children. Either way, you are still my best suspect. Now, do I need to arrest you to get your official statement?"

Silence. The hustle and bustle sounds of my children getting ready to leave had suddenly come to a stop. Mothers of young children know that silence is not always a good thing. I leaned around the Flint wall to see all eyes and ears of my children focused in our direction. Even Corbin held his breath, his mouth set in a frown.

Enough was enough.

Smiling up at him, "Chief of Police Johnathan Flint, I sincerely believe if you had enough evidence to arrest me, you would have done so already. But you don't and never will, because I didn't do it." I put my hand up to stop his interjection. "Now, I really want to do my part so you can find the person who treated Harvey, literally, like trash. However, my children's protection comes first. I am taking them to the Pit Stop Sub Shop to be with their father for a quick lunch. Then I will come straight to your office to answer as many questions as you like."

"I have enough to hold you up to seventy-two hours." The Chief's hazel eyes narrowed, "Why should I trust your plan?"

"Simple." Calling on my teacher voice, I explained, "With this small town's grapevine, there is no place I can go that tongues won't wag. If I deviate from that plan, it would be easy to track me down, especially in that purple monstrosity of a vehicle, which, I am sure, that was your plan all along."

Offering a peace treaty, I added, "Also, you are welcome to join us for lunch if you wish, to keep tabs on me. My husband makes the best chicken salad around."

Skylar suddenly stepped between the Chief and I. "Mom? Should we call Mr. Timberland to meet you at the police station?"

I turned to the Chief, "Do I need a lawyer to sign a statement?"

Jacob Timberland, our family lawyer, was also the mayor of Charlottesville, and the Chief's new boss. A fact not lost on him when he finally responded. "I expect to see you in my office in one hour, no more."

I resisted the urge to salute him as he moved to let me pass.

Hustling five children out the door and into a strange van takes time. I put the breakfast food away and wiped down the counter tops. Every spring we fight off an invasion of ants. I hated using chemicals so clean surfaces was our first defense. While Audrey helped Emily gather a few workbooks into a pink backpack, the boys grabbed their band instruments. Tuesday was band practice day.

To the Chief's bachelor eyes and ears, it must have felt like being in a three-ring circus, though I hoped his stony expression was due to lack of sleep from the night before. Too bad he didn't even try Audrey's strong coffee. That would have perked him up.

Finally, we walked outside with our bags. As I locked the front door, the children began to fight over the seats. Every day, the children rotated who would sit in the front passenger seat and control the radio. Travis hopped in front, while Emily stood looking in.

"Where do I sit?" Emily asked me.

"Good question," I replied, turning to Corbin and the Chief. "State law requires Emily to be in a car seat until she is age eight."

"Don't you have two of them?" Corbin reminded me.

"Yes, but the second on is in Martin's van, which is already at the shop." I turned to the Chief. "Do we wait for it, or will one trip without it get me into trouble?"

The Chief sighed long, as if even he was counting to ten or even twenty. "One trip without it is permitted."

"Yippee! I claim the whole back seat." Emily cried as she crawled over seats to the back.

"I will make sure she is buckled in tight," said Audrey, climbing in after her.

I thanked Audrey as I climbed up into the full-sized van. Mr. Wilson did a great job to maintain his favorite vehicle, but it found ways to show its age. The springs creaked with my weight, and I had to hold the key a full three seconds before the engine would turn over. Once it was started, the purple monster purred like kitten, which changed quickly to a roar when I added any gas. I had Travis turn the radio off, not to hear the engine better, but this van only played one station- the oldies.

By the time we arrived at the Pit Stop, business had slowed to a crawl. We usually had two big groups come through. The high schoolers have an early lunch period, and Martin creates quick lunch size portions at student prices. As the upperclassmen rush back for their next class, the town workers come in for lunch.

Martin had the day's special laid out for us in the upstairs room. Usually he brings home some lunch a little later in the afternoon, unless we have activities that bring us to his side of town. This means we have later dinners in the evenings, when he gets home. The adjustment to fit Martin's schedule is one of the reasons we home-school. With his odd hours, the children would not otherwise be able to spend time with him. No one ever complained about Dad's leftovers, either, as he was a fantastic chef. It worked great for our budget and less food went to waste.

I had heard the Chief's stomach growling as we left the house, but he declined to join us. Corbin accepted the invitation, ostensibly to make sure I meet the one-hour deadline, but I knew he had an alternative motive. He had been around Martin's delicacies enough to know what his taste buds would be missing.

Martin pulled me aside as our hungry crew gathered around the table, "I am wondering if we should call John Timberland to meet you there."

"Has Skylar been talking to you? I don't need a lawyer. I didn't do anything but find and report the body."

"Yes, Skylar and Hunter both have and I agree with them. Chief Flint is from the big city and sees things differently than we do," Martin replied.

"Corbin will be there," I offered.

"But he is already walking a fine line, between his boss and his family. As you well know, this is the exact reason the city hired someone from outside, to prevent favors."

"And I don't want, nor need, any favors. All I did was report a body." Giving Martin a big hug, I reassured him. "But I promise to take all that into consideration, and I will call John if I think I need to."

He squeezed me back, "You know I am just trying to take care of you."

"And I know I do not make it easy for you," I whispered. "There is one way you can take care of me right now."

"Oh, yeah?" He said looking at me.

"Find me some headache medicine. It is not as bad as last night, but I could use some help in that department."

"Glad to be of service to my lady." Martin bowed and kissed my hand before heading to the First Aid cabinet.

Once the food was put away and the table cleaned up, we split into two groups. The girls stayed with Martin while the boys jumped in the van. Hunter claimed it was to make sure they arrived at their jazz band practice on time, but I knew better. The boys were hoping for more details on Harvey's demise. I could tell by the perfect angelic look on their faces. Still, it would save time if they were along for the ride.

Chapter Six

"RAINBOW BAILEY, ALWAYS MAKING an entrance." Mrs. Sheri Dillon, called to me from the front desk. In her thirty plus year career as Police headquarters administrator, she had faced down various disorderly drunks and teenage hoodlums. It didn't matter that she was shorter than most seventh graders, she demanded, and received, respect. "What a way to baptize the new chief!"

I set a smile on my face, accepting the first of many not-so-helpful comments I would receive today now that I was out in the community running errands. "Well, finding Harvey like that was quite a shock. I am here to give my statement so they can catch the killer. But I would also like to make amends by paying for the dry cleaning."

Mrs. Dillon nodded her approval before buzzing us through the lobby door. "I took them to my cousin Kristi's place. Chief wouldn't let me at first. But as soon as he stormed out to find you, my nose led me straight to them. His clothes would be ruined if I hadn't stepped in, and I couldn't let our new town representative walk around looking and smelling like the trash."

"I am very thankful you did that. Please have Kristi call me when they are ready. I would like to pick them up and deliver myself with sincere apologies."

"As it should be," Mrs. Dillon affirmed. "I will let her know."

Polite conversation completed, I asked, "Is the Chief in his office?"

"I think he just stepped out for a moment. But I know he is very anxious to see you, so why don't you wait for him in his office. He won't mind. The boys will follow me and behave themselves in the conference room, I am sure." Mrs. Dillon directed.

"Yes, ma'am." The three boys responded in chorus, though disappointment was written all over their faces. They recognized the firm command and marched behind Mrs. Dillon to the left as I headed further down the hall to the Chief's office.

I hesitated just inside the door, not wanting to be caught in the middle of a power play. The free invitation into his office was probably one of Sheri's little tricks to make her impression on the new Chief. It might take a few weeks, but Sheri would impress on him what she has taught many of his predecessors. Chief Jonathan Flint might be the Chief of Police, but Mrs. Sheri Dillon was the boss of the office.

I applauded when the Charlottesville City Board decided to hire someone fresh, someone unrelated to our fair townsfolk, to the position of Chief. Our town's tumultuous history includes a few long-lasting family feuds. Thankfully, most have died out over the years, but their memories surface on occasion, and we certainly did not need any new ones.

Still, it wouldn't hurt to sit down in one of the two chairs positioned in front of the desk while I waited for him. 'Look, but don't touch,' Aunt Irene always said.

First impression of the new chief said formal all the way. According to the paper, this was his first job as the Chief of Police of any town. He was making every effort to show he was up for the job. The wall behind his desk was covered with awards and citations, carefully positioned in an overall elongated diamond pattern. Adding up the years, the awards covered over twenty years of service to the city of St. Louis. It was an impressive record, revealing his dedication to his job and community. Neat, formal and proud. Coming to our small town with no big awards to hand out would be a big adjustment.

On his desk was an ornate light wood frame, different from the dark wood ones he hung on the wall. The blue flowers carved and painted on the edges piqued my curiosity. I couldn't help picking it up.

It held two pictures. The full-sized picture captured the pure energy of a beautiful dark-haired woman in a simple blue summer dress, standing in a city park, laughing at the person behind the camera. Her smile would hold anyone's glance, but I was drawn to the smaller photo. Tucked in the lower corner was a much older faded photo of a shy girl, leaning against a red barn. Though taken many years apart, it was easy to see they were the same person.

Something was familiar to me, though I couldn't pinpoint what exactly. It was a young girl in cutoff jeans, the style back thirty years ago, and a red barn like all other country barns, and some structure off in the distance.

"Mrs. Bailey," called Chief Flint from behind me.

I felt like a kid with hands caught in the cookie jar, and quickly put the frame back on his desk. Hoping I had found the right spot on the desk, I turned around.

"I see you finally made it into the building. Please sit down." He motioned as he walked over to his desk. Pressing the intercom button, "Mrs. Dillon, please send in Officer Engebrecht with Mrs. Bailey's statement."

"Yes, Chief. Right away, Chief," Mrs. Dillon responded with an extra cheery clip in her voice.

Oh, yes, Sheri was definitely having fun breaking in Johnathan Flint, and I was right in the middle of it.

As 'right away' turned into minutes, I decided to break the monotony of silence. "How do you like it here in our quiet little town?"

"Just fine."

"The city picked a nice house to rent for you." I commented, referring to the small two-bedroom house on the edge of town. "Surrounded by farmed fields will be a new experience for a man used to living in the city.

He nodded.

"Nice picture." I indicated the frame I had been holding.

"Thank you."

Enough of these simple answers. If he didn't want to have a nice conversation, well, too bad. Welcome to small town life: we like to chat.

"That frame is personal, very different from the other on the wall. Must be someone very special. Your deceased wife perhaps? She was very beautiful and very happy." I rambled on, but the Chief said nothing. I started walking around. "Now the certificates on the wall stand out nicely. Many people put their photos up haphazardly, but you took the time to give it order and balance."

His eyes followed me as I walked, but no comment came from the other side of the desk. I tried another tract as I returned to my seat. "Sometime soon you should stop by the Pit Stop for a 'Welcome to the community' dinner. Did you enjoy today's special at the diner down the street? Oh, I should warn you that the tomato sauce and silk ties do not mix. I hope you give it to Sheri for dry cleaning. Her cousin, Kristi, is the best in town."

The chief hurriedly looked down his shirt for tomato spots. Not finding any, his eyes return to me. "Was that supposed to be childish joke, Mrs. Bailey?"

"What? Oh, no, you misunderstand me. I see you have a green striped tie now with your blue shirt. You don't strike me as a sloppy dresser. I have an eye for colors and I am pretty sure it was a blue tie this morning, which tells me something spilled and you changed it quick. Dina's diner serves meatballs every Tuesday, so it was probably her spaghetti sauce." I shrugged, "It helps our business to know the competition's menu, you know."

Mercifully, Officer Engebrecht finally walked in, clearing his throat to break the tension, and handed over a file folder. After glancing at the contents, the Chief handed it to me. "Is this correct?"

"Sad, isn't it," I said after reading the one-page report, "that the ending of Harvey's life could be written down in so few paragraphs. I do hope this information helps you. No one should get away with murdering an odd but sweet man and tossing him in the garbage like junk."

The chief leaned back in his chair. "You said that before. You believed it was murder from the start, and not just an accidental death. Why?"

I thought carefully, "Well, you had to know Harvey. As a mentally challenged person, he was odd by the town's standards, but definitely not crazy. Yes, he liked walking around the community with unplugged headphones just talking to himself, but he was always friendly and courteous. And he was smart enough to dress appropriately for the weather. Last night, though, he was dressed decently in his work pants, not in his old junk clothes that he would use for dumpster diving. And remember that his eyes were open. Also, he seemed wrapped in plastic with many other bags around him like someone tried to cover him up."

Chief was looking at me while he hand-scribbled some notes. "Didn't you report last night that you only glimpsed his leg and face, before you scrambled out?"

"Yes," I agreed, "but that is all it takes to recognize nice khaki pants and that his shirt had a collar."

His pencil hovered over the paper. "Anything else?"

"Hmm." I closed my eyes, focusing in on those precious few seconds. Last night I was too shocked to think on it, but it wasn't as painful now. "Well, there was a dark smear on the plastic around him. Not on his face, but more from his back. I suppose even that could have been from hitting his head in a fall, but why would anyone need to cover that up if it was an accident?"

"I was hoping you might be able to provide that information," replied the chief.

"What do you mean?" I asked, opening my eyes.

"You seem to know exactly what happened." He stated.

"Of course not. I just told you everything I observed." Then I added, "I am trying to help the investigation as a good citizen should. Am I still a suspect?"

Chief Flint shrugged, "Is there something you would like to confess?"

Maybe my husband was right. Maybe I did need a lawyer. But I didn't do anything wrong! I opened my mouth to reply, but didn't know where to start.

He sat there with an encouraging smile. Is this how he earned all those awards, by infuriating people so they blurt out confessions? Well, I had nothing to confess, and I refused to play his game.

"You didn't answer my question, which, as I said at the house, means there is not enough evidence. Especially with my father's alibi, you would need solid evidence." I reasoned out-loud for him. "Also, I believe even in the big city murder cases, a motive is required."

I leaned over his desk, my hands on his pristine desk, "Write this down in your notes: I HAVE NO MOTIVE. Harvey was always friendly to me and my family. In fact, years ago, he helped the twins find the way home when they became lost on a bike ride. As for the details, I just notice them. Always have. It is what makes me a good artist."

"Take Josiah, here." I turned to Officer Engebrecht, "So distracted thinking about Miranda's pretty face, he didn't notice the chocolate sauce from last weekend's ice cream social was still on his uniform."

"How did you know?" Officer Josiah Engebrecht asked, looking down at his shirt. "You weren't even in town."

I turned back to the chief. "In true Romeo and Juliet fashion, and thanks to an old family feud about reasons long forgotten, Mr. Anderson would never let his daughter Miranda date an Engebrecht. Josiah, working the late shift, probably patrolled by the church hoping to see her at the social. She snuck some ice cream out to him, and in saying good-bye the chocolate spilled."

"Nobody saw us, I swear." Josiah turned red, wailed his denial. "You won't tell her dad, will you? I don't want her to get into any trouble."

Ignoring his officer, the chief asked, "You guessed all that on one chocolate stain?"

"Inferred, yes." I corrected him.

"Then, why didn't you report all this about Harvey Henson last night?"

Somewhere in that conversation, I had wiped the smile off the chief's face. I wasn't sure if that was a good sign or not. Preferring not to dig my grave deeper as I tried to climb out of it, I took my time responding.

"I had just fallen on a dead body. Someone I knew personally. Chief, I think your clothes testify to my state of mind about that," I began.

A raised eyebrow was his only response.

Uh, oh. I had better reach my point quickly. "Thanks to farm life, I have dealt with death a few times in my life. Last night was different, and not something I ever want to repeat. Definitely not easy to think about. But today, the sun is shining and I am over the surprise. It is much easier to reflect and focus on the details."

Giving a nod to his wall of plaques, I continued. "And once you have all the right details, that wall of achievements tells me that you have the skills needed to find the culprit."

I reached over to initial his notes and signed my statement. "Here is my signed statement. If you have more questions, I will be at home, at the sub shop, or out doing whatever is listed in my planner. Which reminds me, when can I get my purse, cell phone and others things from the van?"

"Sorry, that is all evidence for now." He stated quietly.

I rolled my eyes while putting on my sweetest smile, "Well, whatever will help you catch the killer. But can we compromise? The purse I can do without, and I can use the twins' phone for now. But I really need a photo copy of my day planner and any loose notes found in it. Without those, my life is a disorganized mess. If I tell Mrs. Dillon what I need, is it possible for her to copy if for me?"

After a slight deliberation, he nodded.

"Thank you." As I walked past Josiah, I pointed out the spot he missed. "Don't worry. You know how I feel about family feuds. I won't tell. But make sure you get that out before Mr. Anderson sees that uniform."

"Yes, Ma'am. Thank you, Ma'am." Josiah sighed relief.

Chapter Seven

I FOUND THE BOYS HELPING Corbin in the police garage, with a guest.

"Good morning, Norman," I greeted the mayor's son, sitting on a stool next to my boys. "Why aren't you in school?"

"Oh, I am. Heard about commotion on the police scanner last night and I just had to be here. Dad made a few phone calls and I am now on a field trip. It will look great on my apps." Norman Timberland was a high school senior, planning on career in law enforcement. Norman winked, "Besides, too many cousins in this room. Best to have a witness."

"Sneaky, and logical," I winked back. "Sounds like a lawyer's kid to me."

"Hey, Mom, look at all this stuff," announced Travis with glee. "Hold your breath though, it stinks!"

"Boo, did you have to find him in the dumpster?" Corbin sighed, leaning against one of twelve tables set up and covered with trash. "I thought I was making a good impression on the Chief, until last night."

"At least you haven't been taken off duty. If it is any consolation, he doesn't seem to like me much either, except as a suspect." I tried to cheer him up.

"Still?" Hunter looked to me.

"Not for long, boys." Corbin reassured them. "That is why I put you to work with this mess, remember? So, we could separate your family things from possible clues."

"Yeah, Mom, there is a lot of our stuff in here." Skylar accused.

"No wonder you got carried away and dropped the calculator." Hunter finished his twin's thought.

"But why did you throw away my Z-top transformer?" Travis complained.

I looked into his sad eyes, "Three reasons. I was tired, it was dark, and if you cared so much, then you should have taken better care of it. Now, let's go. You don't want to be late for practice." I reminded them. To Corbin I added, "I hope you sorted it by kind of trash bag first."

I turned to leave and ran smack into Chief Flint, causing yet another embarrassing moment in the short span of our relationship. He caught me as I bounced backward, but quickly released, once assured I wouldn't end up with my rear end on the floor.

"I'm sorry." I said, trying to walk past him.

"Just a minute. What did you mean about the garbage bags?" He asked.

"The bags? That is simple." I point to the garbage tables. "See the thin, cheap white ones? Janice Peterson, the owner of Power Fitness, insists on buying those even though it usually requires double bagging the trash and usually costing more."

I walked to the next tables, "Those thin black bags belong to Mr. Cummins. A few years back, he plowed into his garage after a night of drinking. His wife kicked him out unless he promised to never drink again. He gave it a good try, but he just couldn't give it all up. Now he drinks in the garage at home. He puts his bags filled with beer bottles in our dumpster at night, trying to hide his drinking from his wife."

"But these black bags over here belong to the Carter family. Some weeks of the year their family of seven children fills their one city approved trash can to overflowing. Mrs. Carter sends the youngsters over after dark with the extra trash to save on the extra trash fee."

Chief Flint asked, "Are these more of your typical observations, Mrs. Bailey?"

"Yes, but you can check for yourself. Though Mr. Cummins will probably deny it, Mrs. Withrow on the other side of the drive can testify to it. Beware, she is the block busybody and will probably give you an earful." I said. "I do hope this doesn't get the Carters into trouble. If you do go asking around, please be easy with the Carters. Mr. Carter is a proud man raising a proud family and Mrs. Carter works to pinch pennies to keep them afloat. I am sure he doesn't even know about the late-night trips."

"And boys," I turned to my sons, "I expect the information told here to go no farther. You know how I feel about gossip. I only told the chief because a major crime has been committed, which trumps minor issues. Now say Good-bye. Time to go."

After proper goodbyes to Corbin, Norman and the Chief, the boys raced down the hall toward the front door. Behind me, Norman confirmed the Carter's bags were indeed on top of Harvey. It sounded like Corbin might soon swap garbage duty for a road trip with the Chief.

By the time I reached the boys, Mrs. Dillon had them starting five hundred jumping jacks for running in the hall. "Mrs. Dillon, I need your assistance in receiving copies of my day planner."

"Chief mentioned that. If you have a minute, we can do that now." Mrs. Dillon offered.

"Yes, please." I replied, at the same time all three boys said, "No."

Hunter added, "Mom, we can't be late again."

"But without my planner, we will miss many other activities this week. It will be fine. Keep jumping." I countered.

I followed Mrs. Dillon as she carried the evidence bags of my purse contents to the copier room. Skylar and Travis finished counting to five hundred, with Hunter soon behind them. The room was a converted closet so I halted them at the door.

"What exactly do you need?" Mrs. Dillon inquired.

I thought about it for a moment. "Any idea how long he is going to keep my things?"

"I have no idea, hon," She replied. "Even if it turns out to have no bearing on the case, it could be months. If it is involved..." Mrs. Dillon let that hang in the air.

"Well, it is not involved," I asserted firmly, before my boys caught on to her implications.

Too late, as Travis questioned, "Mom, why would your purse be involved? Is that why you talked with the Chief so long? He thinks you killed Harvey?"

"Listen, boys, all of you. The police chief has to do his job, which includes looking through all the evidence for clues, interviewing people, and sifting through the facts that will catch a killer. You have seen the pile of trash they have to look through. One little thing in that mess might have come from the killer. So, we just have to be patient as they figure it out."

"Hey, goofus," said Hunter. "The police always have to check with the person who found the body. Their first suspect, but rarely the last. It is just a point to start, right, Mom?"

"Yes, Hunter, quite right," I said, "But watch your language. I have raised you to be nicer than that."

Turning back to Mrs. Dillon, "Let's have the next month of my planner, please, and my phone list from the back. That is four pages long."

Turning back to my sons, Hunter added, "Sorry, Mom. Besides, you can't even kill things you hate, like snakes."

"Thank you, Hunter, for being so reassuring." I rolled my eyes. Again. I was surprised they didn't just stay rolled in my head by now.

My patience and energy were truly waning, between the battle with the chief and the lingering headache.

"Here you go, Mrs. Bailey. This should do it for a little while." Mrs. Dillon called my attention back to the present.

"Thank you, Mrs. Dillon." I replied, glancing at my watch. "Boys, march, double time. Now!"

So excited to finally leave, they didn't see Doc McCarthy coming in the front door. Folders fluttered to the ground as Skylar and Hunter caught the older man before he could fall crashing to the ground.

"Whoa! What is the rush, my boys?" Doc McCarthy had delivered the twin speed demons, as he did all my children.

"Sorry, sir. We are late for jazz band," Skylar explained.

"Not too late to pick up the mess," I said.

"We know, Mom," Travis gathered some of the photographs and flipped them right side up.

"Thank you, boys, but be careful just to touch the edges of the photographs and not the pictures themselves." Doc cautioned.

"Cool! Body parts. Is this from the autopsy?" Hunter placed a pile into my outstretched hands.

I took one look at the pictures and wished I hadn't. My queasy stomach had enough of poor Harvey up close and personal last night.

My male offspring adore the morbid side of life. It started with mummifying a chicken for an Ancient History class. As we studied other time periods, many animals have followed suit at the hands of Hunter and younger brother Travis while Skylar preferred to research dungeons.

Thankfully the girls enjoy creating costumes and cooking delicacies from the same time periods. Not to be one-sided, the girls have helped with mummies and burials while the boys have cooked a few meals. Creative projects that inspire learning is un-schooling at its finest!

To calm my stomach and finish the job at hand, I concentrated on placing in order the numbers in the corner of the pages. Though with some numbers found in different corners, I still had a quick glance of each picture. Ugh!

As I glimpsed Harvey's body on the examination table, my mind raced back to the same question: Who could have done this to Harvey and why?

Harvey was a simple soul. For twenty plus years he had earned a living at the Workshop, a company that specifically hired those who were mentally delayed. In his off hours, we would see him wandering the streets through all kinds of weather, but always making it home in time for dinner.

"Thank you, my dear." Doc said, bringing my mind back to the present. "I need to drop these off for the Chief to fax copies to the state attorney."

"Good-bye, Doc. I apologize for my crew."

"No worries. Learn the lesson, boys, rushing does not equal safe arrival," Doc called as we hurried to the Purple People Eater.

Chapter Eight

THE BAND SHELL at the city park was five short blocks from the police station. The Charlottesville Jazz Band was already practicing when I dropped the boys off, preparing for the weekend fund-raiser. Various bands and choirs would be providing music throughout the day for the hundreds of expected visitors.

For the third year in a row, Hunter played the saxophone and Skylar played the trombone, but this was Travis's first year with percussion instruments. Our house band was rounded out with Audrey on flute and Emily had just started Clarinet but the girls declined to join the jazz band.

At the other end of the park was my next stop, Brummel's IGA grocery store. After dropping off the boys with their instruments, I drove the Purple People Eater into store's parking lot so I could reload the kitchen with some much-needed supplies. Audrey needed more flour if she was to bake cookies for the church meeting, and we needed six gallons of milk to last the week, plus a few odds and ends.

I decided to park in the rear of the parking lot, farthest from the store, for two reasons: The Purple People Eater required a wide turning berth and two parking spaces. Bracing for the onslaught of curious conversation, I headed into the store.

From three different aisles I heard friendly calls.

"Hello, Rainbow, I am surprised to see you out," called Nancy Parker as she checked-out.

"I would still be lying in bed if that had happened to me!" said Lesley, the checkout girl.

"Are you sure you're okay?" asked Mrs. Penant, my retired third grade teacher.

Doing my best to respond in kind to the friendly comments, I replied on the move, "No time like the present. I have a family to feed. Accept for a few bumps, I am just fine."

"I thought you liked surprises," a disembodied voice called from behind the milk cartons, making me jump once again.

"Only when they are good surprises and last night was definitely not good," I said, piling three packages of cream cheese for our breakfast into the cart.

Mr. Brummel, the store owner, came out of the cold, "Here is something that shouldn't be a surprise. You have been the talk of the town by almost everyone today."

That was definitely not a surprise. "I gather all the town cooks made an early run on casserole supplies?"

"What can I say? Gossip and tragedy are good for my business." His shrug belied the sparkle in his eyes. Mr. Brummel himself was a major hub of the well-oiled grapevine. "Well, what is the news? The real news, not stories circulating the grapevine."

While Corbin had wormed a promise to keep the full story to myself, I knew the neighbors had begun spreading the news before my head hit the pillow. Which meant, by now, the rumors must be pretty creative.

Keeping the details to myself, I presented the basic true story, if only to bring the mountainous lies back down to mole hill size. "The real story is that I am a klutz. I was cleaning out my van, but dropped the wrong handful into the dumpster. When I attempted to retrieve the good stuff, I rolled right in, landing on poor Harvey. The police took over from there. It is not a very glamorous story, I'm afraid. And, no, I am not interested in what is circulating."

"And, please," I added. "I only told you the real story to help correct the rumor."

"Who, me? You know I am as quiet as a church mouse." He winked consentingly, as he placed five gallons of milk in the cart for me. "But I think I hear Ruthann in aisle six."

"Thanks for the warning," I replied.

Mrs. Ruthann Marlin was the oldest living descendant of Charlotte Jensen, for whom our town was named. In her mind, that meant offering an opinion on everyone's business and how it reflects on the community at large. Since we didn't see eye-to-eye on those reflections, restocking my chocolate stash would have to wait.

Instead I dashed two aisles over for the baking items for Audrey. While price-checking the brown sugar special, I heard a voice I recognized float over the top of the aisle. "Of course, I would never wish anyone harm, but I, for one, am glad Harvey is gone. He was a creep, always peering over my son's bushes as he walked past. It was like he was looking for something or someone." Judy Thiessen said, evidently more than willing to contribute to Mrs. Marlin' obsession.

"I even caught him once when I was babysitting my beautiful granddaughter Carmen one afternoon. We were outside enjoying the late afternoon sun to help get rid of her cough. She had just fallen asleep on a blanket when I felt someone watching me. When I asked Harvey what he wanted, he said he was looking for my daughter in law, as if they were best friends! But I had never heard her mention his name before."

"Oh," crooned Mrs. Marlin loud enough for the whole store to hear, "That would have given me a fatal scare."

"Not me, thanks to the kick boxing class I know some moves," assured Judy. "And I had my grand-daughter to take care of. I marched over to him and told him I would call the cops if ever I saw him again near their house!"

"Oh, how brave you were," exclaimed Mrs. Marlin.

I placed the last list item into my cart and rushed to check out while they were too busy entertaining each other to notice me. I refuse to participate in that part of the grapevine.

One-sided stories like that only hurt people, especially for Harvey, who was no longer here to defend himself. Harvey was not born blessed to be a rocket scientist, but he certainly wasn't a danger to anyone. Not the Harvey I ever knew.

Their voices moved down the aisle toward the front as I reached the cash register. Time to scoot, as I had neither the time nor energy to fend them off today. Luck was with me, I paid and loaded my goodies into the van before the busybodies realized I had escaped.

Ruthann attempted to wave me down as I drove by the front door. Smiling, I politely returned the wave. Though I didn't like her style, it would do me no good for her to know that. She was a very influential person in our community. I didn't have to like her, but I respected her influence.

Chapter Nine

AS SOON AS THE PURPLE PEOPLE EATER pulled up to the curb on City Park road, my good friend Jill Jensen jumped from her baby blue van and pounced with a big bear hug. "Oh, Boo, how awful for last night. Although, if you don't mind me saying, I am glad it was anyone but me."

I laughed, "Oh, but you didn't see me making a fool of myself. And in front of Corbin's new boss. So, tell me, what story did you hear?"

"One? I have heard at least four!" she teased. "Please tell me the real story."

By the time I finished my condensed tale of woe, including the damage to Chief Flint shoes, she was laughing so hard her eyes were tearing up.

"I am so sorry," she said between giggles. "I know it is not funny, but I could just picture you tumbling in. And then the look on the Chief's face. That had to be priceless."

"Laugh all you want, but you still have your van, purse, and phone, and you are not the number one person of interest," I replied.

She stopped laughing. "Well, that explains why you haven't been returning my phone calls. But you are kidding me about being a suspect, right? You have got to be kidding! Either that or the Chief is nuts."

"Well, I am the one who found the body, much to my family's chagrin," I shrugged. "Has the Chief spoken to you yet?"

"No, not yet. Well, I haven't been available much today, with driving Katie to school, then work at the store, shopping for groceries and now Katie from the school to this." Jill's daughter Katie also played in the Jazz band with the boys. "When he does come to talk to me, I will certainly give him a piece of my mind on that subject. There is no way you could have hurt Harvey. You seem to be one of the few who really liked him."

"What do you mean?" I asked.

"Well, with this event on everyone's lips, I have heard three different type of responses. Some are sad, and some are more relieved than sad." Jill paused. "I am not saying any of these people would have hurt Harvey, but they are glad they don't have to see him walking around anymore."

This was news to me, but then I tried to stay out of the rumor mill. "And the third group?"

"Well, a few seemed very quiet when they heard the story. You know, the usually talkative people being uncharacteristically hush."

Before I could ask more, the children came running with their instruments. Chit-chat time was over, it was time for both of us to go back to our errand lists.

"See you at the meeting tomorrow." Jill gave me a quick hug before rushing off to her car. "But call if you need anything."

"Thanks, friend." I waved, as she drove away first, allowing more space for that big van to pull into traffic. My next stop was to pick up the girls at the Pit Stop.

The kitchen area was a scene of domestic bliss. Martin, Emily and Audrey were working side by side measuring, mixing and rolling dough for tomorrow's Chicken Dumpling soup special.

"Oh, good, you are back," called Martin, his sleeves rolled up past his elbows in attempt to keep them clean. Today his plan wasn't working, but boy, was he cute when he was covered in flour. That attraction was how we ended up with five children.

I smiled, wiping some flour off his cheek. "Oh, did I forget something?"

"No. Just happy to see you returned safe from the lion's den," he said, leaning in for a kiss. "Orange is so not your color."

"Martin!" I scooped a handful of flour and threatened to blow it on him.

Laughing, he quickly spun me around so the flour was aimed at the wall, kissed my cheek, and asked, "So, how did it really go?"

Snuggled in his arms, my temper melted. "Just fine. We reviewed my statement, added a few details I remembered today, and that was that."

"You don't have to worry, Dad. Mom told the chief to leave her alone. `I have no motive'," Travis mimicked my voice. "We heard that down the hall in the garage."

Hunter said, "We even helped Corbin with trash duties."

"And we saw pictures of the dead body," Skylar added.

I twisted around in Martin's arms and gave him a big kiss. "See, no worries."

"Well, in that case," he added, over a chorus of "ewww" from our children, "I do have a job for you. Paula from Harvest House called. She has also been over blessed with food baskets and was hoping we could help her."

I sighed, "Did you tell her we already have plenty of food from the well-wishers?"

"Yes, but she wasn't really offering to share. She wants the food, but she doesn't have the room to store it." He turned me back around to face the kids. "I think we can make the room in our freezer, and we have the workforce to make it happen."

"That explains the old boxes of plastic ware I see on the counter," I said.

"I thought we could divide the larger casseroles into smaller servings, and bring it back here for storage," he suggested.

"Hmm, and after we do all this, we can return part of the food every week, and they end up with almost new meals every day," I said.

"You read my mind," he said. "Oh, and she hopes to share with Hilltop House, too."

Harvest House, where Harvey lived, was a resident home for men with mental disabilities. Hilltop House was the women's equivalent. Each housed about six to eight people.

"That much food! Sounds like I will need an army of help. How many can you spare?" I asked, looking at the mess, wondering who I should put to work before I strangle my beloved children.

Domestic bliss had evaporated. Travis was threatening Emily with a handful of flour over her head, while Skylar and Hunter were trying to steal Audrey's dough. If Martin and I didn't organize them soon, there would either be a revolt, or a food fight.

"You can take them all. Molly will be here soon. She can help me finish and clean up." Martin declared.

Molly Mackan, a high school senior, worked for Martin three afternoons a week and on Saturdays. We all helped at the shop a few hours a week, as necessity dictated, but even for a family business, under-aged children were limited by the number of hours and types of work.

I clapped for attention, "Okay, you heard your father. Girls, wash up. Boys, move our groceries into the fridge here to keep the milk cold and load up the plastic ware. We have a job to do."

Due to the size of our town, nothing is more than fifteen minutes away. In half that time I pulled up behind Harvest House and we knocked on the kitchen door. Johnny Nettles, another Harvest House resident answered the door as if he was just waiting for a knock.

"Come in, Come in, Mrs. Bailey. Miss Paula told me to let you in. She said you would be helping in the kitchen. She said people keep bringing food because Harvey died. But, why? He doesn't need food if he died." Normally solid and confident, Johnny unabashedly collapsed into tears and hugged me tight. "Why did Harvey have to go? He was my friend. Why did he have to leave me?"

"Johnny, I know you are sad." I tried to calm him with words he would understand. "Now is the time to remember going to church with Harvey every week. You know Harvey is now with Jesus, and that is a very happy place to be."

"But I miss him. He was my friend." Johnny sniffled.

"We all miss him, Johnny, and it is alright to be sad, for a little while. But I don't think Harvey would want to stay sad. You have friends like Miss Paula and the other men here." I said, untangling myself from him arms. "Now why don't you take Emily's hand and sit at the table. Skylar, can you fetch Johnny a glass of milk, please? Hunter, find a plate and some cookies. I think we could all use a snack."

The noise of cabinet doors opening in the kitchen was like a beacon to the other men who lived here. Ian Stewart, the youngest of the men, arrived shortly followed by Brian Kress, Matthew Inness, Kevin Preavy and Scott Applestone. Each accepted a plate and glass quietly before heading to their own seat.

Wondering where her men had disappeared to, Paula Newman, retired high school teacher turned house-mother, walked in with arms full of more gifted food.

"I hope the snack is alright with your schedule." I said, accepting the casserole to place with the others. "They just seemed to need a pick-me-up."

"Oh, bless you, Rainbow, and thank you for coming. Our schedule is non-existent today. My boys didn't go to work today due to the incident. And, as you can see," Paula waved her hand at the counter top, "we have had many, many house-calls. No rest for the weary at heart it seems."

She gave Johnny a pat on the back. "Johnny here has been my right-hand man, answering the door if he recognizes the visitor. The others, well, being social is not their strong suit, and while some of our visitors truly care, many just want to gossip."

"Well, we are here to work." I said. "Why don't you pick what you want for dinner, and then sit down to rest with the men. If the doorbell rings, we will take care of it. You can count on the Bailey crew to get this kitchen sorted."

"Umm, just pick something simple for tonight. Thank you so much for this. I really could use a good sit." Paula slumped into a chair. Emily quickly delivered an extra plate of cookies.

"Oh, you are such a sweet-heart," declared Paula.

"Thank you," replied Emily.

"You are all just wonderful to help us today," Paula proclaimed. "I hope we are not too much trouble."

"Not at all. Happy to help," I said, nodding to the children to begin. "We will set aside the chicken casserole and fresh Cobb salad for tonight. Now you sit and we will take care of this in no time."

It wasn't hard to organize my children. They were used to helping at the Pit Stop and church potlucks. Audrey and Emily, with the best handwriting, were placed in charge of labeling and noting the donations. Starting at one end of the kitchen, they wrote down the type of food, the type of container, and who brought it. I planned on asking Aunt Irene to print up some thank you notes for Paula to sign later in the week. They also recorded any special ingredients, in case of allergies, on the freezer labels.

Travis set out containers in front of the twins who divided the food into manageable portions. He also washed the dishes. I put the food in the freezer or the van for transport to the Pit Stop, in between playing butler. To the phone callers, I politely but firmly asked them to call back in the next few days as the residents needed some rest. I said the same to the two people at the door after collecting their donated food items.

Even though this house was overflowing with food already, I accepted every item offered. To refuse any would be an insult, and in this small community, that was trouble in the making. Paula had enough trouble now with Harvey's suspicious death.

In just under thirty minutes, we had the clutter vanquished and counters wiped clean. My children were rewarded with cookies of their own and Johnny even treated them to some of his private soda-pop stash.

One more chime announced the arrival of Chief Flint, as surprised to see me open the door as I was to see him, with the youngest officer Eric Perdale. "You sure get around, Mrs. Bailey. I didn't see Harvest House on your schedule for today."

"Just neighbors helping neighbors. We were asked to help in the kitchen, as their kitchen overflowed with blessings." I explained, as I led the way. "Would you like to join our little cookie party?"

He raised his eyebrow at me, so I amended my statement. "Party may have been too strong of a word." I added quietly, "The men were at wits-end anxious so we all sat down for a snack. Please, join us."

He shook his head, getting straight to business. "We are just here to ask questions."

He followed me into the dining room as I made the introductions. None of the men would look at the Chief, though a few smiled at Officer Perdale. Kevin rocked in his chair, Matthew and Brian pulled their hair, while Ian and Scott stared at the floor. Johnny cleaned off the opposite side of the table, scrubbing at an invisible spot.

Not good. The new chief needed to learn more about Harvey to solve the murder. If only Johnny, the newly appointed leader of the group, would open up. Then the others would give the chief a chance.

As I finished introductions, Paula added, "Boys, Chief Flint would like to be a friend, to us and to Harvey."

Audrey, who understood the social aspects of food as well as her father, accepted the dirty plates for washing and then handed Johnny a new plate with cookies. Coaching Johnny, she said, "Chief Flint only wants to find who hurt Harvey, and he needs your help to do that, Johnny. You can help him."

Johnny shuffled toward the Chief without looking at him. Placing it on the table in front of the guests, Johnny stuttered, "Wo.. wo.. would, you like sssssome of Har.. Har.. Harvey's coo.. cookies?"

"Those were Harvey's favorite kind," Paula added.

For a few moments the Chief continued to stand. Realizing that everyone in the room was waiting for him, he slowly pulled out a chair and sat down. "Yes, thank you. I would love to try Harvey's favorite cookies."

After his first bite, he paused and added, "Would you like to know something, Johnny? Double chocolate chip is my favorite, too."

As Chief took another bite, Johnny smiled and one by one all the men reached for another cookie. Officer Eric pulled up a chair to join them, with notebook in one hand and a cookie in the other. With the ice broken, I decided it was time for us to leave.

As my boys were securing the food in the back of the van and the girls sweeping and mopping the floor, Paula asked for one more favor.

"Rainbow, could you help with one last chore? I haven't had the heart to go to Harvey's room since we learned of his death last night. But Flandan's Funeral Home was asking for some clothes for his burial. Would you help me?"

"Of course." I was not about to leave her in the lurch. "Do you think you are up to it now?"

"Yes, please, while the boys are busy downstairs. I thought of asking Johnny, but you know the boys just don't handle tragedies like this well. He has been a real blessing today, but, well, I think it would be too much for him, where as I have been through this before."

"I remember," I said, thinking back over eighteen years when Paula's husband died shortly after her retirement from teaching high school. His funeral was the day before Martin and I married in the same church.

My girls joined us for the trek upstairs, giving the chief more privacy for his questions in the kitchen, while the boys waited in the living room. Paula had the master bedroom on the main floor, but each of the boys had their own small bedroom upstairs. Harvey's room, the largest because he had lived there the longest, was at the end of the hallway, with a window facing the street.

"Harvey didn't always keep the neatest room, but he did clean it when asked." Paula rambled on as we walked. "And he always put his dirty laundry down the bathroom chute in time for laundry day."

We stopped at his closed door. Paula took a deep breath as she turned the knob.

Based on her description, I expected to see a room like a typical teenager, with bed sheets a mess, socks and shoes scattered, and maybe a dirty dish or two. What we found was much, much worse.

The mattress was half off the bed, pillow shredded, and drawers dumped. His closet had been emptied, with the contents everywhere.

Paula gasped so sharply, I reached out to steady her. "I take it Harvey was usually cleaner that this?"

"Yes. No. I mean I check it every month, but I have never seen it like this," Paula said.

"Do you think any of the other men could have done this?"

"Absolutely not! They have a healthy respect for each other's personal belongings. I make sure of that. And Harvey was like a big brother to them, always caring for them. They would never do this to his room." She beckoned to the mess. "Besides, he usually kept it locked, which is why I brought my keys."

"Audrey, Emily, stay here with Paula. I think we need to get the Chief in on this." I announced.

Chapter Ten

DOWNSTAIRS THE BAILEY BOYS were playing Uno in the living room with the men, giving Chief Flint and Johnny time alone in the kitchen. My determined march through the kitchen door alerted the Chief immediately that something was up. "Is there a problem, Mrs. Bailey?"

"Johnny, would you mind if I talk with the Chief alone for a moment?" I asked.

Johnny was crestfallen that I was taking his new friend away. I smiled at him, "I am sure the Chief will come back to chat again. While you wait, I think Travis would love to see the new train cars run in the living room."

"You noticed!" Johnny's smile lit up the room again. "No one else who came today wanted to see it."

"Of course, I noticed. You have another blue one. Now you have even numbered colors on the train." I shooed him into the living room and turned to the Chief. "I am sorry to disturb you just now, but we have a question upstairs. Did the police search Harvey's room today?"

"I don't believe that is any of your business, Mrs. Bailey," he replied, narrowing his eyes.

I took a deep breath while I quickly counted to ten, "Have it your way. But I was really hoping you could say yes, which would explain the mess in Harvey's bedroom that nearly gave Paula a heart attack."

He raised his right eyebrow at me as he motioned, "Show me."

At the top of the stairs, we found Paula now sitting on a chair in the hallway. As I neared the open door to the room, I stepped back to let Chief Flint have a good view.

After fully surveying the scene, he asked, "Did any of you walk into the room?"

"Maybe a step to see the whole room," I offered. "But I was sure the police officers, even while doing a thorough search, wouldn't have left the room like that. I moved everyone quickly back into the hall and went to find you."

"I see," he nodded. "Ladies, if you would please move back downstairs where you will be more comfortable until I take your statements." He pulled out his cell phone as we headed downstairs.

For the second day in a row I was entertained with red, blue and white flashing lights. Corbin arrived with a haggard look as if he just woke up from a nap. He walked right past me, forensics bag in hand, and headed upstairs. Officer Eric Perdale stayed downstairs with us, asking questions and trying to take statements.

Though the residents knew him, they refused to speak. It was bad enough to be in shock at losing a good friend, but now they had a crime scene in their own home.

Paula didn't know where to begin, as there had been so many people stop by. Audrey copied the list of the food dishes in the kitchen for police records. Paula attempted to put the list in order, but it was difficult when the over thirty different people stopped by and many of the visits overlapped.

Claiming to add to the statements, my twins cornered poor Eric and asked more questions than answered. When they were finished, I wondered who had interviewed whom. Finally, Chief Flint and Corbin returned, rescuing Eric from my boys, for a conference. Eric handed his notebook over to Corbin, before disappearing upstairs.

Acknowledging all the curious eyes, the Chief addressed the rest of us. "Thank you all for cooperating. At this time, it looks like someone was searching Harvey's room for something. I would appreciate it, Mrs. Newman, if you would look upstairs and let me know if anything is missing."

"I'll go with you, if you wish," I offered, as Paula struggled a bit to rise from her recliner.

Paula sighed with relief, "That would be most appreciated."

Chief Flint objected, "Is that necessary?"

"What do you mean?" Paula asked, using her teacher voice that commanded young hooligans' attention for over forty years.

"Well, I would prefer if Mrs. Bailey stayed away from the crime scene at this time."

"And why is that, young man?" commanded Paula.

"Well, Ma'am, this is the second crime scene Mrs. Bailey has found in twenty-four hours."

"Are you saying she is a suspect?"

"Just a person of interest at this time," he conceded, then added, "but the more she stays out of it, the better for her."

"Person of interest? You have any proof of wrong doing? It sounds to me like she has been a law-abiding citizen by reporting these things." Paula continued in her thirty-six-year veteran teacher voice, "Maybe they don't have people like that in the big city, mister, but you are in a small God-fearing American town now. And I know Rainbow would never hurt anyone, especially not any of *my* boys, or she would have me to deal with."

Paula turned to me, "You know that, don't you, Rainbow?"

"Yes, Ma'am." I flashed back to a younger Mrs. Newman, hundred-pound-when-wet English teacher, who stepped into the middle of a fight between a couple of three hundred-pound boys fighting in the hall, grabbed their ears and frog marched them to the principal's office.

"Rainbow, did you hurt Harvey?" Paula asked pointly.

"No, Mrs. Newman," I replied.

"Then that is good enough for me." She turned back to Chief Flint, "Chief, it looks like you need to get to work finding a new `person of interest'!"

From the frown on his face, I envisioned a few choice responses he considered. Realizing this was not a battle worth fighting at the moment, he capitulated.

"I thank you for your input, Mrs. Newman. May I escort you both upstairs to complete an inventory survey?" He asked, intending to keep me in sight.

"Yes, of course." Paula replied.

"In the meantime, Mrs. Newman, as legal guardian of these men, do you grant us permission to take their fingerprints? We need to match and eliminate any fingerprints that come from the household in order to discover any new persons of interest."

"Why certainly, Chief Flint. I will even show them by being the first." Paula smiled at him.

"Tomorrow. First thing in the morning, at the station?" Chief Flint said with a glance at me. "Would that be too early for you?"

"Nonsense, Chief, we start early as part of our routine," Paula replied. "A good routine helps us deal with the unexpected."

Chief nodded, motioning a clear path to the stairs. As the three of us traipsed upstairs, I detected a half victory smile on the Chief's face. He can have his early bird's skinny worm. Night owl's rabbit soup for me.

Eric greeted us at the entrance to the room. "Mrs. Newman, we need to know if anything is missing, as it seems the person or persons ransacked the room fast looking for something. Knowing that would greatly help the investigation."

"Can we move anything?" Paula asked.

Chief replied, "Yes, we finished processing the room for fingerprints and recorded the damage with photographs."

Paula and I stepped carefully into the room, afraid to trip over or break things buried in the mess. I centered the mattress and made the bed just enough to create a workspace. Paula began working with the boxes from the closet. I rehung the clothes while Chief Flint watched my every move.

"Oh, I don't know," sighed Paula after filling five shoe boxes with twenty or more still sitting empty. "All my boys seem to be little pack rats. As long as they found places to store it all, I usually didn't fuss at the amount, but right now this is just too much. It will take days to go through it all and even then, I might not know if something is missing."

"The real reason we came up here was to find funeral clothes," I stated. "I suggest this gray suit with the white shirt and his favorite tie." Then, inspired by the mouth-watering smells that wafted up the stairs, I added, "Break time, I think. Dinner will give you strength."

In the hallway I inquired, "Chief, could Paula finish cleaning this up tonight and call with a list of anything that is missing?"

"That would be fine. Eric will be here to supervise." He consented, offering his arm to Paula. "I know it has been a long day."

We found Paula's boys actively setting the table.

Audrey explained, "They were starting to get hungry again. Hunter found the chore chart for this week and Johnny read the assignments. Skylar, Emily and I will have the food ready in a few minutes."

Paula perked up instantly, "That is just wonderful, Audrey. Thank you so much. I didn't realize how late it was getting. And, please, everyone, we have plenty of food. You all must join us."

Chief Flint declined, "No, thank you. We have to get these reports in."

"Well, a man has to eat, too, but suit yourself," stated Paula, as she lined up her boys to receive a plate of food.

With Officer Perdale left behind to supervise the Bailey activities, the Chief drove off with Corbin, but not before I managed to sneak him a doggy-bag of his favorite chicken casserole. Chief Flint might work well on an empty stomach, but after growing up with Corbin, I knew my cousin functioned best on a full stomach.

Using the landline, I called Martin with updates so he would not worry about us, nor pack a dinner home that night. After dinner dishes were washed and put away, Paula and I headed back upstairs, with a plate of food for

Eric standing guard. With the residents retiring to their own rooms for the evening, my crew joined us. Under Paula's supervision, I put my girls in charge of the dresser, while the boys restocked the closet with all the knickknacks and collectibles.

Paula was right, Harvey certainly had plenty of things in his room. There were large items such as airplane models and basic items like marble rocks. It was pointless to try to put all the things back in their places. Even Paula didn't know how Harvey had held on to so much. We just wanted to make his room nice out of respect. Knowing how much would be given away soon, I sent Skylar and Hunter to retrieve a few boxes to hold the various items Harvey held dear. Besides, the other residents would probably choose a few mementos over the next few days.

We all worked pretty quietly on the sobering job, lost in our own thoughts. What could Harvey have that someone wanted so badly?

"Mrs. Newman?" asked Travis, breaking into our thoughts. "Does this part of the train belong up here?"

Paula took the train Travis held out and gripped it tight. "Yes. It matches the coal car downstairs. Harvey always played with this car so much that it caused some fights with the boys. So, I bought him another one for his very own on his birthday three years ago. He kept it in his room when they weren't playing."

Paula handed it back to Travis to put in the box. It slipped out of his hand and bounced on the floor, knocking the coal door open.

"I'm sorry," said Travis, "Did I break it?"

"No, that was the reason Harvey liked it. The back-coal door opened," explained Paula.

In a short time, we were done. The room looked much better. According to Paula, it looked cleaner than it had in years.

"Can you tell if anything is missing from the room?" Officer Eric asked Paula.

"I have no idea. It looks like it is all here, but I didn't know about every little thing they owned. As long as it wasn't an animal or food, they could have it up in their room," she explained, as she locked the room on our way out.

As we headed downstairs, I couldn't believe how dark the night sky had become. The Pit Stop had been closed for a little while now. Martin would be headed home soon, probably just putzing at the shop until we arrived with the divided food containers. Officer Perdale headed back to the office to report no missing items.

On our way through the living room, Travis stopped by the other train set to see if that long coal car opened up.

"Hey, Mom, look what I found."

As I walked over, Travis pulled out a piece of paper from the hidey-hole. He unrolled it on the train table. Drawings on the paper looked like a map to somewhere. There were markings that looked like trails, with houses and such on the way. But some of the lines trailed off the edge of the paper where it seemed to be torn from the pad.

"Oh, that Harvey", laughed Paula, "always making little hunts and games. He loved secret messages. Of course, they were easy for me, but they stumped the other boys for a while."

Skylar came to look. "It looks like part of our town, going out a little farther towards the Emerson Woods. See, here is the highway. That is the north stoplight."

"No, that is the stoplight at Miller street. But the map might continue up to the North stoplight," added Hunter.

"Are you talking about near the cemetery side of Emerson Woods?" Audrey asked. "We went hiking with my Girl Scout troop that way last year. Remember that, Emily?"

"Yes, we were letter-boxing. I remember you found a black box looking thing, but the location was off. Mrs. Connor looked at but said it wasn't the right kind of box. So, we went on until we found the right box," answered Emily.

Hunter asked, "Did you look in it?"

"No," admitted Emily.

"Do you think you could find it again?" insisted Hunter.

"Why should we want to do that?" I wondered.

"Yeah, Mrs. Connor said to leave it alone since it wasn't the gray box we were looking for. This one was black. I know she opened it, frowned, and then put it back quickly." Audrey explained. "Why? You think it is important?"

Skylar, agreeing with Hunter in their silent twin way, replied, "Because it might mean something to Harvey."

"Oh, I bet this is just part of his silly games he played," Paula indulged. "I doubt it means anything."

Hunter turned to Audrey, insisting, "Well, can you find it again?"

"We could try," she said, looking at Emily.

"But not tonight. We need to scoot with the food." I declared. The food was stored in coolers from the Pit Stop, but it would spoil if we did not reach the deep freezers soon. "Let us continue the discussion at home."

We said our good-byes to Paula and the boys and quietly left.

Chapter Eleven

AFTER DROPPING THE HARVEST HOUSE FOOD at the Pit Stop's walk-in freezer, we hurried home. Though it was bedtime for most families, our evening work was just beginning.

Skylar and Hunter's assignment notebook for the day was a disaster. They were too busy being teacher in the morning, and musicians, detectives and household butlers in the afternoon. All the children had been tremendous help without complaining, and that good character development counted more to me than any grades. Still, the work needed to be done, so I sent all three boys to the school room with math and science books.

Audrey and Emily joined me in the kitchen to make Pecan Supreme cookies for tomorrow's meeting, since they finished more schoolwork in the shop while the boys had band practice.

Martin joined the boys. Excited voices floated down the hallway, indicating more talking than studying. I would have to ask Martin for those stories later. The twins' favorite subject was Formal Logic and its practical applications in life. They loved to get separate answers from us parents, then use it against us in a logical battle of wits. It was almost a daily struggle, but Martin and I worked to stay on the same page as parents. Our battle plan goal was to be fair, but firm, which required communication.

When the cookies were finished and the dishes washed, I lit the stove under the kettle. The children put on their pajamas while I set out the hot chocolate mugs.

"So," Martin chose the oddest shaped cookies from the cooking racks to serve as a late snack, saving the best for the ladies tomorrow. "A map in the caboose?"

"I thought the boys were giving you an earful instead of doing their schoolwork."

"That is not an answer," Martin rebuked. "The boys want to follow the trail. Your thoughts?"

I leaned against the counter, trying to pin down the words that reflected both head and heart, "This whole experience reminds me of Sunday's sermon on Jonah and the whale."

"You told me you were in the dumpster less than two minutes before you spit yourself out," he laughed.

"True," I admitted. "But the point implies. Given the choice, I would not have gone in the dumpster, and by default I would not have found Harvey. By now he would be buried under a week's worth of garbage at the dump, reported missing, maybe never to be found. That is not right either."

"Agreed," Martin sighed. "What happened to Harvey was horrible, and someone compounded the issue by trying to hide it. I just wish it wasn't you that found him. And now the boys want to dive into Harvey's business."

"Dive in? Cute," I rolled my eyes.

"Sorry, no pun intended," Martin frowned.

Just two steps for me to gather him into my arms. "Look, this hike tomorrow. We might not find the supposed treasure. It might not mean anything if we do. But one positive in this adventure: we will have safety in numbers."

"And you think it is worth it?" he asked.

"I do. Harvey was dishonored in the trash. I think the boys want to do something to help me, and in the end, maybe to honor Harvey." I explained. "Also, they are enjoying a bit of the mystery. I believe you were the one who started reading the Hardy Boys as a bedtime story years ago."

"You approved, if I remember," Martin smiled. The kettle whistled as pairs of feet thumped down the stairs. "You agreed it would teach them logical reasoning and creative thinking."

"It did encourage them to think outside the box, just like we hoped." I said, mixing the hot chocolate and adding ice cubes and two marshmallows in each. "Only in this case, they are searching for a box."

In a few minutes, we were all comfortably sipping in the living room, gathered around a map of the county, comparing it to Harvey's map.

"Here is the service road through the back entrance," explained Skylar. "It looks like the road on Harvey's map here. See where it crosses the creek?"

"That makes this direction North. Which way did you come in?" Hunter asked the girls.

"We parked in the main parking lot here, and headed down Tiptop trail. The rest of the markers that we followed I will have to see to remember," said Audrey. "Or, I could try to call our leader, Mrs. Connor, to see if she remembers."

Martin interjected, "No can do. Mr. Connor came for lunch mentioning his mother-in-law was having problems with kidney stones, so Mrs. Connor left for the airport at five this morning. Probably not the best time to be contacting her."

"Sorry to hear that," I said. "Add the Connor family to your prayer list, kids."

"Well, I believe she printed the directions off some website, though." Audrey added, getting us back on track.

Hunter and Skylar ran to the computer to see if they could find it.

"What about you, Emily? Do you remember any more?" asked Travis.

"Not really, sorry," Emily frowned.

"That is OK." I consoled her. "I still think this is a wild goose chase. But we can make the time for it tomorrow, if we all get an early start." We would miss more school book time this week, but exploring the real natural sciences is better than books.

Martin turned to me, "Are you going to invite Corbin to join you?"

"If we find something, we will call him," I promised. "Oops. Almost forgot I don't have my phone anymore."

"We will bring ours, Mom" called Skylar from the computer in the school room.

"We think we found it," said Hunter, as the printer started up.

"Good. So, the schedule tomorrow is to go for the hike in the morning, then drop you kids off at home while I go to the church fund-raiser meeting, and you tackle more school. In the evening, I go clean Power Fitness," I organized the day.

Emily shuddered. "Are you sure you want to go back there? I mean, what if Harvey was killed there and the killer comes back. I wouldn't want to be there."

"That is because you are not as brave as Mom. You are a chicken when it comes to anything." Travis teased his sister.

"Travis!" scolded Martin. "Apologize right now."

"Sorry, Emily," Travis mumbled.

"Well, Emily, if truth be told," I smiled at her so she wouldn't worry. "The memory of that night does not encourage me to go back, but I can't let that stop me. Though, I will definitely make sure I do not park next to the dumpster again. Over all, I feel perfectly safe being here in our town."

I looked at everyone and added with more perk than I felt, "Now place your order for sandwiches, and we will have a picnic while we are in the forest preserve. Then put your cups in the sink and head to bed. Say your prayers and lights out. We want to get an early start."

By the time all the children were in their rooms reading or sleeping, I was ready to climb in bed myself. I might have slept half the morning away, but this day sped by fast and furious. I could barely keep my eyes open as I washed the dishes. Martin dried the cups and led the way towards the bedroom.

"Now tell me, how are you really doing?" He asked as I spread toothpaste on my brush.

"I guess the main shock has worn off. Other than that, I am dead tired. Oops," I replied. "My turn for a bad choice of words, I guess."

Leaning back against the bathroom counter, waiting his turn, Martin said, "I am still worried you are still the number one suspect. I think the boys are, too, based on their recounting the day’s events."

"Grumfff!" I choked on the toothpaste in my mouth. After coughing and spitting the rest I turned to question him. "Why?"

"Things the new Chief said or didn't say. Beside the fact that he wouldn't release your purse or cell phone, now you were found at a second crime scene. If I had known, I wouldn't have sent you to Harvest House."

"I understand that is basic police procedure to look into anyone near the body." I dismissed their concerns as I got ready for bed. "Anything else?"

"Families do not make good alibis, especially since your father spoke to you before talking to him," he paused. "The boys learned time of death was around an hour before class. Only your fast food receipt counts as a strong alibi. The rest is from family members. Adjusting for that could put you in town just in time."

As I considered this, Martin continued, "Corbin has not been very reassuring in answering their questions."

"I will have to speak with my dear Bro/Cous tomorrow." I said, referring to Corbin by my pet name for our relationship.

Martin put his hands on my shoulders, "Hey, I am just the messenger. But it does make me concerned. That is why I thought you might want to take a witness tomorrow."

I considered his implications. "Correct me if I am wrong but according to your assessment, even if we find something, the chief will believe it was a set up, and if I use Corbin, also my relative, as my witness, validity would still be in the question and he would be definitely caught in the crossfire. I don't want to do that either."

"I understand that," Martin agreed.

"On the other hand, I suspect that even if the girls' memories are correct, I don't think we will find anything having to do with Harvey. Then we would be also wasting valuable police time. But if it makes you feel better, you can let him know of our plans." I consented, then changed the subject as we climbed into bed. "Did the boys tell you anything else important or concrete?"

Martin smiled, "Not specifically. Just that this afternoon, they requested a lot of gelatin."

"Whatever for??"

"Oh, it seems that Doc reported that Harvey was stabbed in the back with something, but he doesn't know what. They remember some TV show using thick gelatin as a mold or model for something like this."

"Oy, these boys! I know we encourage them to use experiments to learn for themselves, not that I ever could stop them anyway, but what do they think they can do that the police can't do?"

"They are afraid the police will stop at you and look no further." Martin pulled me into his arms. "I am inclined to let them do this. Look, we don't know this police chief and he doesn't know you. I do know sometimes the police latch on to one person and stop looking for other suspects. The best way to prevent that is to find new evidence. I don't know how else to protect you. Besides, what do you think the boys will really find? If anything, they will just have fun with gelatin."

"I suppose it won't hurt, only make another mess for them to clean up." I laughing at that vision. The idea brought memories the twins at six years old deboning a chicken for the first time. We had to wash the counters, the floors, and the walls when they were finished.

Snuggling into my husband in bed, I reveled in his fresh baked bread smell. Having worked in a sandwich shop all his adult life, making pasta and other bread mixtures, his skin radiated a permanent yeasty aftershave. I felt safe in his arms.

"Martin," I said.

"Hmmm?" He replied, holding me close.

"I don't want you worrying about me."

"I always worry about the love of my life," he said. "But why shouldn't I?

"To convict anyone of murder, there has to be a motive. That is the key to this whole case. I don't have a motive to kill Harvey," I explained. "And I used to believe they would have a hard time finding a motive for anyone." Turning out the light, I added, "Unless you really stretch it, like in Judy Thiessen's case."

Martin was interested in that, "What do you mean?"

"I overheard her in the store today. Something about how Harvey would come by to talk to her daughter-in-law on his walks. Judy thought it was creepy and told him to leave. Even told Ruthann Marlin in the grocery store that she was glad Harvey was gone. Can you believe that? Harvey wouldn't have hurt anyone."

"You believe that because you took the time to get to know him. Not everyone cares that much," Martin said.

"Did the boys tell you about Paula shouting my innocence at Chief Flint?" I asked.

"Yes, I would have loved to see little Mrs. Newman starring nose to chest with Chief Flint," he laughed.

"So, you can see why I am not that worried. Now turn off your light and roll over so I can hug you."

I was asleep the minute my arms wrapped around the love of my life.

Chapter Twelve

"OOHS", "NOT QUITE" AND "TRY ANOTHER ONE" squeals emanating from the living room ushered in the morning sun. The great gelatin experiment was underway. I groaned, rolled over, and buried my head in my pillow. Memories of Harvey, dead in the morgue and my up-close discovery floated behind my eyelids. Not an auspicious beginning to another day, but I decided I might as well go see how the experiment was progressing. My only hope is that it wasn't blood colored gelatin.

"Good Morning, Mom." All five of my children gleefully called as they watched Audrey plunge a screwdriver into a tall extra thick rectangle of pale-yellow gelatin. Ugh! Yellow was better than blood color, but couldn't they have colored it a non-body color like blue or purple??

"Are you alright, Mom?" Emily asked as I leaned over and grabbed the counter quickly.

The three boys measured the depth, took a picture with the digital camera and recorded the notes on a big sheet of newsprint.

Martin came over to me, "Good morning, dear."

"Yes," I whispered, swallowing the lump in my throat, then repeated in a firmer voice. "Yes, I am fine. Good morning to everyone. Are you having fun? Did you learn anything yet?"

Travis pointed to the chart hung on the wall for family messages and assignments. "We have several pans of gelatin and gathered a variety of household and simple garage tools. We have listed what tool makes what size and shape of indentation."

Hunter continued, "We decided that just one person should do the stabbing so we can try to exert the same force each time." He stopped, then added, "That still isn't fool proof, as a measured machine would provide more consistent results, but it is the best we can do at the moment."

Skylar took it from there, "We started first using household tools, because we think there is a high chance the perpetrator came from kick boxing class, which usually consists only of women."

Everything they had reported up to that point sounded logical, but I still didn't like it. I felt aghast at the thought that my fellow kick boxers could have been involved. I knew all those ladies, and couldn't picture any of them doing this to someone. "Those are my friends you are talking about."

"Sorry, Mom, but the facts don't lie," apologized Skylar. "The class members had the best opportunity to move the body to the dumpster in the time between death and discovery, since sticking with their normal routine would create less suspicion."

Emily said, "Audrey is doing the stabbing, as she was the logical choice to represent the women. I am too small."

"But before you limit your suspects too much, don't forget how much Harvey weighed. It wouldn't have been easy to lift a full-grown man over the edge of the dumpster." Corbin said as he walked into the room.

"Good Morning, sleepy head." Corbin said to me, "Martin called me about your plans. No chief this time so I just came in."

"You are welcome anytime. You know that. So, are you going to join us? And are you sure you want to? You look like a zombie." I declared.

"Right back at you," He waved his hand to dismiss that idea. "I will be fine as soon as this case is wrapped up. Unfortunately, I can't go on the hike with you. The Chief and I have a list a mile long of people to interview, but do call me if you find something."

"Thank you, Corbin. I still feel better knowing you are aware of the plan." Martin shook Corbin's hand. "Now I need to go to work. Stop by for your picnic. Your orders are the first on my list." Martin gave me a hug as he left.

"I also came by the house because Martin said you were working on something else that might be case related." He turned to the kids and the experiment on the counter, and laughed "Interesting choice of color for the gelatin."

Corbin usually liked to see their science experiments, whatever the topics. He would join in like a kid himself.

While the boys explained their plan to him, I took the time to get dressed for the hike, and laid out a second set of clothes for the afternoon meeting. Knowing my family meant I probably would not have much time at home between events. When I returned to the kitchen, they were demonstrating thrusts of the most likely items.

Hunter explained, "We accidentally saw the pictures doc had taken of the wound. It wasn't a pin point like a screwdriver. It was more of flat slit. Here, Skylar and I drew what we remembered. Our samples seem to indicate that it could have been caused by scissors, or pruning shears. We know we haven't tried all the possibilities, but these are a sample of the most common items found in a house."

Corbin asked, "Why something from a house? Why not a tool from a particular type of job?"

"Well, the only suspects we know for sure in the area of that dumpster are the ladies from kick boxing. Women would most likely use a kitchen tool. And since Harvey was moved, it probably wasn't something from Power Fitness." Skylar continued.

"Interesting theory. How did you know he was moved?" Corbin said.

Hunter picked it up from there. "While at the police station, we could hear Mom mentioned seeing the dark stain of blood on a tarp, which was probably wrapped around him to hide Harvey and protect the vehicle used to move him. Now considering estimating time of death and when Mom's class starts, there are a couple of time scenarios...."

"How do you know when he died?" I asked.

"That fact was on page one of the autopsy report." Skylar rolled his eyes at me, like how could I have not noticed that fact. "Doc reported that Harvey died somewhere between six and seven that evening, but lawyers could argue slight variance to that. Now since we didn't arrive in town until about seven due to bathroom breaks, the chief probably still has you on his list, Mom, especially since arrival time is a little vague. We also could have sped along those roads and conceivably arrived earlier than that."

I sat down on the couch fast, before I fell over. "Are you trying to get me in trouble?"

Audrey came over to hug me. "That is what I thought when we talked about it last night. We are just trying to protect you, Mom. Really. To do that, we need the facts we can refute it."

"Did we guess right, Uncle Corbin?" Travis asked.

"Chief Flint hasn't said much, but that is one possible theory, and he has probably thought of it," Corbin hesitated. "However, he would still have the same problems. There is really no shred of evidence that proves anything, one way or the other. And, as I heard your mom pointed out to him, she has no motive."

Emily joined me on other side of me and snuggled in. Looking at her older brothers, she said. "You better come up with another theory, because Mom would never hurt anyone."

"Hey," called Corbin, getting down on his knees to look her in the eyes. "Who is the policeman here? Do you think I will let anything happen to my best cousin? I know Rainbow didn't do it. Damn if I am going to stop looking for evidence until we find the killer."

"Corbin!" I exclaimed. He knows I don't like swearing around the children.

"Sorry, Rainbow, but it is true." Corbin apologized.

"Besides, Emily, we have other, better theories, remember?" consoled Travis.

"No, she was sleeping during our conversation." reminded Audrey.

"What conversation? When?" I asked.

"After you went to bed, Travis and I got together with the twins." Audrey admitted. "We couldn't sleep after talking about it. That is also when we made the gelatin."

"Oh!" I was flabbergasted. I didn't realize they were that worried. And how in the world did Martin and I sleep through it?

"Just wait until you hear our other ideas," Travis fairly bounced in his seat.

"Yes," said Hunter, "Where was I?"

"Relocating the body," directed Travis.

"Yes, thank you." Hunter went on, "If Harvey had been killed in one area and the murderer could relocate the body, they would pick some place familiar. The killer had to come to Power Fitness often or is familiar with the area enough to know about the dumpster there."

"If that is true, that still includes half of everyone in town," I said.

"We think we can safely narrow that down, at least for a while, to active members of the Power Fitness class. To narrow it down ever further we need a possible motive, which we hope to find in the woods today," concluded Skylar.

Corbin clapped, "Excellent presentation."

"Are we right?" Travis cut in.

He looked at me, then spoke seriously to the boys, "I am not at liberty to discuss an active case, but since you are making some pretty good deductions, and I don't want you stepping all over our investigation, let me say this much:

"Yes, we believe he was moved. And, yes, he was stabbed, deep enough to penetrate his heart. We don't have the murder weapon yet. The professionals we have consulted have given us a list of possible objects. The rest of what you have here is pure conjecture." Corbin summarized.

Emily raised her hand, "Conjecture?"

“That means `good guesses', Emily." Corbin explained. "You are using very good reasoning skills and I can see you have listened quite well when I have discussed police procedure. I applaud your interest, but as you do your experiments, don't forget that this is an ongoing case in which someone died. It is a matter for the police. It is not a game."

"We know," said Audrey. "We are just concerned about Mom, that she is the only suspect. And we liked Harvey too."

Corbin nodded, "Well, the chief hasn't let me in on all his thoughts because I am related to Rainbow, but I can tell you from my experience that just her proximity to the body and the ransacked room would not be enough evidence to convict her. She has an alibi, though, as you pointed out, it is not 100%. Without a murder weapon or motive, we don't have much to connect her to the murder. So, what the police have as evidence against your mom is circumstantial at best and easily refuted.

"Does that make you feel better?" Corbin asked.

We all nodded, except for Emily, who frowned and raised her hand again, so Corbin added, "Circumstantial means that the facts that we know are not enough for anyone to try to claim that your mom did anything wrong."

"Oh," she smiled brightly at him, "Okay."

Hunter asked, "But you don't mind if we still try to follow that map?"

"No, I don't mind," Corbin agreed. "I agree with Paula that it is probably a silly game of Harvey's for the people he lived with. You found the map in the common area, right? Not in his room? So, have fun on your hike. Could I have a copy of it first, though, just in case?"

Skylar handed Corbin a piece of paper. "We thought you might want one."

"And we better get going soon, or we will run out of time." I added.

Corbin said goodbye to the kids. I walked him to the door while they found their boots and water bottles for the hike.

"Thank you for reassuring them." I said.

"Anything for my favorite nieces and nephews. Don't tell them, or it will go to their heads, but they are spot-on as far as our investigation. We have already asked the neighbors if they could list who came in during that time. And before you ask, no, I can't tell you what the neighbors said."

"When would I ever ask that?" I laughed.

"Well, even if you did, my lips are sealed," Corbin said.

"You already said a mouthful to the kids," I teased him.

"I only verified facts the kids had already figured out. But call me if you find anything at all in the woods. I mean it. Anything possibly connected to Harvey, the chief will want to know about it, ASAP." He gave me a kiss on my cheek. "Please be careful. We don't know why Harvey died. It could have been a complete accident, and someone just panicked instead of reported it. Or he was murdered, which means there is a killer out there."

With that announcement, he closed the front door behind himself.

'Thanks for the warning, Cousin,' I thought.

Chapter Thirteen

THE BOY SCOUT LEADER TRAINED my sons well, requiring a backpack for all hikes that included water bottles, notepads and pens, compass, personal first aid kit and pocketknife. All three boys had their backpacks and Audrey had one ready for us girls.

"Here's your boots, Mom," Travis placed the hiking boots in front of me.

"Everyone ready to go?" I asked. "Phones charged?"

Hunter had the twins' cell phone they share and Audrey had hers. With five kids, including three of them old enough to be a bit independent, I needed a way to contact them if plans changed. For this reason, our family owned four pay-as-you-go phones for basic communications only. This kind of plan also taught just how much time and money was spent on their phone. If the kids want to talk to someone for hours, they can do it from home, or they pay for it themselves.

We headed out to the Purple People Eater, picked up our lunch at the Pit Stop, and drove the short distance to the Emerson Forest Preserve main entrance on the edge of town. The Interpretive Center and Ranger Station had been the starting point for the girls' original trail. Their plan was to walk their memories while the boys kept an eye on Harvey's map.

"Hey, Mom, let's get a map of the trails as a reference," suggested Skylar.

"Hello, Frank," I called out to the park ranger awaiting visitors inside. "We need a map of all the trails."

"Oh, good, the Bailey crew is here. I heard you are hunting hidden treasures today. Mind if I tag along? I would love to find some new treasures in the woods."

"Aw, who told you?" asked Travis.

"Your father mentioned it when I called in an order for our Rangers meeting next Tuesday." Frank leaned over the counter to whisper to Travis, "Sorry, was it supposed to be a secret?"

"No. Well, maybe?" Travis whispered back. "It all depends on what we find, I think."

"Yes, Mr. Winter, you can come along." said Hunter. "Maybe you will see some trail markers we don't. Do you know about Letter-Boxing, and where some might be? We only have half of a map, and the girls' memories to go by."

"Yes, I know of five or six different letterboxes in the woods here. I don't have them marked on any maps because people enjoy the hunt by following the owner's instructions. Plus, from time to time they get moved by the owners. As long as the woods do not get tramped too much, it is a fine game for people to enjoy in the woods."

As Frank taped a sign to the door indicating he would be back in an hour, I quietly teased, "Did my husband put you up to this, maybe by offering a special on the food?"

"Not at all. Well, he did offer, but I turned it down." Frank explained. "Love my job with its many opportunities to get out of the office. And I, too, am curious if Harvey had his own box-hole here. I would often see him here. I just never thought to ask why. Now I might get the answer."

"Well, girls, which way do we go?" I asked the girls. "Lead the way."

Audrey and Emily led the way down Hump Back Trail. Along the way, Audrey saw a forked tree that looked familiar, a fallen tree, and the small waterfall. Hunter and Skylar marked our progress on the ranger's map and attempted to match it with the part of Harvey's map.

When we came to the large rock, Audrey paused. "I don't remember which way. We stopped here to look for a sign, but this is where I was dive-bombed by a bee, so I really wasn't paying attention."

My treasure hunters spread out, looking around in all directions. Both Hunter and Emily called out at the same time, but from different sides of the rock. Hunter found an X carved in the rock, while Emily found a star shape. While they were discussing which way to walk, Skylar found a half moon shape on another side.

"Now what do we do?" Travis asked.

Skylar laid the maps on the rock. "I see where we are on the trail map, and I think this rock is this large circle on Harvey's map. But Harvey didn't mark cardinal directions and these other bumps could be any hill on this trail."

"At least we are on both maps," Hunter replied.

Emily said, "I think we had lined up with the star and followed it out, but I don't remember how far."

Unanimously the kids decided we had one-third shot of finding it in either direction, so we might as well follow Emily's direction.

In single file, Emily, then Audrey, then the rest of us headed out from the star. After about fourteen paces, the girls came to a dirt patch.

Suddenly Audrey remembered, "It had been really wet and muddy that day, so I veered to the right, climbing over some fallen trees."

"I followed you, but the moss was slippery over one of the trees. I slipped and fell. You came back for me, and that is when you thought you had found something." Emily finished for her.

They went around to the right to climb over and then looked under all the fallen trees. Hunter and Skylar made a little wider walk doing the same thing. Frank and I waited on the trail with Travis watching the maps.

After the fifth tree, when they were almost around the mud pile and ready to get back in line, Hunter called out, "I see something. Over here. There is a hole in the crook of this tree, where these two branches meet."

Audrey joined him and agreed, "That is about the right height for the hole."

Ranger Winter cautioned, "Careful, boys, do not just reach inside the hole since it could be used by an animal now." He left the path, heading cautiously over the vegetation to help the boys.

Skylar found a stick and poked it in the hole. We heard a soft metal clank as it did.

Audrey reached in, as her leader did months ago, and pulled out a black metal toolbox, as Travis and I climbed over there to see. Inside we found a few knick-knacks and newspaper clippings, but the first clue that this belonged to Harvey was his initials "HH" etched inside the box lid.

Hunter dug into his pack to get out his phone to call Uncle Corbin, while Skylar dug into his to get out some latex gloves and the camera. Once I had Corbin on the phone and explained what we found, I handed the phone to Ranger Winter to give directions. Together they decided it was still best for Corbin to go to the main parking lot, since we were actually closer to where the end of the trail meets parking lot than from where we had started the trail.

"The Chief and I will be there in ten minutes." Corbin said. "Don't touch anything," he yelled as he hung up the phone.

Luckily for everyone involved, Corbin wasn't there to see all three boys just roll their eyes at him. They knew better than to touch it with their bare hands. They had already put on gloves to hold the loose objects as they moved them out, snapped a picture front and back and replaced it.

Frank just laughed as he watched the procedure. "Watch enough detective shows in school?"

"Just make sure you put everything back in the order you found it!" I cautioned. Ignoring their second eye roll that indicated they already knew that, I offered to go escort the police back here. The girls came with me, because if that really was an important crime scene, we didn't need to be trampling it up. Frank stayed to supervise the boys.

By the time we had walked back to the parking lot, we could see the flashing lights of Corbin's police cruiser coming up the drive. At least the siren wasn't blaring so as not to scare the fauna in the forest. They parked closer to where we exited, on the other end of the parking lot than the Purple People Eater.

No friendly greetings graced Chief Flint's lips. Just a gruff, "Lead the way, Mrs. Bailey."

Upon arriving back to the big rock in the middle of the trail, we could see the three boys lounging around off to the side, attempting to look innocent, drinking from water bottles. Chief Flint and Corbin headed straight into where Ranger Winter was standing guard over the box treasure.

The happy hiking mood was gone. My children sat quietly, straining to hear what the police were saying. There was a mumbled discussion as the Chief's eyes glanced at us often. I don't think he was too happy at the situation, but I couldn't decide if it was the box, or the fact that it was us Baileys who found it.

Ranger Winter demonstrated how we used a stick to feel for the box. The men must have heard something because suddenly Corbin was getting out his flashlight and peering down the hole. He stopped to put gloves on, then reached down inside the hole and pulled out small yellow scraps of paper with blue writing. Could Butterfingers individual size candy bars have been Harvey's favorite kind of candy bar?

Hurray, Hurray! Finally, the Chief found something I didn't. That feeling didn't last too long for me, though. The Chief frowned again, when Hunter offered a plastic bag to hold the wrappings, realizing we had come prepared for clues.

Deciding we had overstayed the chief's patience, I announced, "we are returning to the Interpretive center to have our lunch."

Chief Flint gruffly left Corbin bagging everything up and walked with us on the trail. "It is getting to be quite a habit to see you and your family every day, Mrs. Bailey. I would rather not, to be truthfully honest."

Not sure how to answer that, I said nothing.

"Can I just ask you one simple question, Mrs. Bailey." Chief Flint asked. I nodded my head to him. "Didn't I politely ask you to report anything you found from Harvey's house?"

"I believe, sir, you wanted to know if anything was missing from Harvey's room. The map was found in the common living room of the house. Paula believed it was some silly game that Harvey had set up." I explained, leaving Corbin's knowledge out of it. "There were no indications that the two things were related. We didn't even know if we could find it. The map is vague and ripped in half. Only the slim chance that Audrey had seen the treasure spot last year gave us the ability to follow the half map anyway."

Arriving at the parking lot, the Chief paused a moment to talk to the boys about what they had touched, while the girls and I headed for our lunch. Audrey opened the back door for the food in the cooler, while I went to the drivers' door for the chips.

Note to self: never reach into things I can't see. Too bad I didn't make that note until it was too late. I reached over the seat, down towards the floor of the van and .... screamed.

Instead of grabbing the handles of the grocery bag holding the chips, I grabbed a wiggly, scaly, cold-blooded creature that immediately tried to wrap itself around my hand.

I screamed, letting go of that nasty creature and jerked back, and screamed again as I turned around and ran with tears in my eyes. I didn't care where I was going, as long as it was away from there.

Panic blinded, I tripped and sprawled face first on the road. As I scrambled to get up, I felt hands trying to grab me. I kicked back, connecting with something flesh and bones and heard an "oaf", but the arms just wrapped me up in a bear hug tighter.

"Mom. Mom, Calm down." Audrey and Emily ran in front of me calling, "Mom, Take a deep breath. You are okay, now. It is gone."

I hate snakes, truly despise snakes, to the point that I am desperately frightened of them. While on vacation at age five, I tripped over a snake hole in a field. Four baby rattlesnakes came out and slithered around me, and bit me. We had to rush to the hospital for anti-venom, less than a year after my mother's death, reaffirming my dislike of hospitals.

Snakes are the one creature I will not let my kids have as pets. We have had worm farms, rabbits, and insects. You name it, we have probably had it for at least a week. But they know how much I dislike snakes. Thanks to the town grapevine, the whole town knows I dislike snakes.

All the energy just drained out of me, my screams turned to sobs and I went limp. I was so happy to see my girls safe, standing there in front of me. Whomever was holding me, slowly lowered me to the ground and let go. I grabbed my girls and gave them a big hug.

Audrey whispered tightly, "Mom, you are choking me."

"You girls okay?" I gave a weak, shy laugh, still trying to catch my breath as I loosened my grip a bit.

"We are fine, Mom. We were in the back, remember?" said Audrey, as she slipped out of my grasp. "Now I am going to go to Uncle Corbin's car and get his first aid kit. Your skinned hands and knees are starting to bleed all over Emily."

I smiled and laughed a little again, letting Emily go, "I am so sorry, Emily." I looked at her worried face. "I didn't mean to scare you. I am so, so sorry."

"It's okay, Mom." Emily smiled sweetly.

Chief Flint, who must have been the one holding me, crouched down next to me.

"Would anyone care to tell me what the hell just happened?" asked the Chief.

"Mom!" Skylar, Hunter, Travis, Frank and Corbin all came running up the path at full speed. "Rainbow?"

"There is a ..." Emily, showing more wisdom than her years, stopped before saying the actual word. "S. N. A. K. E. in the van," she finished telling the boys.

Audrey called, "Mom grabbed it, thinking it was the grocery bag."

As a group, the guys trooped to look in the van.

"Stay away from it, boys!" I yelled.

"I take it you don't like snakes, Mrs. Bailey?" the Chief asked.

"Mom was bitten by rattlers when she was little and even ended up in the hospital." Audrey explained to the Chief, as she began to wash the dirt and blood off with a wet wipe.

After they had taken a quick glance inside, I heard what were supposed to be appreciative comments, I am sure.

"Whoa, Mom, you touched it?" Hunter called.

"That explains it," Travis said. "It's big."

"Girls, stay here with your mother," Chief Flint commanded, as he went to view the snake.

"It's harmless," called Frank.

Chief Flint asked, "Officer Cross, what are you doing here?"

"I heard the scream and thought you might need back-up."

"As you can see, Mrs. Bailey will be fine now. Get back to the evidence. Do you understand." Chief commanded.

"Yes, sir." Corbin glanced at me as he ran, back down the trail.

"Ouch!" I said. Audrey slapped dabbed antibiotic ointment the last band-aid to cover my knee.

"All cleaned up, Mom," said Audrey.

"Kids, stay back, out of the van. Mr. Winter, you said it is harmless." Chief Flint continued to take charge of the situation. "Does that species like to crawl into vehicles?"

"Well, it has been known to happen in winter, though rarely, if it senses some heat buildup and finds a hole to crawl in. But this is late spring, on a warm sunny day. Not much reason to need that extra heat." Ranger Winter explained.

"Thank you. Do you have a cage available for it? Please bring it out here so it is ready. Skylar?" Chief Flint pointed to one of my boys.

"I'm Hunter, sir," Hunter tried to correct him politely.

"Sorry, Hunter. Are you bothered by snakes?"

"No, sir."

"Good. Would you keep an eye on it and call me if it tries to move."

Chief looked at our lunch cooler that Audrey and Emily had dropped in their haste to get to me. The lid was ajar, showing the jug of lemonade we brought from home, running as a stream across the ground. Then he glanced at me with Audrey and Emily.

"It's Travis, right, son?" Chief pointed.

"Yes, sir, I'm Travis."

"Good. Do you know if there is a vending machine nearby?"

"The lower level of the Interpretive Center, on the outside deck, sir."

Chief reached into his pocket, "Here is some money. Go get your mother a soda. You know what she likes?"

"Yes, sir."

Crackle, crackle went chief's radio. He stepped away slightly to respond.

"Chief Flint?" Corbin's voice floated through the tiny speaker.

"Here, report," Chief responded.

"Uh, it is gone, sir," Corbin announced.

Chief barked back into his walkie- talkie, "What do you mean it is gone?"

"I am at the hole in the tree, but it is gone, sir. The black box is not here where we left it."

The Chief swore under his breath. "Stay right where you are. I'm coming back. And radio in for back-up."

Pointing to my other son he said. "Skylar?"

"Yes, sir." Skylar's back straightened to attention.

"Is it right to assume you have a camera in your backpack."

Skylar managed to look only slightly guilty when he replied, "Yes, sir, I do."

"Then I want you to take a few pictures of the snake. Do you boys know how to handle snakes?"

"Yes, sir. Mom doesn't know, but we move them out of the yard before Mom sees them." Skylar replied.

"Good. After the pictures, boys, if the snake decides to move to a new location, you have permission to put it in the cage," Chief directed.

"Will do, sir," The boys said together in that eerie way the twins had sometimes.

The Chief came over to Audrey and I. "Audrey, how bad are those cuts."

"Just basic abrasions like we clean-up on the boys all the time. Nothing serious. I have already cleaned them up."

He looked me over and asked me, "I would like to get you more comfortable before I check on Officer Cross. Will you throw up on me again, if I help you into the Interpretive Center?"

I saw Travis coming around the building with a soda and wryly smiled at his attempted joke, "No, I think I will be fine."

He insisted on helping me up and got me walking, blocking my view of the van on the way into the Center.

On the way he played twenty questions. "Was the van locked?"

Getting tired of all the questions and still shaken up, I responded, "Of course it wasn't. Contrary to the last few days, we don't have rampant crime in our town. And who in their right mind would try to steal the Purple People Eater anyway?"

"Mmmmm." He grunted his opinion of that. "Then tell me about this distraction."

"Distraction? Have you ever been bitten by a poisonous rattler? I almost died. I think my phobia counts more than a distraction." Just the thought of how that felt made my head start to spin a little. It was a good thing I had Audrey on one side and the Chief on the other.

"Mom, you are okay now," Audrey reassured me, holding on just a little tighter. She explained to the Chief, "Mom usually doesn't react this bad, but she hasn't touched a wild snake since that incident. Most of the time she just squeals a little at the sight and walks away."

Frank unlocked the door to the center, and his back office. Once I was settled into Frank's chair and Travis presented the soda, the chief disappeared quickly out the door dragging Frank with him, calling more instructions to the boys and into his walkie-talkie on his way out the door.

I drank half the can in one gulp. As I started to feel better, the whole scenario seemed to dawn to me. Everyone knows I am afraid of snakes. My family and friends all came running and now the black box full of Harvey's treasures was gone.

That meant two things. First, the map and the box of stuff either had something to do with the murder, or at least someone thought it did. Second, most likely that same someone planted the snake in the van, hoping for the distraction, or to make me look foolish again. Possibly both.

Well, the plan worked. Corbin left the scene and now the things are missing. And I truly went hysterical, again, in front of the Chief. Three horrendous events in less than forty-eight hours.

Always trying to find the bright side of things, I was just thankful it happened to me, and not my children.

Chapter Fourteen

TEN MINUTES LATER the small parking lot was almost full. Two more police cruisers had arrived. Eric Perdale cordoned off the area with yellow tape, and Josiah Engebrecht dusted the van doors for fingerprints. Sammy the snake, as my boys were starting to call it, was safely placed into the cage and transported to the County animal control office until further notice. Our lunch was part of the "crime scene area" so we called the Pit Stop to have something, anything, delivered.

Martin decided to deliver it himself, placing his lunchtime assistant, Millie Parker, in charge of the shop. "I needed to see myself that you were really alright this time."

I was so happy to see him, as were the children. They were learning, as I had two nights before, crime scenes on TV or in books are much more exciting than living through one. There was a lot of just waiting around for your turn to do something. Having a new audience for today's story was exciting for Hunter and Skylar, who were able to report how their camera pictures, taken of the items before the police got there, were now considered evidence.

The chief had made a few encouraging comments as he collected the camera into an evidence bag about the details the boys captured. Their pictures, after all, were now the only record of the items in the black box.

"He took the whole camera, Dad," complained Hunter.

"But he said he would give it back once they downloaded the pictures from the memory card," said Skylar.

"Does the camera still have the rabbit mummification pictures on it?" Hunter asked Skylar.

"Oy, I hope not," I said.

"And Frank found the hide-out." Travis chimed in.

"What hide-out?" Martin asked.

"I heard Corbin talking to Eric..." Travis started to tell his tale.

I cut him off. "Use his title while he is working, young man."

"Sorry, Mom. Uncle Corbin told Officer Perdale how Ranger Frank used his old tracking skills to find a trail that made a beeline from Harvey's tree to the nearest road, which is only about a block away hidden by the trees." Travis explained. "They even found a matted down area where the perpetrator had been hiding when we came down the path looking ourselves."

"The person must have been following their part of the map." Audrey spoke what we were all thinking.

Skylar thought it through. "The box was closer to the end of the trail than the beginning. He or she could have put the snake it the van after we started the trail."

"And then hid when we arrived at the box, maybe. It could be he or she had the X that marks the spot, but not enough clues to find the right tree? Or the snake took too long, and we beat the perpetrator there." Hunter finished thinking out-loud.

Emily looked at me with a question in her eye. I offered, "Perpetrator is another word for villain."

The Chief's arrival prevented any more discussion. "Mr. Bailey, with your permission, and attendance, I would like to interview the children concerning the recent events."

One, by one, the Chief questioned each of the children, with Martin as their parental supervisor. As another witness, I was not allowed to be the children's chaperone. Finally, it was my turn. For the third day in a row, I received the third degree by the Chief. When did we arrive? Was there anyone else here at that time? Did we lock the van doors? How long was our hike? Who knew we were coming here? Martin had brought my favorite fountain soda drink with the lunch. Even so, the whole process was tiring and monotonous.

The chief also seemed to acknowledged that fact. "Three days, three crime scenes. Tell me when the next one is, and I will come prepared with your favorite soda- my treat."

My mouth dropped open, then closed. Did he think he was being funny, or was he being serious?

"How should I know? Unless, you still believe I am involved in this case?" I asked.

"Why shouldn't I?" He leaned back in his chair and crossed his arms.

"Because whenever I find something, I call the police right away."

He brushed that off, "Just a way to cover your tracks."

"Because I am patiently co-operating and answering all your questions."

"Again, just a way to cover your tracks."

This argument wasn't working. Time to change gears. "I didn't have to report the body."

"Actually, the law requires you to report a death." He stated.

"But a killer wouldn't report the death, but let the it go to the dump. And, why would I tell you about Harvey's room, why would we have reported the map from the train? Why would I have called when we found the stuff. OR even taken the pictures? Or invited Frank along?" I fired questions back at him.

"Those are valid questions." Rising to his full height, he glared. "Or, you could have planted this whole thing so we would look for other people. Officer Cross told me all about the kids' experiments and why they were doing them. Maybe they set the whole thing up to protect you. And, of the items in the black box, you could have quickly taken something out that belonged to you."

Most people towered over me in height, so I refuse to be intimidated by it. "If it wasn't for my family, you wouldn't have found the black box in time or even have the pictures." I ended, realizing I was leaning across the desk and was yelling at him.

"If it wasn't for your hysterical screaming making your WHOLE family run to you, we would still have the black box." He leaned right in at me and whispered. His meaning was clear: not just my family's safety, nor my freedom, but Corbin's job was in peril.

In the ensuing silence, floorboards creaked just outside the office door. The crescendo of our voices had drawn an audience. The thought knocked the wind out of my sails, bringing the tension inside the room down a notch or two, but I was too mad just then to completely back down. We just stared at each other eye-to-eye.

I broke the silence. "Are you going to charge me with anything?" I inquired as calmly as I could.

"Not yet." He admitted, though the threat hung in the air. Stepping over to the door, he added, "We are not finished here."

He opened the door to reveal shoes I recognized. My short stature restricted my view over people's shoulders, so I relied on other views. Three pairs of skinny legs wearing gym shoes belonged to my boys. Behind them, one pair of custom ordered high arch black loafers, lightly dusted with flour, belonged to my husband. Off to the side, a pair of black shiny dress shoes with uniform pants implied one officer awaited next instructions.

Officer Engebrecht said, "The van had a faulty passenger lock so Mrs. Bailey couldn't have locked the door if she wanted to, making it easy for anyone to break in."

Accepting this information, Chief Flint replied, "In that case, if you are finished dusting for prints, release the van. Mr. Bailey?"

"Yes, sir?" I heard Martin reply.

"May I suggest you use the purple van to take your children home? I don't believe your wife would be comfortable driving it just now."

My whole family started speaking at once giving the Chief some fuss about leaving me here.

He waited until their rant calmed, "No criminal charges will be filed today, I promise. I just have a few more questions, and then I will personally deliver Mrs. Bailey home safe."

"He is right, Martin." I added, coming to the door. "Can you take the kids home in the Purple People Eater? I will be fine here."

"Are you sure, Rainbow?" Martin pushed past the Chief, hugged me and slipped a phone number along with the spare keys to his van into my pants pocket. He whispered, "Remember even the innocent need a lawyer sometimes, to help navigate the system."

"I will remember that. I promise," I whispered back.

His touching concern was one more reminder that this situation was turning serious. Evidence, without a few true witnesses and a smoking gun, was a set of incomplete facts that could be mis-interpreted.

I could see from an outsider's point of view that the fact that I reported a body, knew my town well, was in the house with the ransacked room, and now unwittingly distracting a police officer certainly weighed heavily in my direction. But that wasn't what worried me the most.

My main concern? A murderer was out there today. He or she was following my family because I fell into this mess. Shuddering to think how close my family was to harm because of me, I need to do something about it now! Think, Rainbow, Think! I must find a way to work with the new Chief so he could arrest the true criminal.

They left and Chief Flint headed back around Frank's desk. "Now, where were we?"

"You were going to tell me that you don't want to arrest me, because deep down inside you don't think I did it."

That made him stop in mid-step. "Where did you come up with that idea?"

"Do you want the actual event that triggered that thought, or the reasoning behind it."

"Both, if you don't mind," he said, leaning back into the chair, crossing his hands behind his neck. "I want to know why you think you can read my mind."

"Let me start with the reasoning. First, as we have discussed, I have no motive."

"That we can find yet. But you might have just covered up some evidence," he cut in.

I ignored him, counting on my fingers, "Second, you saw how I reacted to finding Harvey."

"I have witnessed many criminals fake all kinds of emotions if they thought it would get them out of trouble."

"I didn't. And I could have just as well reported it without falling on him". I shuddered just to think about it again. "Third, yesterday. If I was responsible for the search, I could have blamed the mess in Harvey's room on the police looking for evidence. Paula would believe me, as on TV the police searches are always messy. Instead, we reported it straight away to you."

"Officers under my command would never destroy a room like that."

"Fourth, if I had created that mess, I would have had the missing part of the map. After living here most of my life, I could have followed the map easily, picked up the treasure box without anyone being the wiser. Especially not the police. Instead we told you, through Corbin, where we were going, included Mr. Winter as accompaniment, and called in the find."

"Taking the time to open the box and handle the items."

"My kids did that, with gloves on, and took pictures..."

"Which you could easily delete a picture before handing it over."

"... while supervised by Mr. Winter. Ask him if you are worried."

"I did."

"And his account matched the pictures." I smiled, knowing I had him.

He brushed away that fact. "He is a friend of yours, which makes his testimony questionable."

This man was incredibly exasperating! I rolled my eyes at him. "And finally, we come to the creature. The whole town knows how I hate those things. Emily told you the story, and I have the hospital records to prove it. I would *never* have willingly touched that, that...abomination of a creature. *That* reaction was not fake."

I waited for him to claim the whole town was in on the ruse, but he sat mute.

Continuing, I added, "But your belief in my innocence peeked through when you put various family members in charge of the creepy evidence before rushing off to the next crime scene. If you believed there was probable cause of me working with accomplices, you would have put me in cuffs in the cruiser. We wouldn't be having this conversation here."

"Perhaps that was just an error in judgment," he stood up and walked over to stand in from of the window.

"That you would have rectified a long time ago, if you really believed that."

"I concede," he offered, crossing his arms, "that I do not have quite enough concrete evidence. Yet. Besides, your children would have objected quite strenuously."

I only raised my eyebrows at that statement. Really? "The children of a suspect wouldn't have stopped you in St. Louis, so I can't believe that would stop you here."

He sighed, walking to the office door, "I think it is time to take you home, where I suggest you stay, so I have time to look for a new suspect."

"Finding a new suspect is a good idea, though I am afraid I can't stay put. At this rate, I am going to be late for the Ladies Aid meeting allowing the tongues to wag freely." I joked as he opened the front door to the Center.

Chief Flint had the decency to look aghast. "What?"

"Oh, come on Chief. Don't look so surprised. It will be all over town by now that Martin took the kids home, while we chatted here. Welcome to small town life."

"Mrs. Bailey, I ...."

I held my hand up to stop the protests. "I never said you did anything wrong. Nor would I spread any rumors as such."

He shut the door, thanked Frank for the use of his office, and we walked to Martin's van.

"But you are an intuitive man, so let me paint you a picture. What happens when you mix a small town, with old ladies, and a good-looking bachelor who just moved into town to work a respectable job?" I let that sink in for a half a minute. "You are, and will, continue to be the talk of every ladies circle in town for quite some time."

"So, this is a very talkative town, after all?"

"Hmmm, that statement implies that people are not talking to you much?"

He nodded.

"Let me ask, just how many invitations to people's houses have you received since you arrived?"

"A few," he admitted hesitantly, opening the passenger side door for me.

"And how many have you accepted?"

"None."

"Why? Do you refuse to stay out of small-town politics? Or just consider yourself a private person?"

He considered the question, "Both, I guess."

I shook my head, "Refusing the invitations is not always a good idea. If you seem anti-social, you will not receive much co-operation in town."

I sat in the passenger seat of the Pit Stop catering van, after taking a good preventative look around and under the seat. I have had enough scares in the last few days to last a lifetime, thank you very much.

"I noticed." He said under his breath. Closing my door, he walked around the front and got in the driver's seat. "Yet, you haven't stopped talking since I met you."

"Shall I take that as a compliment?" I smiled.

"Just stating the truth." He teased, "Usually it is the guilty suspects who prattle on, trying to save their own skins."

I mockingly frowned before explaining. "Welcome to small town life, Chief Flint. Locked doors, uncommon. We may not like everyone, but seeing as we bump into each other often enough, we have learned to live with them, flaws and all. Complaining about neighbors can be a favorite hobby, but we would give the shirt off our back, if they needed it. However, just moving next door doesn't a neighbor make. It takes days, months, years to make the connection. Unfortunately, with the Harvey situation, you didn't get much time."

"What about you?" Chief Flint asked suddenly, after a quiet mile down the road.

He caught me off guard. "Me what?"

"You started talking since the minute we met. What do these 'little old ladies' say about you?"

"Oh, me?" I laughed. "I don't care. I have been a rabble-rouser since I began to walk." When the Chief quirked an eyebrow, I added, "I simply don't play by society's rules."

"Explain." Chief demanded.

"Easy example? I had the audacity to marry a Maurey."

"First marriage?" Chief asked.

"No." I laughed, "I take it that Josiah didn't explain the Big Feud, yet?"

"Are you referring to the chocolate stain? I didn't ask."

"Yes. Big feud between the Jensens and Maureys. Some love triangle family feud started before, but exasperated by, the Civil War. The stories on either side do not match, so no one knows how it started exactly, but the implications reign to this day."

"I am afraid to ask, but was are these implications?"

"First, think Romeo and Juliet. Marriage between the feuding families simply doesn't happen."

"But you and Mr. Bailey?"

"Martin is a Maurey on his Grandma's side of the family tree, while I am a Jensen. We have had eighteen wonderful years of marriage together, and I pray every day for more. But the rules are still there in the minds of most of the town residents."

"At least your story didn't end like Romeo and Juliet." The Chief frowned, "Same for Josiah Engebrecht and Melissa Anderson, then?"

"Yes," I declared, "this is also why we need you, not Corbin, to be Chief. Too many still follow the rules."

"There are more rules?" He asked.

"Yes, we also broke the second rule." I tried to explain, "You see, handing down the family farm or business to the next generation is not just a happy occasion, but assumed and expected."

"And you are against this?" Chief asked.

"No, but I believe people should choose to be what they want to be, and work at a job they love for the rest of their life."

The Chief nodded.

"Martin, as oldest male, was expected to take over his father's pharmacy, but his heart wasn't in it. I encouraged him to dream instead. Owning a restaurant has had its ups and downs, but we work through them together." I continued, "You see, long ago I decided to be myself and be proud of it. When I make a mistake, which we all do from time to time, I own it, apologize and do my best to make amends." I turned to the window, "And then I started doing 'strange things' according to the neighbors."

"Give me an example."

"Well, I have a large family, with five children. And I gave up my art career to be a stay-at-home mother. Most people understood that one, thinking I would go back to work when the kids were in school. But to top that off, I decided to home-school them. That was the big one right there. People felt I was turning my back on the community that raised me after my mother died."

Turning to the Chief, I added, "But I bet you have heard all the tongues wagging about me already. Surely you were checking up on me."

"There are no complaints on public record." He responded vaguely. "So why do you home school?"

"Ah. That is the question I am asked all the time. There is an easy answer, yet it is very hard for people to truly understand."

"Try me," The Chief said encouragingly.

"Well, basically, it is a lifestyle that fits us. By staying up later and getting up later, the children spend more time with Dad. They learned to work together, with people of all ages, as they helped with catering jobs. Also, I can tailor to each child's individual needs without sacrificing other lessons. It started with the twins, who could read chapter books by kindergarten, and loved checking out science books from the library. We did send them to school for a few weeks, but they didn't fit in. They asked too many questions, and couldn't sit still when told. So, we brought them home. All of our children have developed curiosities that never end. I personally think it is a good thing."

The Chief pulled into my driveway.

"So here we are," I spoke a little brighter, "my house, school or crazy zoo, whatever you want to call it. I don't mind. It fits our family, and that is what matters."

Chief Flint put the car in park. "Of course, you are aware of and following the state laws concerning homeschooling by reporting to the right people and testing."

"No required testing in our fair state. Homeschooling laws vary quite a bit from state to state. There should be a printout of the state laws already on file at the police station. I made sure of that when we started this journey so everyone would be aware of the legalities," I reported, bringing out my 'Momma Bear' voice again. "I might be a horrible cook, and inconsistent housekeeper, but when it comes to protecting my children, I am spot on."

"How do you know if they are doing well in school if you don't test them?" he inquired, turning off the engine.

"Ah, the age-old question. I believe that excessive testing is bad for students. There are other ways to know the children are learning without regurgitating the facts onto a piece of paper. Too many schools are having to teach to the test. That is not my goal. I wish for them to grow up to be happy, healthy and productive members of society.

"Through homeschooling, they have learned to work with people of varied age groups and enjoy doing it. As for actual school work, we have a math program, a writing program, and a phonics program. After that, all we need is a library card, and a healthy curiosity. When they had a question, I didn't spoon feed the answer to them. Instead I taught them how to research the answer, by interviews, reading, and doing experiments."

"Are you sure everything is being covered?"

"Chief Flint, I might be unconventional, but I believe in responsible behavior. I do the standardize tests every three years since third grade, just for people like you," I winked. "Every time, each one of them scored at or above grade level in all subjects. So, yes, I think our style is working."

I looked at the faces that popped in the windows as we arrived. "Speaking of learning, why don't you come inside the house while you wait for a ride. The kids can show you, first hand, what they have been working out. I know you will probably hate it, infringing on police procedures and all. But they are only concerned for me, and have always loved a mystery."

He only grunted a reply before opening the van door.

Not seeing the other van in the driveway, I knew Martin was back at the shop, which was fine with me. After all, we have a business to run. Opening the door for us was my Uncle Arlis Cross, Corbin's father and the man who helped raise me.

"Is Aunt Irene here?" I asked, after introducing Chief Flint.

"Naw," Uncle Arlis answered in his slow country drawl voice. "She dropped me off and ran with the cookies for the meet'g. She would have given you a ride, but thought it better to make sure the ladies were fed on time."

"Martin called us," he added, glaring at the Chief. "To protect the grandkids."

"Thank you for coming over," I gave him a hug.

I lead the way into the rest of the house and I found all the children around the dining room table, creating pencil drawings of Harvey's items. The twins jumped up quickly when we entered the room.

"Hi, Mom," announced Hunter, looking as if I caught them with their hands in the cookie jar. "And Chief Flint."

"What do we have here?" the Chief asked.

Skylar cleared his throat after a moment of silence. "Well, sir, we didn't think you would let us have copies of the pictures we took. So, we are creating drawings of what we remember."

Smiling, I went over to have a closer look. "Oh, what excellent details we have here."

I could see the name of the casino coin. River's Luck Casino sounded familiar, I just couldn't think of where.

Audrey had a good eye for jewelry and did her best to recreate the bracelet. She showed me the inside writing. "I know there was writing inside. I think I have the names correct, but not positive. I didn't realize I needed to memorize them."

Hunter had a skill with numbers, "I wrote down the dates from the newspaper articles we found. I thought we could go to the library and look them up."

"Good idea. Or we could check with the newspaper microfiche also," I agreed. "But I am sure Chief Flint has someone already doing that and we don't want to get in his way. How about we put that on tomorrow's schedule? Meanwhile, I brought him in to see the gelatin experiment. Why don't you explain that to him while I change clothes."

Eager voices echoed down the hallway. Being able to logically communicate their experiments to friends and neighbors has been an important part of our home-school education. I figured the family would keep the Chief occupied for a full five minutes, giving me a chance to get ready for the next event.

Once in my room, I tore off my clothes and threw them in the general direction of the laundry basket. Luckily, I had laid out a better pair of jeans and a pullover blouse. Add a new pair of socks and viola: a new me. I used a comb through my hair as I walked to the door to put my shoes on. I did not even bother to look in the mirror. No time for a beautiful routine today.

I grabbed a notebook and pen off the side table to replace the one sitting in the Police station lock-up. I would miss having those notes from the last meeting, but I have helped with fund-raisers for so many years, I could probably do it in my sleep.

Emily caught me as I re-entered the room.

"Does this mean the Chief likes us now?" she whispered to me.

I looked to Chief Flint, who turned at her question, for the answer to that one.

As he looked at all those expectant faces, he cleared his throat, then crouched down to talk directly to Emily. "Not all the evidence for this case has been found and analyzed yet. What we do have concerning your mother is circumstantial and tenuous at best. The police department, especially myself, would appreciate your continued support. Please report anything you see or hear concerning Harvey to be communicated back to me." He added, "Personally."

I nodded my thanks to him. My family would love to hear that I am off the hook and not a suspect anymore, but I also appreciate the fact that he didn't lie or sugar coat the facts. The older children looked a little relieved.

Emily asked, "What does Circumstantial and Tenuous mean?"

"Circumstantial means 'Pointing indirectly toward someone's guilt but not proving it.' And Tenuous means 'slight or weak connection'," he replied.

"Is that a good thing?"

"It means your mom has been at every crime scene, so far, but just being there doesn't prove anything," Chief answered.

"Speaking of crime scenes," Uncle Arlis started, "the boys here told me about this morning. About my son, Corbin leaving the scene."

I cut in, "Boys, how could you! That is Corbin's story to tell."

"Sorry, Mom. But we couldn't tell the whole story to Grandpa without it," Travis explained.

"No excuses. You will apologize to Uncle Corbin later," I told them.

"About my son," Uncle Arlis continued, "I just want you to know that Irene and I raised our family to be God-fearing Americans, who put family first. Rainbow and Corbin were raised together like brother and sister, so of course he ran to help her. Now, I know he didn't follow big city procedures and such, but he is still a good police officer, a hard worker, and a quick learner, which ought to count for something."

While Chief Flint took a deep breath, considering what he was going to say, Corbin knocked as he walked in the front door, calling "Hello, Rainbow?"

"Come on in," I responded.

Walking into the dining room, he saw the whole crew. "Oh, Dad, hi, uh, you met Chief Flint."

The Chief took advantage of this way out. "Mr. Cross, it was nice to meet you. Children, I will check on your progress tomorrow. Mrs. Bailey, walk with us to the door, please."

"Certainly."

At the front door he paused, "Humor me, Mrs. Bailey, where are you going to be the rest of the day?"

"Of course. I am definitely late for the Ladies Aid meeting. By the time I get there now, all the cookies and coffee will be gone." I smiled.

"Any place else on your agenda?" He asked.

"Oh, tonight I have kick boxing class at seven o'clock at the Fitness Palace." I frowned. "Not looking forward to that like I usually do, but I also have commitments there. I will do my cleaning chores, and then I need to finish painting the men's bathroom afterward. Will probably be there until midnight." I explained.

"Will anyone be with you?"

"Not usually. But the Palace owners rent out keys for 24-hour access. People can get in with their own key, at any time."

"I will send a patrol car to drive by frequently then."

"That would be a comforting thought for me and my whole family. Now I better get going. Excuse me." I said, leaving Corbin to walk the Chief out.

Turning back to the living room, I gave some last-minute instructions. "Work hard to keep your Grandpa out of trouble." I said as I grabbed the keys to Martin's delivery van.

"Very funny, Rainbow, " Uncle Arlis fussed.

"Be careful, Mom." They called as I ran out the door.

I decided to slow down as I got close to the van. I couldn't help myself, but spent a few moments inspecting it for more surprises. Finding none, I pushed the speed limit all the way to St. Matthew's Lutheran Church on the other side of town.

Chapter Fifteen

THE PARKING LOT WAS FULL, so I had to park a block away and hoof it. I still arrived twenty minutes late, but with the large crowd, it had taken them that long to process through the coffee and cookie table, and take their seats.

Aunt Irene spotted me and waved me over to her table. "I saved some of Audrey's cookies for you."

"Have I missed anything yet?"

"About the auction? No. But many people were looking for you. And I heard Harvey's name in the midst of various conversations," she replied.

Bang, Bang, Bang. Grace Montgomery, wife of the congregation president, hitting her great grandfather's gavel on the table. She loved to proclaim, to anyone new in town, her descendance from the first judge our town had back in Charlottesville's horse and buggy days. In fact, I would bet she was one of the first people to present the new chief with a food invitation. And if he turned her down, that would make her mad as a hornet. God forgive me but I couldn't help it; I smiled at that thought.

Aunt Irene patted my hand, "Rainbow, I know you have a happy disposition, but that smile is going to get you in trouble."

"What? Oh! Sorry, I was lost in thought. What did I miss?"

"Only a prayer and dedicated silence for Harvey Henson, while you were grinning like the Cheshire Cat. That is not good for a suspect in his murder."

Thoroughly brought back to the present, I frowned.

"Sorry, Aunt Irene. I am trying my best to get out of that position." I whispered.

"Shhhhh!" came from a few directions so I ducked my head down and opened my notebook to at least look like I was paying attention.

Friday marked the birthday of Charlotte Jensen, the name-sake of our town Charlottesville, Illinois. Her husband, Raymond Jensen, was a largest landowner in the area one hundred fifty years ago, when the government scouted the area for the placement of a railroad. He donated the land on which our town now stands, claiming the right to name the town after his beloved deceased wife.

One hundred years later, many smaller towns surrounding Charlottesville were hit by a devastating string of tornadoes. To raise money to help our neighbors, the ladies St. Matthew's Lutheran Church held the first ever Charlottesville Auction of fine linens, baking and handiwork sewing. The Lutheran Ladies' Aid and many other church groups opened not just their wallets to pay for the rebuild, but their hearts and homes to eleven newly orphaned children.

This auction became a tradition, held on the first weekend in May in honor of the original Charlotte's birthday and grown into the largest all-day auction in the mid-west. Five different denominational churches in

Charlottesville, each hosting a different auction ring around town and each raising money for their own local causes. Other churches and groups help support this endeavor with their own booths spread around town selling food, providing and organizing parking, and a delivery service for the items bought.

The purpose of today's meeting was to verify all the different group's schedules. The town was expecting five thousand extra people, an almost fifty percent increase in population. To accommodate all the people, many community services prepped and braced themselves for possible emergencies. Sheri Dillon was there to report on the police plans for traffic control and patrolling the area. The sanitation department marked the map for the extra garbage cans and port-a-potties. Even the banks were planning on being open with extra staff all day for making change, deposits and withdraws.

Grace controlled the speed with her gavel, banging every five minutes or so. Once all the business reports finished, Grace called out a reprieve, "Thirty minutes, planning time before we begin the volunteer group reports."

As the last bang came down, Aunt Irene whispered, "Get ready, here they come."

I didn't need the warning. I had lived here long enough to be prepared. Normally Grace herself would have led the charge of questions, but she was in the front of the room and I was in the back.

Irene's friends began the various questions, "I can't believe you are still standing here. I would have died to touch a dead body."

"Boo, what a horrifying thing you went through."

"Did you really throw up on the chief's shoe? How embarrassing!"

"Rainbow, how are you doing, dear?" asked Mrs. Culter, head nurse at the hospital, who helped deliver my babies at home due to my nosocomephobia.

"It was not a pleasant experience, obviously, but I am working through it."

Suddenly a voice boomed over everyone.

"How dare you send the police to interview my husband and disturb him at work." demanded Mrs. Cummins. "Because of your insinuations, my husband's reputation has been sullied. He does not drink. If it weren't for my friendship with your Aunt Irene, I would sue you over defamation of character."

Her voice carried across half the room, causing a sudden quiet.

I opened my mouth, but for the second time today, I didn't know what to reply to that diatribe. The smart defense would be laying it on the new police chief just doing his job asking questions where the evidence led him. While that would take me off the hook, it would be throwing him to the wolves. Or I could simply reply that I was assisting the investigation into a community crime. That would garner some sympathy in the crowd, but since I have learned Harvey wasn't as loved as I thought, I wasn't sure anymore.

Before I could formulate a reply, Sheri Dillon placed herself between Mrs. Cummins and myself, "I sent him to the job site, dear sister. Would you rather the Chief visit at your house and investigate what is really in your trash can?" Sheri leaned in, lowering her voice to a whisper to add, "Or see what is in your cupboards? You can thank me later."

"There is nothing illegal with my cupboards contents." Mrs. Cummins squeaked.

"Hmm, *still* best to keep it under wraps, remember?" Sheri replied. "But if questions are asked later, just keep in mind it was you who yelled across the room just now."

Blessed Aunt Irene corralled the now shaking Mrs. Cummins and lead her towards the food table for more refreshments.

Sheri leading me in the opposite direction, "Don't you listen to her, dear. Everyone already knows he drinks like a thirsty camel."

"But not always beer?" I tilt my head to look at her better.

After a side wards glance to me, Sheri admitted, "Let's just say a few ninety-year-old recipes have been handed down the family line to Brad Cummins."

I counted back through history and found myself in the age of Prohibition. "Ah."

Sheri led me three tables over. Mrs. Withrow hailed for me to stop. "I heard that Mrs. Cummins, and don't you pay any mind to her. That nice new policeman came to see me, too. I was happy to talk to him, even though he politely refused some of my chocolate pie." To Sheri she added, "Is he on a special diet? I have never known a bachelor to refuse my chocolate pie."

"Not that I know of," said Sheri. "He seems to eat all kinds of foods."

To me Sheri asked, "What do you think of him? Has he eaten at the Pit Stop yet?"

"Honestly, this week has been such a blur" I said, deflecting the answer.

"Oh," Mrs. Withrow shrugged. "It was still a wonderful visit. He was such a gentleman. He sat when I sat, arose when I stood up. I haven't been treated like that in years." She giggled. "You know, he reminded me of that old TV show, Dragnet. 'Just the facts, Ma'am.' He wanted to know what kind of trash bags I used. That was the second time he came around. The first time was the morning after that dreadful night when you found poor Harvey. Little Corbie came with him then. Oops, I mean Officer Cross. My, these youngsters grow up fast."

"What did he want to know?"

"Well, Corbie knows I keep a keen eye on the neighborhood. Gotta do my duty and keep them youngsters in line. He asked if I remember who drove in the parking lot the night before and when. Well, I go to bed at nine sharp because you can take the cowgirl off the farm, but you can't take the farm out of the cowgirl. I still like to get up before the cock crows. But I had the numbers written down from the night before. I handed it right over."

"What numbers are those?" I asked.

"Well, the license plate numbers of course. As far as I recall, the ladies from kick boxing were the only ones who arrived between seven and nine Monday evening. Rainbow, you came in last and as usual still there when I went to bed. Running a little late, this week, weren't you?"

"Just a bit," I admitted, then asked, "No other car came in after me?"

"Sorry, Dearie. I didn't realize it would get you in so much trouble, but I told him what I just told you. The ladies drove in, it was quiet until class was over, then in ones and twos, they slowly drove away until only your van was left."

Break time was over and Grace began hammering us back to order. "Ten minutes ladies and gentlemen. We must keep moving as all have much to do before this weekend."

I excused myself from Mrs. Withrow's table and sat with my church group buddies: Nancy Pickler, JC Bancock, Cassie Stasik, and my best friend Jill Jensen.

"Oh, Rainbow, I am so glad you are alright. I couldn't believe what I had heard Tuesday morning on the radio," said Cassie.

"To think we were that close to a murderer." Nancy shuddered.

"Now I wish I had been able to stay and chat, Boo, but Bill had such a headache, I had promised to come straight home and put the kids to bed." said Jill.

"I understand," I told her. "There was no way you could have known. Now let us get down to business."

We tried to focus on the arrangement of the tables for our part of the auction and bake sale. Friday at three was the earliest time we could all get to the church for setting up the rented tables and food. We wouldn't have much time, as we needed it done by seven for the preview lookers. But after years of practice, we felt we could almost do it in our sleep. Plus, we would all bring our own manual laborers, AKA our children. After all, the next generation needed to be trained to keep this running as smooth as possible.

Our group, used to working with each other, completed assigning tasks quickly. Soon the conversation circled around again to the main topic of the week.

"Does anyone know when the funeral is going to be?" Jill asked.

"I don't care," said Nancy. "I am glad he is gone. He gave me the creeps always walking around. He seemed to be everywhere I looked. I was starting to think I would wake up one night with him in my house."

"That is what Judy Thiessen is saying. She didn't like him around her granddaughter," Jill mentioned.

"He was always digging in my garbage. And talking to himself. I would be resting outside in the peaceful quiet afternoons, and he would walk by just jabbering away into that old Walkman radio like it was a cell phone. Creepy!" complained Nancy.

JC changed the subject. "Enough about Harvey, what do you ladies think about our own Joe Friday? He could come get my facts any day. He has been with you the longest, don't you agree, Boo?"

"He is easy on the eyes," I agreed.

JC laughed with glee, but Cassie gasped, "Rainbow! What would Martin think to hear you say that!"

"I love Martin with all my heart, and we are happily married. He also knows I am an artist, and look for the beauty in all God's creations." I laughed, reassuring Cassie with a hug. "JC has no competition from me, though she might from Mrs. Withrow."

"Oooh," Nancy winked at JC, "I am not sure if that is a compliment or an insult."

"Neither, I would think," said Cassie seriously. "She is old enough to be his mother. And the poor guy hasn't even had a chance to tour the town, before this happened. What do you think, Rainbow? You have spent the most time with him. I heard you are the main suspect, not that we believe you had anything to do with Harvey's death."

"I think the only thing on his mind is finding the killer." The fun conversation was over. It was time to refocus their attention. "He seems to be a good police chief, just trying to do the job we hired him for: following the trail of facts, without bias, until he finds the truth. But back to Harvey. I never heard anything bad about him before."

"That is because we all knew you were his friend, Rainbow. You always stick up for the underdog, and you don't like to hear bad things about people," explained Jill. "That is also why we love you. We know you won't repeat any rumors, or believe any rumors about us."

"Yeah. I never liked that he always seemed to be spying on me. But didn't he spy on you, Boo?" whispered Cassie.

"Well, sometimes we would see him by our side bushes, but we just invited him into our yard then. I figure he was lonely."

"How could he be lonely when he lived in that house with all those men? He had friends there," Cassie said.

"Just think about when you went to summer camp. Did you get along with everyone in your cabin?" I explained. "Maybe Harvey felt the same way. And those men have different abilities. Harvey was higher functioning and just wanted to be able to use those abilities. We enjoyed talking to Harvey."

"Better you than me. That is all I have to say. I have had enough odd men in my life." JC was always the outspoken member of the group, a skill developed dealing with all the men in her life. Not only was she a single mother of two boys, she took over her father's construction company, efficiently running three crews, when his health declined.

Our conversation halted at that point as, again, the hammer of Grace called all our tables to order. The high school departments and after-school clubs reported who would be working, when and where. As each department finished, poster board work schedules were posted on the wall. Seemed like a bit of overkill, but we had to co-ordinate now before conflicts created vacancies. It wouldn't be good to have the trumpet player miss his solo because he was stuck serving ice cream at the chess club's booster booth.

Next, the church and community groups posted their schedules, as family members often helped out in more than one booth. The churches auction money goes to help families in the community or food bank and their bake sale money goes for their own church projects. The high school clubs designated their money toward the plans for the new high school gym and pool.

The Bailey family would mostly be busy with serving food at the Pit Stop, but I was also part of the club the Power Fitness ladies formed a few years ago.

I was nominated from our table to report. "We are all ready for set up on Friday at three. Otherwise, each of us just needs to finish our own contributions to the bake sale and bring them prepackaged on Friday."

"Good to hear it," Grace, with her sugary-sweet smile, capitalized on this opportunity. "I wanted to speak to you about that, Rainbow. We all know you are so busy every day, with being a wife, mother, and teacher to your large brood of children. I simply don't know how you do it all.

"And now you are called to spend so much time serving the community by working with the police. I believe I speak for all of us about the fear that runs deep in this community, and will continue until the dreadful villain is apprehended. I am sure our new chief is well trained for this duty. But I, for one, am grateful that such a well standing citizen like Rainbow has been willing to give up so much of her time to assist the newcomer."

Delivering the *coup de grace*, Grace offered, "I am willing to help lift some of your burden and prepare your cookie contributions myself, so you can more fully devote your time to our great community. I promise to guard your secret family recipe carefully. I am sure your fore-bearers would understand this is a crisis."

Not one chair rustled. Not one cell phone beeped. Not one eye blinked. All awaited my response.

Chapter Sixteen

"WHAT DID YOU SAY to that, Mom?" asked Hunter.

"I would have told her to stuff it," said Skylar. I frowned at him, because I knew I should, though that had been the first thought to cross my mind.

I had finally made it home after the long meeting, steaming mad. I tried so hard the rest of the meeting not to blow up at the people of my beloved community. It seems all they could talk about was Harvey and the new Chief. And when their tongues start to wag, most were negativity guised as "trying to be helpful". If only they spent more time on working with our police force instead of talking about the new boss, the whole situation could be solved and in the past.

One consensus: Chief Flint had not made any friends. It seems every time he had dinner in a restaurant, members of the community or the owners tried to give him a free meal as a welcome gift, but he refused their generosity and insisted on leaving his own money. This made it hard for anyone to accept the Chief and talk to him. Yes, they answered his questions, but didn't volunteer any helpful details.

As for Harvey, the views were mixed. About half the people liked him. The other half thought he was "sneaky", which meant different things to each of them.

At the top of my list of all things sneaky was Grace Montgomery.

"Mrs. Montgomery just wants Grandma's secret recipe because Mom always wins at the fair for her sweet soft cookies," Audrey stated. "It makes Mrs. Montgomery mad to lose to anyone, especially Mom, because everyone knows Mom can't cook."

"Thanks for the vote of confidence, I think," I said wryly. "You do know that you wouldn't starve to death if I had to take over the cooking, right?"

Audrey came and hugged me, "Oh, Mom, we know that. It is just the best division of labor and time to have Dad cook for us, since you teach us. It is just a plus that it tastes better, too." She smiled, running around the counter, ducking back out of my reach.

My children know all about the secret family recipe and helped to bake it every year. Thursday afternoon we would work together to mix, bake, cool and wrap them individually for sale at the fund raiser. They also knew not to tell *anyone* the secret to the recipe.

"What did you tell her?" inquired Emily.

"I was as polite as I could be." I started to lecture about manners. "Sweetness is the best defense at times like these. Getting angry is just what they want."

Travis cut in, "Mom, we know! What did you tell her...please?" he added sweetly, attempting to prove he already knew the lesson.

Nodding that I recognized his effort, "I said thank you so much for the offer. However, it was our whole town that was assaulted by this event, and our new chief will need *all our help* to solve the crime. I felt confident that if everyone assisted the police by answering their questions, our duly trained and professional police force will bring justice to a quick end on the perpetrator. Therefore, I had plenty of time, with my beloved family's help, to do my duties to the fund raiser and the community."

"And did she understand that speech?" laughed Hunter.

"Yeah, that was probably above her grade level." echoed Skylar.

"Boys, is that how I have raised you? To be so critical of your elders?" I snapped.

"Sorry, Mom," said Hunter. "But she is always putting you down, whenever she can."

"And everyone else for that matter. I'm surprised she has friends," stated Skylar.

"Only because her husband is the richest in town and donates to every cause," added Audrey. "She mentions his generosity at every opportunity she gets."

"Shame on you, all of you. I know I have raised you better than to talk about other people like that."

Oh, bless my children. I had been rather mad at Grace when I arrived home, and it probably showed. I wonder if they goaded me into that speech to remind *me* that I should play nice. That is how it works sometimes in homeschooling. I learn as much from them and their interests as they learn from me.

"Besides, if I let her bother me, then I am giving in to her bullying. By fighting back, I am stooping to her level. Remember the Golden Rule? Treat others as you would have them treat you. Then all of God's children can get along, even if we have different styles and opinions." I stopped to changed direction. "Now, I declare the end of this conversation. I would rather you show me what you and Grandpa were working on."

My creative children delivered a neat stack of drawing papers. One by one, we laid them out on the school table to discuss. Art has always been a big class at home. While Martin's love is cooking, my love is painting. I don't create my own work as much these days due to the challenge of running a school and a home, but I enjoy fostering the ability in my children any chance available.

"We remembered six things in Harvey's treasure box and drew them with all the details we could remember. See? What do you think?" Emily asked.

Hunter handed me the pile of sketches. "First we have a recipe from the Springfield newspaper from twelve years ago. It was submitted by an Abby Ford."

"Well, that could just be Harvey's favorite food." I responded, slowly spreading the pictures on the table.

"Here we have a coin from the River's Luck Casino," said Skylar.

"I never thought of Harvey as a gambler. Or much of a traveler. Funny, I know I have heard of this casino, but I don't know why."

"You will think of it, Mom, I know you will," Emily encouraged.

"Thanks, sweetie," I gave her a squeeze. "What else was there?"

"Here was a silver ring, not that old of one, either. I think it was small enough for a woman. Inside it said 'Caroline & Carl'," Audrey pointed out.

"There are at least five Carolines in town." I thought. "I don't know of any married to a Carl. It could be from one of his distant relatives or it just might be from someone outside of town."

"Here is the drawing of a dog whistle. Did Harvey ever have a dog?" Emily asked.

"He could have, even a long time ago. It could be just a fond memory."

"We also have a 4-H ribbon from six years ago, and here is the charm from the necklace. And finally, we have some newspaper articles. We didn't get to read it much then, but we remembered the dates and papers they came from," Travis pointed out.

"While you were at the meeting, and with Grandpas' guidance, we searched the Internet for more information. This one is an article from twenty years ago on Harvey," Travis said

"You are not going to like it, Mom," Audrey cautioned. "It says he was on trial for robbing a bank."

Skylar began the story, "The good news is that he was just the assistant. He plead guilty but mentally incapable and therefore not responsible."

Hunter finished it, "The real planner, Joe Carson, whom they knew of, but hadn't caught yet, was the instigator. According to the newspaper, Joe befriended Harvey and asked him to "help". Harvey didn't really know what was going on, he was just the distraction."

Travis added, "After the trial, he was put into the Harvest House program and as far as we can tell, has stayed out of trouble."

Ah-ha! Another possible suspect. I asked, "So who is this Joe Carson? Did you find any info on him?"

"Joe was a career criminal in various states. Or at least many jobs were attributed to him. He was finally caught twelve years ago and sentenced to life in prison in two states," Hunter answered.

Skylar burst my bubble. "But before you think he is a suspect, he died in a prison fight three years ago."

I frowned. That was a dead end. "Well, we now know more about Harvey. Anything else?" They all shook their heads. "No, OK. This is what I think. It looks like a box of old memories to me. I don't know why anyone would need to steal his memories. But first Harvey is murdered, then his memory box is stolen. It has to mean something. There must be a clue in here somewhere."

Changing directions, I offered, "Sometimes the best way to find a solution to a problem is to forget about it for a while. Let's get back to our regularly scheduled work and hopefully our subconscious will make a connection."

The children moaned as I added, "Now, let's see the school assignment list."

The rest of the early evening was spent on some of my favorite and not-so-favorite things. Cleaning, laundry and school work wasn't my joy in life, but those activities took care my family, my first priority. My children's priority was their school work, but it required everyone's effort to tame the dust and germs in our active household, since being their teacher took up most of my time. When they needed a break from their school work, there was always laundry to fold, floors to wash or furniture to dust. General picking up was a daily routine at night.

For the next two hours, I listened to Emily read, taught three math lessons, and helped Travis with his history homework. Together we threw in a couple of loads of bed sheets, and scrubbed the kitchen counters and floor, and dusted the piano.

The twins shared a room with two loft beds, complete with desk and dresser under each. Audrey and Emily also share room, with a split twist bunkbed style bed. Travis was the lucky one who gets his own room, though it was the smallest room in the house. The children's bedrooms and one full bathroom we added upstairs years ago when we raised the roof on our ranch house soon after Audrey was born.

We converted the second bedroom on the main floor into a school room with an old blackboard and dining room table from the discount store. I had envisioned all of us working, learning happily together in one room. Though, as the years past, the children found their favorite places to work in private, including couches, beds, the floor, and the front room window seat. The official school room became little more than a repository for the books that were currently not in use, and current science experiments.

At around six in the evening, I hauled the last of the sheets out of the dryer and sent the children to make their beds. Meanwhile, I rummaged through the fridge for snacks. Martin usually brought dinner home by half past eight, but it was time for me to go spend some "Rainbow time" at Power Fitness. It started with the kick boxing/dance class, where I shimmy and shake away the stresses of the day with fun music and great friends. Cleaning four hours a week was my way of earning free membership classes.

Excited at going tonight, I was not. Downright scared stiff? Not really. The events of this week made me leery of venturing out. However, I was *not* going to teach my children to let their fears rule their lives.

With my workout bag in hand, I grabbed the keys to the Pit Stop van. Travis blocked the door and offered to go with me. Then Audrey offered. And then the twins. I turned them all down.

"Harvey was placed in the outside dumpster, not inside the building," I tried to reassure them. "Okay? Now you lock the door behind me, and don't open the door for anyone. If they don't already have a key to the front door, then they can come back when Dad is here. Dad said he would come home early tonight so he should be here soon."

"See," said Skylar. "You are worried."

"Not worried, just cautious."

Closing the door on the worried faces, I waited for the click of the lock. I could go back to the scene of the crime by myself. No, I had to go back, by myself, tonight, or I was afraid I never would.

Chapter Seventeen

I HEADED OUT THE DOOR with a flashlight to check for critters, the boys' phone and a healthy dose of determination. Raising a large family was hard work, and my brain and body craved fun Mommy time. Gathering with friends twice a week to shake and shimmy to upbeat music really worked out the strains of running a household.

I arrived early, careful to park in the front of Power Fitness, and not around back by the dumpster. Once inside, my first stop was the washer and dryer. The towels were washed all day long, but there was always another load to be done. I had time at night to wash, dry, and fold two loads if I start right away. Then a quick change, and I dashed into class as the first beats began to pulsate through the stereo.

The class dances were lively, alternating between Samba, Rumba, Flamenco, and even some country line dances. Some steps were easy, while some required concentration. Most of the regulars were there, led by the instructor Janice, who challenged and pushed us to the physical limit. Usually, my mind forgot everything else in life and just concentrated on stepping in time to the beat. Being at the scene of the crime again hauled all kinds of thoughts to the surface. I spent the whole hour tripping over my feet, and off balance as my brain would shut off the questions.

Could it have been one of these women around me, one of my friends who had caused all the trouble? After all, these classmates were the only ones known to be in the area Monday night. But why would anyone? What could he have done to any of them to elicit a stabbing? Or if it was an accident, why would any of my friends throw the body in the trash?

An hour later, my brain hurt, along with my body. My very good friends, JC, Tammy, Nancy and Jill, all crowded around after the last stretch.

"I lost my bet," JC announced. "Didn't think you would come."

"Why wouldn't I be here?" I asked.

"Splat. Hissssssssssss," she barred her teeth in a half grin.

I smiled back, "Well, no better time to wiggle away the stressors than here, surrounded by people who truly care."

JC laughed, "Good for you, Boo. Have a good night!"

She handed out five-dollar bills to the other women before she walked out the door.

"And we won the bet. I knew you wouldn't let someone frighten you away," Jill backed me up.

"We also thought you might like these," Nancy and Jill, each pulled a 2-liter bottle of my favorite soda out of their gym bags. "Jill's idea."

Jill shrugged, "What are friends for?"

"You ladies know me so well," I laughed whole heartedly, for the first time in days. It felt so good. "Where is Samantha tonight? I hope my 'discovery' didn't chase her away."

"Ugh, no. She wishes it was that," claimed Jill, Samantha's cousin. "Her son Jamie brought home the stomach flu Sunday night. It waited two days and now the other brothers and husband all have it. She is refusing visitors for now, but I am heading over in the morning to help disinfect and nurse the family back to health."

Janice called from the hallway after changing clothes, "Hey, Rainbow, how are you doing? I haven't been able to see you since Monday night. Are you okay?"

I excused myself from the ladies, to follow my "boss", Janice, the owner of the Power Fitness for the last three years, through the snack shop into the office. "Yes, I am fine now. It was a bit freaky at the time, finding Harvey like that." I added, "And of course you probably heard the story of the chief's shoes by now."

“An unforgettable introduction," she teased. "I hate the idea that a murderer was using our dumpster. Especially with all those ladies there that night. I am very glad no one else was hurt, but I sure hope our reputation isn't tarnished from this. To think that if you hadn't fallen in, they might not have found Harvey's body."

"I don't know about that," I protested. "His disappearance would have been reported eventually. Our police force would have looked in the landfill eventually."

"But would they have found him in all that trash? I don't know," she countered. "Do you know if they will arrest anyone soon?"

"I'm leaving that up the professionals," I stated simply.

"But I thought you were helping them,” she protested.

"I am only answering their questions."

"And this morning's hike? Did you really find something that belonged to Harvey? How did you find it?"

"Oy! The grapevine in this town is fast!" I rolled my eyes, exasperated. "Harvey simply liked to play games with his roommates, and we followed what we thought was his last game on half a map. It turned out to be just a box of his old treasures, trinkets he collected over his life. Even a newspaper article about his past. Just things in his life he wanted to remember," I explained.

"It is too bad someone stole it."

"Yes, it is too bad. That box would also have been a great thing to show at his memorial, whenever the body is released." I said. "Now, if you will excuse me, this week has been exhausting already and it is only half over. Faster I get to work, the faster I can get to bed. Laundry is calling for a switch."

"Have at it. How is the painting coming?" Janice inquired.

"Fun to have a paint brush in hand again. Boring to do only one color. But it is coming along. I will get another wall or two tonight," I said.

"Thank you for adding the painting to your busy schedule," Janice called as she walked out the door. "And, ah, make sure you double check the locks tonight? I am nervous with the body dumped here."

"No problem," I replied. "Good night."

While the women ran through the showers after class, I switched laundry and then I began my rotation into the open room where all the exercise classes are held. I kept a bottle of bleach spray to wipe down as many handles as I pick up, disinfecting and straightening up all the balls and ropes and such. Public places like this are a hothouse for germs to grow and spread. After picking up, I vacuumed, and then wiped fingerprints off the mirrors.

The free weight and exercise machine room was the next big job, where I repeated the process. The people who used the room were supposed to wipe down after their usage, but that only happened half the time. I wiped down handle grips and seats, but vacuuming was tricky, trying to get around all the chairs and benches that didn't move. This was also one of the smelliest rooms so while I am in the building, I lit a scented candle from the little shop by the office.

After that I switched laundry, and quick folded the load of towels. The last two rooms, aerobic machines and the women's only resistance room, were easier to wipe handles and seats and vacuum the floors. I also wipe down a few spots in the tanning booths located between those two rooms, checking under all the benches. It was amazing what people dropped and left behind.

"Almost finished," huffed Bob Flanagan, riding the stationary bike in the aerobic room, as usual on Wednesday nights.

He was usually there until nine, which was why I did my cleaning in that order. Everyone who pays an extra deposit receives a front door key to use the facilities twenty-four/seven.

"No worries, Bob." I said. "Just make sure you holler when you leave the locker room. I plan to paint in there tonight if empty."

Bob nodded as a reply.

Tidying finished, I rounded up the paint supplies from the cleaning closet and headed into the woman's locker room. I heard a voice while edging the wall.

"Rainbow? Where are you?" called Corbin from the hallway.

"Women's Locker room. I will be out in a minute." I said, putting a few last brush strokes on the baseboard and gathering my stuff to take to the next room.

“Hey, Corbin," I said, and after verifying the police chief was not with him, I quickly gave him a hug. "What's up?"

"Oh, I just thought I would see how you were doing."

"Checking up on me? Did Martin send you, or Chief Flint?" I accused him.

"Nobody sent me. I just wanted to see how you were doing,” he said with a smile.

"Officer Corbin Cross," I cajoled. "You know you don't have to check on me. I can take care of myself."

"I am not here as a police officer. Can't I just visit my almost sister?" He said a little cryptically.

"What do you mean by that statement? What happened? Are you in trouble? Were you fired? Is it because of me?" I prattled off at him.

"Whoa," he said holding up his hand. "Alright, sheesh! I never could get anything past you. No, I am not fired. I should be fired, because I know better, but I am still on the force."

"Tell me all about it while I paint." I walked back into the woman’s locker room and picked up the paint brush.

He walked in, hands over his eyes, "All clear?"

"Perfectly," I said. "Now sit yourself down and make some noise."

He sat down on the bench, and sighed, "Sheri had some calls waiting for the chief, so I wrote my reports, and delivered them personally when I saw he was off the phone. Figured I might as well get it over with. He read the reports, signed them and called Sheri in to file them. Then he handed me a new shift schedule. Speeding ticket stuff. I am working early morning shifts, and pulled the double duty this weekend."

"Is that it?" I smiled.

"Oh, there is one more thing. He told me to specifically tell you that I am off the case though, so, and I quote 'If your sisterly-cousin finds anything else, call me directly'. Here is his card. Because of that, I am off for the night. I report for regular duty tomorrow." Corbin ended with, "You happy now?"

"Full pay, not downgraded? No suspension?"

"That is right."

"Yes," I smiled at him. "I thought it would end up okay."

"What made you think that?" Corbin asked cautiously, trying to connect the dots. "What exactly did you say to him back in the Interpretive Center?"

"What do you mean?" I shot back.

Corbin tried to use that 'I am going to wait the suspect out' trick, but I wasn't taking the bait. I just finished the edging on the wall.

Finally, he broke down, "At the Interpretive Center, he was questioning you, almost yelling, and suddenly the tone changed. At the house, you seemed to be best friends. And on the trip back to headquarters he didn't yell at me, just sat lost in thought.

Corbin demanded, "So I repeat, what did you say to him?"

A knock on the door made us both jump.

"I am heading out, Rainbow. Locker room is empty." Bob called. "And I found this bracelet. I will leave it by the office door for the lost and found."

"Thanks, Bob. See you this weekend," I replied picking up the painting supplies and heading out the door.

"What did I say, word for word? I don't know. And you know how I don't like to gossip," I continued once Bob left. "We just talked. About this week's events. About the different points of view on the evidence. About adjusting to small town life. Actually, I didn't plead your case at all, just that I believed he would be fair."

Putting the spray bottles into his hands, I gave Corbin a slight shove toward the men's locker room door. "Now, if you are going to hang around here protecting me like a big brother, here is the cleaning supplies for the men's room. You have to help or neither one of us will ever get home tonight."

"Yes, ma'am. Your wish is my command."

I followed, reminding him, "And clean it like Aunt Irene taught us. No smudges on the mirrors! I will be checking on you!"

He just laughed.

While I washed the paint brushes, I allowed Corbin the job of taking out the trash. I wanted to switch the jobs and take the trash myself. I mean, eventually I would need to face that dumpster again. But Corbin insisted, and I was too tired to argue at that point. If he wanted to be a hero again, I wasn't going to fight it.

Though Bob couldn't enter the office, I had a special key because the laundry room is located behind the office. I put the last of the laundry in the dryer, passing the lost and found box on my way through the office, which was where Corbin found me examining the gold bracelet Bob left behind.

"What'cha got?" he asked.

"Just another lost item. Real gold. This bracelet is worth a lot to someone. It has some initials on it. CKT. I was thinking of looking at the membership logs to find the owner. Then I can call them to see if they are missing anything. Want to join me for some old-fashioned detective work, Detective Cross?"

He just shook his head at me. "Just Officer Cross, now."

I smiled, encouragingly, "But you will be again, and this has nothing to do with Harvey. So, let's go solve this mystery together."

No one in the membership roll-a-desk files under the "T"'s matched it.

"Maybe the initials are in monogram form, with the K beginning the last name, not the T." Corbin said.

"Of course, how stupid of me. See, the Chief will soon learn just how smart you really are," I said looking up the K's listed.

There was one Caroline Teresa Kepler. I didn't know any Caroline Keplers, but I did know a Teresa Kepler. I gave the number listed a call, anyway.

"Hello, Kepler residence." said Teresa when she answered.

"Hi, Teresa, this is Rainbow. I hope I am not calling too late."

"No problem, Hun. I finally got little baby Toby down to sleep and was just watching a little TV. What's up?"

"Well, I was cleaning up at Power Fitness and I was wondering if you were missing any jewelry. I might have found it for you," I mentioned.

"Oh, did you find my gold bracelet. Fred bought it for me last year, and I absolutely love it. I know the clasp was getting loose from Toby tugging on it, but I hadn't had a chance to get it fixed. Did you find it?"

"Could you describe it a little more?" I asked, wanting to verify.

"Well, it is a gold bracelet, with lots of swirls etched into the band. In the center is a plate with my initials, CTK, only in monogrammed style."

"Bingo, we have a winner. I will leave it here on Janice's desk for you to claim tomorrow. Is that alright with you?"

"That sounds great, Rainbow. I am so glad you found it. Fred doesn't know it is missing yet. He thinks I am getting it fixed. I will take it straight to the jewelry store tomorrow."

"Good plan," I said, then asked, "I didn't know Teresa was your middle name."

"Oh, yes. I didn't grow up in town, so you wouldn't know that. I am one of the Smithingtons," Theresa replied.

"Now I remember." The Smithingtons were out of Mapleton, fifty miles away. It is a tradition in their family that all the first-born daughters were named Caroline, but then used their middle name. We have about three or four of them that married into our community now. I added, "Well, enjoy your quiet time. Good night."

Finished for the night, Corbin turned off lights, and I blew out the candle in the weight room.

"Are you going to follow me home, too? Or are you going home and get a good night sleep for once this week?" I asked.

"It is only a few blocks out of my way," he admitted.

As I locked up the building, Corbin searched in and around Martin's van again for me. I hugged him as I got in and buckled up. I wanted to argue against him following me. However, I knew this was his way of showing he cared, so I let him.

Martin met me at the side door from the garage with a big hug as he reached around me to lock the door.

"Are you sure you didn't send Corbin over to baby sit me?" I smiled. I might tease him a lot, but deep down inside I was ever so glad to have Martin as my partner in life.

"No, I didn't send him, but he had called to see if you went to work tonight. How is he? Not in too much trouble I hope," Martin asked.

"Well, he is off the case, which right now means back to traffic duty. But he still has his job and I am confident he will move back up."

"That is good to know. He didn't say much to me. I had a suspicion you could pry the story out of him," he smiled at me.

Lights blared through the doorway from the living room. "Kids still up?"

"Yawning like crazy, but they all wanted to see you home tonight and I didn't have the heart to say no."

The kids were busy looking at the drawings they made of Harvey's treasures.

"Think of anything yet?" I asked. They all shook their heads, no.

"I have a thought about the ring." I offered, as six pairs of eyes swiveled in my direction. If we weren't talking about a murder, I would have laughed out-loud. "The Caroline on the ring could be one of the Smithingtons, who named their daughters Caroline, but most used their middle names commonly instead. I can think of a few of these ladies right now, But," I cautioned, "I don't know of any of them married to a Carl."

"That is a great thought, Mom," said Skylar.

"I wonder how we can research that?" wondered Travis.

"Right now, I have no idea. A general Internet search is not possible. We would have to look at hospital births or marriage records. That can be done if we have a particular person in mind, but not on the general public of our town," described Hunter.

"The other question: Does this ring even have anything to do with Harvey's murder?" Martin pointed out.

"Good point," I said to him. "Let us forget about it for now. Maybe something will come to us again. For now, go get ready for bed! I will check your school work before lights out. We need to see where we are in this week's assignments and plan accordingly. Remember tomorrow is a big day. School and errands in the morning, baking in the afternoon."

"Speaking of baking," Martin added. "You need to get the recipe out so we can verify we have the quantities correct."

Digging down to the bottom of my bedroom closet, I found the big box of all my mother's cookbooks. This recipe was saved for special occasions only, hidden away until used. I had so many wonderful recipe books from her. I don't know why I kept them; I don't cook enough to warrant the time looking in them, and Martin makes his own recipes. Every time I thumb through them looking for my recipe, I consider donating them to the rummage sale, but I never did. I had so few memories of my mother, and hope someday to pass these on to the girls. I had books from church fund raisers and Girl scout activities, and ... wait a minute. That type setting looked familiar.

I had tucked my recipe into St. Matthew's church cookbook published five years ago. I flipped through and found a recipe from Samantha Stone's prize-winning asparagus casserole.

I brought the recipe and the cookbook back to the living room with me to show Martin.

"Did you find the recipe?" asked Martin.

"Yes, but also I thought this looked familiar. Have you ever cooked this recipe?" I asked.

"I have made something like it, but I don't use the heavy whipping cream. Why?" Martin replied.

"I don't know. Let's have the kids look at it." One by one, they came back from brushing their teeth, dressed in robes. Emily had her fuzzy slippers on.

Audrey looked at it and said, "Here, Mom, look at our drawings." She pulled them out of the side bar and laid them out on the table. "We don't have the whole recipe down, because we didn't recall all those details, but the main ingredients are here. I wonder if it is the same recipe."

"Did Harvey's copy have Samantha Stone's name on it anywhere alongside Abby Ford?" I asked.

The twins said together, "I don't think so." They looked at each other and Hunter added. "I think we would have remembered it if it had a second name on it."

Skylar added, "I wish we could look at the pictures we took. Then we would know."

"Do you think we could ask?" wondered Travis.

"I could try to ask the chief when I run my covert shopping mission tomorrow," I offered. "For now, I'll make the Last-Minute list, while you all head to bed. And lights out now, no reading. Busy day tomorrow."

People in small towns had a hard time keeping any secrets. The only secret I had was this recipe, which I made just one time a year for the town auction weekend. Every year someone tried to figure out exactly what was in it. If someone ever did figure it out, well, I would be disappointed as it would mark the end of an era. But until that day came, it was a fun game my family played. We all enjoyed baking day and purchasing the ingredients was part of the fun.

To make the one hundred dozen cookies we sold at the fundraiser, we needed a lot of supplies, as did all the other bakers in town. For the last two weeks, townspeople had placed orders with the grocery store for butter, flour and sugar and other ingredients. I also placed an order, for the basic ingredients, only. To keep everyone guessing I ordered different amounts each year. This year I ordered fifteen pounds of butter, while last year I ordered seventeen.

During the year, I also mail ordered other ingredients that can sit on the shelf, like vanilla and spices. The special ingredient I use comes from the original company in New York, ordered through Martin's wholesaler, and is mailed to my father's farm two hours away, which necessitated last weekend's trip to the farm to pick up those supplies.

I found the grocery list for the week, including breakfast items, fruit and raw vegetables for snacks. Martin helped double check the sugar, flour, vanilla and baking soda on hand against the order I placed to make sure there was enough. Then we added a few things like food coloring and shelled nuts, just to keep the community guessing.

Once the list was made and Martin put it safely in my wallet, we headed to bed ourselves.

Chapter Eighteen

THE ALARM SOUNDED EARLIER than normal Thursday morning.

"Morning already?" Martin asked, eyes closed.

"Shh. Go back to sleep." I replied, resetting the alarm. He could sleep another hour and a half before getting ready for work.

I hoped to finish the errands before he left, so the children wouldn't be left at home alone. Usually they are fine on their own for an hour of errands, but with the crazies that happened this week, I wanted to keep their home alone time down to a minimum for their safety.

I barely waited until the school buses had finished their rounds before revving up the Purple People Eater and headed through town. I still hated driving the monstrosity, but there were no other vehicle options within a thirty-mile range.

I had a list of errands a mile long. My first stop was the police station, hoping the Chief would be there. Sheri gave me a passing nod, and buzzed me right in.

"Back so soon," she said. It was a statement, not a question.

Not quite sure how to best respond to that, I just nodded, continuing down the hall.

Chief Flint stood up when I entered, but did not look happy to see me. "I see you survived the rest of yesterday without mishap, Mrs. Bailey. To what do I owe this pleasure?" Chief Flint asked formally.

Boy, he was grumpy today. Time to lighten up our relationship.

"It's Rainbow," I announced.

"Excuse me?" he asked, surprised.

"Rainbow. My first name. My mother named me after God's promise sign to Noah. Her first girl after two boys and many miscarriages. It is so unusual that newcomers take a while to get used to it. In our town, we are pretty informal. We reserve titles for pastors, doctors, and those old enough to be our parents. You don't strike me as that old," I smiled at my joke.

He just raised one eyebrow which I took as a sign to go on.

After taking a deep breath, I explained, "Yes, well, I came across an idea last night concerning Harvey's collectibles, and you did request that I come straight to you. Would you please allow me to look at the pictures my sons took?" I asked.

He thought about it for a moment. "Tell me your theory."

I hesitated, "My children are very good at drawing, so I think I am right, but I would like to verify a few details before I explain it to you."

"I insist you will share this theory with me either way," he commanded.

I paused, carefully considering my options, as I didn't want to get anyone in trouble. Yet by closing this line of questions it could help point to the murderer. "Fine. But I am trusting you to treat it with the utmost caution. I can't see the person in question harming Harvey."

"That is for the evidence to decide," he assured as he paged Josiah Engebrecht to sign the pictures out of the evidence locker.

"Let's go to the conference room," he gestured toward the hallway. "After you."

Once down the hall and seated, I thought we would wait in silence, Chief Flint's preferred method of waiting, but he surprised me.

"What about my title of Chief?" he asked.

"Excuse me? Oh, you mean like Doc and Pastor? That falls into that category unless you say otherwise." I gave him a hard look, "But you don't strike me as someone who would want to be called by your first name."

He seemed pleased with that answer, until I added, "May I give you some advice, though? Don't fuss too much if Sheri calls you by your first name. It is her way of saying she likes and accepted you. And since she basically runs this building and keeps it running smoothly, you'll want to stay on her good side."

His face turned hard as he grit his teeth. Not sure if that meant he didn't like my advice, or in this case, he thought he already blew it with Sheri. Before I could ask, Officer Engebrecht arrived with the photos.

The Chief spread them out on the table, "Just look."

Wow, if my boys weren't thorough in their picture taking. I found three pictures of the recipe alone. One farther away and two close ups at different angles in case the sunlight created shadows.

"See this recipe? You can see the date on this recipe as from twelve years ago, printed in the Springfield, Illinois, newspaper. It is accredited to Abby Ford, and there is her picture." I dug into my make-shift bag to pull out a cookbook. "Now I present to you a copy I own from the County fair cookbook from eight years ago. See the recipe by Samantha Stone? It is the exact same recipe, using a certain kind of creamed milk."

"What exactly are you saying here?" the Chief asked.

"This contest Samantha entered is for newly invented recipes only, not copies or family heirlooms. She won that year. It wasn't until the next fall, it was decided a special 140th anniversary cookbook including all previous winner recipes was to be compiled for sale. The county fair made money off the collection of recipes, not Samantha."

I continued, laying out my thoughts, "Here comes the conjecture. Did Samantha copy the recipe, or just happen to come up with it herself? Since Harvey obvious knew about Abby's recipe, did he put the two together? Did he tell Samantha?"

The Chief finished putting the pieces together, "If Mrs. Stone did in fact own the recipe before, at the very least she would be embarrassed among her friends and family. At the worst, she could be sued by the original owner."

"For the $50 prize money? Not worth the cost of the lawyer to file the suit. No, in small town like ours, there would be a smear campaign of shame and embarrassment that leads to a family feud. Samantha could be the thief, to keep this hidden, but I really can't see her killing Harvey over this. Besides, the newspaper and the cookbook are old. Wouldn't she have done something before now?"

"Criminals don't always act on a proper schedule, Mrs. Bailey. I am going to keep this cookbook for a while."

"I thought you might. And you're going to visit Samantha, aren't you? Be aware that the Stone household is fighting the stomach flu, which means it would have been hard for her to be the thief from yesterday anyway." I said, adding, "Please be gentle. I really don't think she is involved, but at least you will get some answers."

Chief Flint asked, walking to the door. "If there is nothing else, Officer Engebrecht will walk you out."

Looking over his shoulder, Josiah watched the Chief walk into his office before he asked, "Rainbow, will you tell Corbin I am really sorry he is on traffic duty?"

"You know my opinion on that," I frowned. "You should tell him yourself."

"I know. I know. But I don't see him now," Josiah sighed. "Chief is running me crazy."

"Must be nice, learning from someone so knowledgeable," I offered.

"Don't get me wrong. I mean, I am happy for the opportunity to move up for a while. But Corbin was better at working with Chief Flint," Josiah said. "I am a better street cop. No good with questions and taking notes."

"Don't worry, you will get the hang of it. Mistakes and practice. That is how you learn," I offered. "As for Corbin, he knows this situation is tough for everyone, yet no one's fault. But I will deliver the message next time I see him."

The next stop was just two short blocks east. The month of May is such beautiful weather, I decided to leave my van safely ensconced in the center of town parking lot. Walking face to the sky, the sunshine worked to relax my worry lines. While my mind wandered, searching for some elusive answers, my insides wiggled and squirmed, disappointed that I had to sic the police on my friend.

Why would Samantha use someone else's recipe for this contest? There had to be some other reason those recipes matched, some good reason. As with any recipe, there would be similar ingredients such as flour, sugar and salt. The differences came with the type of each individual ingredient, such as white vs wheat flour, that make each combination unique. Perhaps Samantha and Abby had the same tastes in basic ingredients.

Samantha was a great cook in her own rite. During some busy catering seasons, Martin would sub-contract with Samantha for her peach cobbler. Her personality was as sweet as her cobbler. Never in a million years would I believe Samantha would have killed Harvey, and especially not after all these years.

Harvey had wandered around the town weekly. The community was used to seeing him so much, he just blended in with the scenery. It is conceivable he would stumble over a secret or two over the years. But Harvey as a cold hearted, calculating blackmailer did not compute. Blackmailing entailed a vicious intent to hold hostage and humiliate the victim. That kind of hatred was the opposite of Harvey. He was simple, open, friendly and helpful. At least that was the Harvey I knew and loved, despite what some grapevine rumors have said these past few days. While I couldn't deny the evidence of the candy bar wrappers in the same tree as the treasures, the pieces still didn't fit tightly together.

The neighbor's reporting that no other vehicles came in during class time limited the suspects down to just the ladies in class, which included Samantha. But she had nothing to do with Harvey's death, I was sure of it. Only the killer would chase down the treasure box, but her family was too sick yesterday for her to sneak off to the woods. I hoped reporting this information would eliminate her from the potential suspect list, and bring the Chief one step closer to the killer.

Arriving at my next stop cut off my sunshine musings. I had a package awaiting me at the post office. Sally Maurey, the postmistress, hailed me the moment I stepped through the door.

"Oh, Rainbow, I am so glad we finally got it. Here is the box you were waiting for from the spice company." She said with a knowing smile.

Well, she thought she knew. I did order some more spices for Martin, but I did that every year at this time. And if anyone figured out how to peek at the packing list, they would find a variety of spices. All part of the fun game to keep the community guessing.

I had to stop and chat for a while. Small town life, after all, dictated at least a five-minute conversation per person met. The main focus continued to be, of course, Harvey's death and my role in the discovery.

"Rainbow, I have never known you to be so clumsy before. Are you sure you are alright? Do you think you might have an inner ear infection? My cousin up in Lambert had one and was falling over all the time. She never knew she was sick until her husband dragged her into doctor's office where they diagnosed it..." Sally went on and on.

I did my best to reassure her that I was just fine. "Sally, I am just fine. I promise."

"Are you going to be able to cook for tomorrow? Oh, but you have all that help, and your husband is the best chef I have ever met. Do you think he could give me the recipe for his meatball soup? It was just divine last week."

"Someday we will print a cookbook for everyone to purchase," I evaded the question. "Now, sorry to run, but I need to hurry or the baking will not get done."

I backed away from the counter as Janice Peterson came in. "Rainbow! I see you are still driving the Purple People Eater."

"Much to my dismay," I replied.

Janice laughed, "Yes, driving must be a challenge with the wide turning radius and all."

"That it is," Smiling, I agreed.

"Any hopes of getting your van back? Or are you still the prime suspect?" Janice joked.

"That is all for the Chief to decide," I said. "Now, please excuse me, I best be on my way. Cookies to bake, you know." I waved good-bye and hustled out the door.

I ran into Nancy Pickler two steps out the door. Knocked her stack of neatly organized envelopes into the air.

"Oh, I am so sorry, Nancy. Let me help you with those." I bent down to pick them up.

"Rainbow, you never could watch were you were going, always rushing off somewhere," She scolded.

"That is what happens when you have to raise twins that go in two different directions at once." I explained, re-stacking the envelopes as best as I could, when I noticed the return address label. It said Caroline Nancy Pickler above her address. But her husband's name is Jeff Pickler.

"Nancy, I didn't know you were one of the Smithington Carolines."

"Yes, silly tradition, isn't it?" she laughed.

"Good, then maybe you can tell me how I can get a hold of a Carl?" I smiled.

Nancy turned as white as a sheet and started to shake.

"Nancy," I grabbed her before she fell down. "Come sit down on this bench. You look like a ghost just crossed over your grave."

"How did you know?" she asked, but didn't wait for an answer. "It is the damn ring, isn't it? You found it. I always wondered what happened to it. Oh, Rainbow, what am I going to do? It is all over, I promise."

"Calm down, Nancy. Yes, I have seen a ring with Caroline and Carl on it. It is yours then?"

She looked around the area to see if anyone was nearby. "Yes, it is, was, mine. It was given to me years ago. Jeff and I were having a rough patch and I, well, I made a mistake. I met Carl when I was vulnerable and things spiraled out of control. Carl gave the ring to me, asking me to leave Jeff. But I didn't really want to do that. The last time I saw Carl, I noticed Harvey out walking around. He had seen me with Carl! I was so scared that I called Carl that night and said no more meetings, and then I buried the ring in the back yard. A few weeks later, Jeff and I were back together after some marriage counseling and things were improving. I went to dig it up so Jeff wouldn't ever find it, and I couldn't find it. For weeks I panicked about it, but finally I gave up. It has been four years now. And I swear I never talk to Carl anymore. You won't tell anyone about this will you?"

"Is everything alright?" asked Sally, from the front door. "I saw you sit down, Nancy, and you looked a little ill."

"She is fine," I announced. "I just ran into her and we decided to sit for a chat."

"Well, Ok," sniffed Sally, offended that she missed some gossip. "Just let me know if you need anything."

"I am fine", affirmed Nancy. Once Sally had closed the door and walked half way back to her counter Nancy squished me with a big hug. "You promise, oh, please promise not to tell Jeff, Rainbow."

"Nancy, I would never blab to Jeff or anyone. You know that. But you do need to tell Chief Flint. The ring was found in Harvey's treasures. Chief Flint will find out sometime, and it would be better coming from you than him asking around."

"He won't tell Jeff? Will I be a suspect then?"

"I can't make promises on Chief Flint's actions, and since we were there around the time Harvey was dropped off, we are all suspects anyway. Hasn't Chief Flint been asking you questions?" I asked.

"Yes. Twice. But I was afraid to say anything. Taught not to trust a stranger, you know?" she replied.

"That is his job, to ask questions. And why not answer his questions? You think he hasn't had to deal with old affairs and indiscretions before? Just think, Nancy, until this is solved, he will have to keep asking questions. What if he asks you about the ring later, in front of Jeff? Wouldn't it be better to take it to the Chief first?"

"I wouldn't know what to say. You know the Chief. Can you tell him for me?"

"No, it would be much better if you tell the Chief yourself. I don't know him that well, but he has been quite fair minded so far. Plus, he might have questions, better done all in one swoop, wouldn't it? Best to talk to him on your time, not wait and wonder if he coming around again."

"I'll think about it," Nancy promised.

"Good." A quick hug as the sun glanced off my watch. "Oh, my, Tempus fugit. Sorry to leave, but I gotta keep moving.”

Chapter Nineteen

I DROPPED OFF THE SPICES in the purple van, then walked the one block north to the Newspaper office.

"Hello, Thomas, how are you doing, today?" I asked, as I closed the door behind me.

"As busy as usual just before 'Fundraiser Day'. Extra busy right now because Tammy is gone," replied Thomas Brubaker, current owner of the family run town newspaper.

"Oh, yes. Any news on her mother?"

"She finally passed the kidney stone, and is doing much better. In fact, Tammy plans on coming home sometime today, but it has really crunched my deadlines," Thomas paused while he pulled out a note pad. "Now tell me all about this week and your adventures. I want to run it on the first page tomorrow."

"My lips are sealed," I put my hand up to stop him. Then added, "as usual."

"But Rainbow," Thomas pleaded, "this is the biggest event in over six months. The whole town is talking about it. Don't you want to set the story straight?"

"Even if I wanted to, Chief Flint requested that I not talk about this case. When the police have it solved you can ask me again, and I might, stressing the word *might*, reconsider it," I insisted.

"Alright, alright, don't help a fellow member of the community struggling to make a living around here," he grudgingly gave in, having lost battles like this before. "Now, did you bring me next week lunch specials?"

"Yes, we also have an ad for Saturday's special edition, if you still have the room. With Harvey's death and all, we didn't get it over here earlier."

"Well, you are in luck. I still have the room. And, while you are here, maybe you can proof-read Harvey's obituary? It sounds like you knew him pretty well."

"Are you still trying to get some information out of me?" I asked sweetly.

"I wish I could, but I know you better," he admitted. "Actually, with all the stuff for this weekend, I am swamped and could really use some help since Tammy isn't here."

"Paula would probably be the best choice for his life history, but I can take a look at it for grammar issues," I said.

"Paula sent me over a listing of what she knew." He led me to Tammy's work station. "Here, you can use Tammy's computer. I will bring it up on the screen for you to read. Make any notes about changes on this pad of paper and I will fix it."

Often viewed as a walk down memory lane, one of the more popular sections in a small-town newspaper is the obituary column. Thomas Brubaker was an expert at weaving the simple birth and death dates, and everything in between, into a simple beautiful life story.

Unfortunately, the article had to include the blight on Harvey's life: his small robbery career.

"So, Paula knew about his brief career in crime?" I asked.

He shrugged, "She must have."

"You know more than that," I said. "You wouldn't print this if you didn't double check the information."

If Thomas was anything, he was thorough in researching facts, as was his father and grandfather before him. Some people have tried to sue for slander, but he has always won the court cases with his background checks and impeccable notes.

"Yes, I checked the court records. Anyone with my dedicated investigative skills can do it."

"And your connections in the courthouse records department," I reminded him. Thomas' sister worked at the courthouse. She didn't break privacy rules, but if the court records were not sealed, she would find the information for him.

"That is true."

"Could I see what you have?"

"Sure," he said. I smiled and was about to say thank you when he added, "I am willing to assist with your investigation, only if you give me something in return."

My smile turned into a frown, "I am not investigating anything. The police have that well in hand."

"That is not what I heard," he dared, attempting to stare me down like we were children again, daring each other to look away.

"You should not believe everything you hear," I replied. This was a game we used to play for a whole recess period in junior high. I should have known he had given in too easy earlier.

"Then tell me what should I believe." Thomas said.

Without a school bell to end it, I knew this stare down could go on indefinitely, but I had many other things to do today.

I sighed, "I fell on the body, accidentally of course. Yes, I threw up on Chief Flint shoes. I am not investigating, as that is the police's job. I am just merely curious about part of Harvey's life I didn't know about. End of story. Now hand over your file on Harvey." I put my hand out.

Seeming to give in, Thomas walked into his office, opened a file cabinet and returned with a file. As I put my hand on it and tried to take it, though, he held on. "Are you still a suspect?" he asked.

"You know the one who reports the body is first on the list." I tried to pull it away, but he still held on.

"Do you have an alibi?"

"Yes, I was on the road driving home from my father's house".

"What about Harvey's ransacked room?"

"Ask the police," I said. This had gone on far enough. He waited in silence for a few moments. So did I.

With a deep sigh, he gave in. "I want another interview tomorrow."

I shook my head. "No more until the murderer has been caught. I do not want to hinder the police nor mess up the evidence."

"What about your hike in the woods? That was a family hike, right? You can talk about that."

I shook my head no, as I felt I said too much already.

"Come on, Rainbow, throw me a bone. I know you are investigating. My sources have seen you with the police nearly every day this week."

"Investigating? Hardly! Here is a direct quote for you. 'I am being a concerned citizen and doing my best to help the police by truthfully answering any and all questions.'" I stated.

Thomas used his free hand to write it down as I continued. "Which is what you should be doing, too. Don't you want a murderer to be caught? Have you turned this file over to them to help them help Harvey?"

That shut Thomas up. I knew he wouldn't give up these sources, yet he lives in this community too. He let go of the file and I took them back to Tammy's desk to look at them.

"Read all you want, but no copies are to be made," he called, wanting to keep his sources close.

Thomas' files were not organized. Once I put them in a proper order, I was able to see a complete story. First were the court files with the summaries of the court proceedings.

Harvey had been duped into helping Joe Carson perform some basic gas station robberies. But he wasn't caught for those. He was caught in the bank robbery trying to run away with a bag of six thousand dollars. Joe Carson escaped with twenty-four thousand dollars. Harvey was on the cameras, red-handed. He had a trial, where he plead guilty with diminished mental capacity. Neighbors testified as character witnesses that Harvey was very helpful and too trusting by nature. They all believed he was scammed into helping in the robbery.

The newspaper articles were a little more interesting. They had actual pictures of both Harvey and Joe Carson. I took a good look at Joe. He seemed familiar somehow, though I knew now I had never met him. Joe was strong as a bodybuilder, with clean cut hair. He looked like a nice trustworthy man in a clean suit.

One newspaper had a picture of him in a tank top, being put in a police car. I took a good look at that one, my eyes focused on the tattoo on his arm. Thomas had said no copies, but he didn't say no drawings. I quickly drew the tattoo on a piece of paper, and a sketch of Joe Carson to show the kids. They have shown an aptitude for making connections. They might be able to help in this matter.

"Are you done yet?" Thomas called from his office.

"Just finished, thank you. Now I will help you with his obit."

I re-read the obituary, jotting down a few notes on sentence structure requiring correction. It was a thorough history, but I felt it was missing something. Remembering a quote in a picture frame in Harvey's room and started to add it when the pencil lead broke. I rummaged through Tammy's desk, looking for another pencil.

In a bottom drawer, I found a collection of pencils and a half bag of Butterfinger candy bars. They were just like the ones in the tree holding Harvey's treasures. What could that mean?

Tammy, the girls' Girl Scout leader, who had looked at the treasures and told them it was nothing. She might have thought it was just a kid’s box, and if it hadn't been for Harvey's death, I wouldn't have thought otherwise. But at least two of the other items from the box were connected to other townspeople.

Bits and pieces began to click into place. One of Tammy's columns, called News Notes, included short-clipped sentences about people's interactions around town. Some of the news stories mentioned in the past six months included references to a hit and run with a little dog, and a controversy over a 4-H project judging. Harvey had both a dog whistle and 4-H ribbon in his treasure box.

If Harvey loved these candy bars, as much as the number of wrappers in the tree indicated, did Tammy, too? Or was something bigger going on?

"How well did Tammy know Harvey?" I asked Thomas as he walked through the office to grab a memo.

Curious, Thomas paused, "Why?"

"Well they seem to have the same taste in candy bars."

"Candy bars? Not likely. She is borderline diabetic and watches what she eats." Before Thomas could make any connections of his own, Tammy walked in. "Tammy, so glad you are home and your mom is doing better. Sorry to rush off, but could you watch the front while I call back a few advertisers?" Not waiting for an answer, Thomas disappeared from sight.

I closed the drawer as Tammy came over to me. "Oops, you weren't supposed to see those."

"You knew about Harvey's treasure box," I stated.

Tammy sighed, pulling another chair over to sit down. "I might as well tell you my side. It is true, Audrey accidentally discovered Harvey's box of secrets that day on the hike. I didn't really make any connections then. But after comparing the gossip grapevine to my memory of the items, I knew Harvey was a goldmine of information from his little walks. I took some walks around town myself and started to piece some of the items to the owners. I used this information to added it to the paper. "

"Didn't Thomas ask for confirmations of the information?"

"You know how much he protects his sources. Thomas never asked where I got my stories from, as long as I could verify the story itself. Since it was already in the gossip mill, it didn't matter so much. My tidbits just added a little more detail. Soon I noticed readership was up. With the Internet these days, it is hard to keep a paper running. Harvey's notes just added a little more spice to read. I would leave him some candy bars as a treat. I only figured out some of the stuff that was put in there recently. Other items, I have no idea yet what they mean. They must be old news or just personal memories."

"Have you told the police any of this?" I asked.

"No. I haven't had the chance. No need to really, I didn't kill Harvey. Just heard about it on the morning news as I drove to my mother's house. Besides, why would I 'kill the golden calf'? I was just trying to help Thomas keep his family newspaper alive. Please don't tell anyone. Not even Thomas knows."

I thought about her words and countered with a plea. "Thomas might not need to know. That is between you and him. But you have to tell the police now. They are involved in this. Especially since someone walked off with the actual box."

"You don't think I did that? I have a good alibi, I left town for my Mother's early Tuesday morning. She lives three hours away. I was with her until this morning. I couldn't have been the one who took the box."

"Then tell the police that. The more info they have, the less running around they do. Then they can focus on the other people they have on their list. Harvey has been dead for three days now." I implored, "As a reporter, you know better than anyone the longer it takes to get the killer, the less chance it will happen. I don't know about you, but I will feel much safer when the killer is caught."

"So, who is on the suspect list?" Tammy jumped into reporter mode.

I visibly rolled my eyes at my old friend, "Funny you should ask. At first everyone from Zumba, including you, were on the list based on proximity."

"Proximity means you, dear." Tammy threw it back at me.

"Not funny." I replied, shuddering at the memory.

"No one would every believe it was you," my old friend backed me up. "Do you think I was really on their list for the killer?"

"Probably not anymore, because you were gone and a few other things have . happened. But whatever information you have to offer will help them narrow down their list."

"All of our friends and fellow members of our fair community," she frowned.

"I know. I can't believe it either. Yet, someone wasn't being fair, were they. Or we would be seeing Harvey walk right through that door. I am probably still on the list. But only for circumstantial reasons. Still, I can't wait for this to be ended."

Bing! Went the bell over the door as it opened to let in Josiah, wearing a crisp, clean uniform. "Tammy, I heard you just got back. How is your mother?" he asked, so obviously leading in to asking for an alibi.

Tammy and I looked at each other and giggled with relief.

"Something I said?" he asked.

"No, Officer Engebrecht. Just girl talk." I said, gathering my things to leave. I reached out to Tammy's arm and whispered, "Please?"

Thomas, hearing the commotion, came back from his phone call.

Tammy barely nodded to me before hailing her boss at his office door, "Thomas did you get a hold of those advertisers?" Tammy asked, "Because I think Josiah has some question for me about Monday night. Down at the station, right?"

Officer Engebrecht caught on quick, "Yes, if you please, Mrs. Connor."

"Lead the way," she said sweetly, joining me near the door.

Thomas ran to his door, calling out, "Don't give up your sources! If you need a lawyer, call me. The paper will cover it."

Adding to the distractions, I pointed Thomas to the desk, "I left some notes for corrections. Happy printing."

While Tammy and Officer Engebrecht headed left, I turned right to collect the purple van. It was taking way too long to check errands off my list. Hopefully, Martin was supervising the list of school for the kids, but he needed to leave for work. I could call Aunt Irene or Uncle Arlis to cover for my absence, but today was baking day and Aunt Irene would be keeping both of them busy. Using the boys' cell phone on my way to the grocery store, I touched base with Martin. Since all I had left was the quick pick-up stop at the grocery store, the kids would be fine alone for a few minutes.

Chapter Twenty

MY QUICK SHOPPING PLAN hit a speed bump upon arrival. By this time of the morning, the line was usually down to the last of the shoppers. Not this year. The line in Mr. Brummel's grocery store stretched the width of the store, from the front cashiers to the back coolers. Baking day was Mr. Brummel's best sales day. From the four corners of the county, the bakers of the weekend's goodies arrived early in the morning to pick up their special orders of milk, butter, flour and sugar.

"What is the hold up?" I asked Trina Dunstin, the lone cashier manning the tills.

"Three of the trucks arrived late. Just a few minutes ago, in fact. Something about the scheduled drivers called in sick and they had trouble finding a subs," she said. "It shouldn't be too long now."

The front of the line moved slowly, as each line item on the orders was double checked before being loaded in the customer's car.

"I hope he doesn't rush too much," I replied.

Several years ago, Mr. Brummel didn't count it out separately before people picked up their orders and there were shortages for the last in line. Mr. Brummel had to call grocery stores from forty minutes away for extra supplies. Not only did that put some people behind in the baking, it almost started a few feuds, as ome of the die-hard bakers accused others of sabotage. No one wanted to repeat that again. Since then, each customer, along with Mr. Brummel, double counted the items as they were placed in the carts. There hasn't been a problem since.

"He remembers, which is why he called everyone but me to the back to help count," Trina said. "Someone had to watch the front for other customers."

Oy, the line was long. What a bummer! Usually by the time I arrived, most customers had come and gone.

Twenty minutes later, after having to rehash my adventures with the ladies in front of me in line, I finally neared the cooler to collect the perishables. A cell phone rang, causing some of the ladies start looking around, digging in purses to check their phones. Not me, because I knew the police had my phone.

"Rainbow, I think you are ringing," hinted Mr. Brummel as I handed him my order sheet.

Oops, I forgot. The twins' phone sings some weird outer-space ringtone.

"Hello," I answered the phone, quickly, as my grocery count began.

"Hi, Mom," responded Audrey. "Mrs. Dillon called to tell you the dry cleaning was done. If you pick it up soon, you can deliver it to the Chief at his house. I guess he was headed there soon for an early lunch."

"Will do," I agreed. "As long as everything is okay at home."

"We are fine. We have the counters cleared and scrubbed. Just waiting for you."

"Delivery trucks were late today. I will get home as soon as I can. Meanwhile you can start on the homemade sprinkles. We should have everything you need at home."

"We will get on it. See you soon," Audrey signed off.

Mr. Brummel signed the order, assigned Craig Maurey, one of his college-aged workers, to help me load the Purple People Eater full of milk, butter and eggs. "Mr. Brummel working you hard this morning?"

"Yeah, but it is worth it," said Craig. "Every extra dime helps pay the college bills."

"Doing well in school?" I asked. "What are you majoring in?"

"Chemical Engineering."

"Oh, tough one," I admired his choice.

"Yeah, but school work has always been easier for me than Chris. Thanks for helping my brother when he was struggling with his EMT prep. I was knee deep in organic chemistry at the time."

"No problem," I said. "He was a joy to work with. He makes a fine paramedic."

"He loves doing it," replied Craig, as he closed the back door of the van. "Heading straight home for baking?"

It was a beautiful spring day. With cool air blowing through the windows, the food should stay cold enough for the errands before reaching home.

"Yes," I said, "as soon as I pick up the dry-cleaning."

"Have a great day." Craig called, reaching for his phone on a slow walk back into the store. I shook my head. Kids and their electronics these days.

Diverting from my planned route, I drove to Kristi's Dry Cleaning. Sheri's cousin ran her business out of one side of her side-by-side duplex house. I parked in the back under some trees for shade, and headed to the front of the house. Kristi was waiting for me in the kitchen, with coffee and some Hostess boxed muffins. Kristi was not one of the 'town bakers' for the weekend, as she claimed she burnt everything that touched her oven. Her expertise was sewing and dry cleaning.

"You have time for coffee while I find the Chief's clothes for you?" Kristi invited me into the kitchen.

I entered with a smile and grabbed a muffin, passed over the coffee in favor of orange juice. I could only spare a few minutes, but to refuse the offer would be insulting.

"Bless you and Sheri for cleaning up my mess," I called down the hall.

"It is my specialty," she replied. "Though you sure know how to make a mess."

She returned with the clothes inside plastic bags.

"Wow!" I said. "Those pants and shoes look as good as new."

Kristi laughed, "Just some simple homemade mixes and scrub-a-dub."

"You have a magic touch, no argument there. What do I owe you?" I asked.

"Nothing. First cleaning for the Chief is on the house. Nice to get new customers."

"I am paying for this one. It is my mess," I insisted.

"Well, how about a great deal. I heard you were given a few gifts of food."

I laughed, "Overrun is more like it. How many meals would you like?"

"Well, my parents are coming in next week..."

"We can deliver a few casseroles Monday morning. How does that sound?"

"You are a lifesaver, Rainbow. Thank you so much."

Finishing off the orange juice, I excused myself, "No problem, but I better get going, so I can get my baking done."

That was a blessedly quick ten minutes. I hoped my next stop will be as fast. Baking time was slipping away.

The Chief's rental house was a short mile and a half away on this side of town. The cold food in the back would still stay cool enough, thanks to some old blankets that Kristi provided for insulation. With a snap on my seatbelt, I was on my way.

It wasn't until the second stop sign that I noticed a slight problem with sluggish brakes. Attributing it to my current hex with vehicles, I made a mental note to call Wilson's garage about getting that checked out, but continued driving.

Three blocks farther down the road, and I realized I was in more trouble than I thought. Coming up on one of the four stoplights in our small town, I pumped, and pumped the brakes. Nothing happened.

Instead of slowing down, the heavy long van, filled with three gallons of milk, twenty-five pounds of flour, thirteen pounds of sugar, and ten pounds of butter, put on speed on the downhill slope, until I was going over forty miles per hour. Kristi's house was on the uphill side of town, while I was headed down hill to the Chief's house. Horn blaring and bracing for impact, I watched as three cars crossing the intersection cleared before my arrival. Blessed be, my light turned green with no one in front of me.

With the biggest obstacle out of the way, I calculate there were five more stop signs between me and the chief's house. Blaring the horn, I blew through another intersection, gaining more speed.

I had been lucky so far, but how was I going to slow down? The boys had an auto mechanic class in Boy Scouts once. What did they say to do? Down shift! Grabbing the knob of the automatic transmission, I pulled down on the gear shift. The engine screeched and strained, but complied to slow down a little, but not enough. Luckily traffic was light, with all the children in school and the town bakers heating ovens at home.

I could try to turn up hill, but that would send me back towards the busier center of town. It was better to drive out of the city limits. Near the Chief's house was a large corn field. I knew that would slow me down fast, if only I could reach it in one piece.

I had to manage a wide right turn at the next stop sign first. Honking my horn as I came near, I drove into the opposing line of traffic. Sounding like a train whistle shrieking helped, as the two oncoming cars pulled over and stopped.

Only one obstacle stopped middle of the road: Mrs. McMillian, in her shiny gold Chevy Malibu, was hard of hearing and was probably confused why the other cars had pulled over. I had no choice but to zig-zag around her, to the left, grab the wheel and yank hard right to follow a big arc path around the edge of the intersection, bouncing on curbs and sidewalks.

Just a few more blocks, to go. I tried downshifting again, all one hundred fifty horses that powered the engine screamed in strained agony. The Purple People Eater slowed just enough to help in my last turn, as I swerved from right to left, scrapping the side of a tree, sending trash cans flying. Three blocks to reach the edge of town. I turned the wheel left, spun the tires, and burnt rubber to straighten the van, on to the last downhill in the final stretch to my destination.

Ahead was one more stop sign, and I was still going over the speed limit. My horn honking alerted two cars as I flew past that last octagonal red sign.

Two blocks, One.... I turned the wheel sharp to swerve left, crossing the traffic line. Once I aimed toward the field, I turned off the engine, waiting until the last second, knowing I would lose the power steering. I gripped the wheel as I plowed down twenty rows of half-grown winter crops before coming to a shuddered stop.

Chapter Twenty-One

BLISSFUL SILENCE AS I LAID exhausted against the head rest, but the silence didn't last long. My front door yanked open in mere moments and Chief Flint's blazing eyes popped into view.

"Are you alright, Mrs. Bailey?" He gave me the once over.

"I think so," I whispered back, still not willing to move much.

"Stay put," he said and turned to the phone in his hand. "Driver is responsive. ETA? Good." To the small crowd of drivers who pulled over to help, he added, "Everyone, please go back to your cars. Clear a way for the ambulance."

Turning back to me, he verified, "Are you sure you are alright?"

"I am just fine." I said. As I reached around to unbuckle, I could feel where the belt had tightened against my body, pinning it in place. Taking a deep breath, I flinched.

Chief Flint caught my grimace. Reaching in, he stopped me, "Whoa, not yet."

I slapped at his hand, glaring. He grabbed back and held my hands firmly. I could almost see him counting to ten, giving me that same look I had often given him, before speaking again.

"You want to tell me why you decided to plow a field with a van?" he asked trying to distract me from moving.

"Brakes stopped working." I growled at him through my teeth.

He stopped in mid-thought and just stared at me. "What do you mean the brakes stopped working?"

I rolled my eyes, the only part of my body that still worked without complaint. "I have been running errands all morning just fine." I breathed in and out slowly, carefully. "Five blocks out of Kristi's Dry Cleaning, the brakes became sluggish and then stopped working."

"Stay put, I want to check something," he ordered, reaching in to pull the hood release lever. I fought the urge to stick my tongue at him like a naughty child, but it must have shown on my face. He decided to add, "Please, stay put?"

Acquiescing, I nodded. Though I would never admit it out loud, I really was feeling too weak physically to move yet. Emotionally, I was tired of everything that happened this week. Not just tired, but sad, angry, disappointed, and furious all rolled into one! This had gone on long enough, circling closer and closer to me.

First the tragedy of Harvey's death Monday night. The killer could have been a passing stranger, for all I knew. That thought was scary enough, but preferable to the alternative: the killer was someone from town. But then someone, most likely the killer, walked right in to Harvey's room, meaning it was someone that Paula or her boys knew. The snake stunt sealed that line of reasoning. Anyone who had lived in town for a few years had probably heard of my Ophidiophobia.

At the time, I thought the snake was meant just as a distraction. Now I wondered if it was a warning, aimed straight at me. It was a harmless prank then, but this was not harmless. Brakes failing so suddenly was definitely a planned attack to stop me by injury or death, of myself or my children.

My thoughts must have frozen me in place because I heard in the background someone calling my name with increasing urgency, cutting into my monologue of thoughts.

"Mrs. Bailey? Rainbow? Are you alright? Help is on the way. Rainbow!" Chief Flint's voice forced me back to the present.

"Help?" The anger at everything this past week came crashing down, daring me to race into action. I locked on his eyes, I unsnapped that buckle and, after kicking at him to move, slid out of the van. "No, I don't need your help, here, now. I need you out there doing your job. I need you to arrest whomever out there is doing this to me, before anything else happens to me and my family."

I emphasized, jabbing him with my finger. The crowd was looking at me, but I was on a roll. "What are you doing standing here? Go chase some clues. Hunt some criminals. But no, you stand here looking at me like I am crazy. That maybe I planned this. Well, look somewhere else, buster."

Placing both hands on his chest while I ranted, I pushed harder and harder against his body wall standing in my way. The last shove knocked me backwards instead. He caught my arms, twirled me around and scooped up my legs, to carry me off through the crowd and into his house. "What are you doing? Let me go. Put me down. Ouch! Are you crazy? Help!" I yelped in the end.

"Clear the way, folks. Engebrecht, Cross, secure that van. Send the paramedics to my house. Clear the way," he yelled over my voice.

No one stopped him. Over his shoulder, I watched Josiah and Corbin just stared at him for a few seconds before following orders. A few of the crowd followed us to the door of his house. He slammed the front door shut cutting them off.

He stomped into the living room, lowering me to the couch. I suppose he tried to do it nicely, but my stomach flopped and neck jerked backwards. I was beginning to feel all the bruises now, but I was still mad enough not to care. I tried to jump up, but he firmly pushed back down on my shoulders.

"Stay here. Don't try to move off the couch or I will be forced to handcuff you to it," he commanded.

I have never listened to commands very well, as Corbin, my aunt and uncle, even my husband could attest. Moving a little, I shifted forward. He retaliated by whipping his handcuffs from his belt pocket. Dangling them in my face, he challenged, cocking his eyebrows: he would follow through on his threat.

Frowning back at him, I tried to control my impulses, but it wasn't working very well. Furious at the world, I started to tremble, dreaming of kicking and punching my way to the door.

"Rainbow. Please" he got down on one knee, eye-to eye, and pleaded. "Trust me."

Was it his use of my first name? His words? The fear in his own voice? Or the pain building from the stress and bruises, I don't know, but the anger rolling deep inside simmered down. I blinked, turning away, and carefully leaned back into the couch for a less painful position. He still didn't leave my side.

"What?" I snapped.

He just tipped his head, questioningly.

"Alright, I will stay here," hands up, I surrendered.

Grunting his acceptance, he kept an eye on me as he walked back to the door to bark orders.

Only when he switched his focus to Josiah at the door, did I acknowledge the pain coursing through my body. The quiet room let me hear every screaming sore muscle, bump and bruise. Tears welled up behind my eyes, threatening to fall. I tried to hold them back as long as I could, by leaning my head back. My eyes closed of their own choice, as I was exhausted from that wild ride.

Pop! Fizzle, Clunk. My eyes opened to see the Chief sit down across from me, gesturing to the generic diet lemon-lime soda can on the table between us. "Sorry, not your favorite, but this will have to do for now."

A moan escaped as I leaned forward to reach for it. Too tired to fight anymore, tears started rolling down. The Chief picked up the can and handed it to me. He also passed over a box of Kleenex. I sipped, graciously, happily feeling the carbonation bubbles cool down my throat, until the metallic taste of artificial sweetener kicked in. Without the caffeine and sugar rush, it really wasn't the same.

A knock on the door announced a new set of visitors, these in dark gray uniforms. Paramedics work twenty-four hours straight, one day on, two days off. Lucky me, it was Todd and Chris's day again.

"Hey, my favorite patient," said Chris.

"Go away." I said, blowing my nose.

"My most stubborn patient" echoed Todd.

I attempted to throw my Kleenex at him, but full range of motion wasn't available just now.

"I see it is hard to move. What hurts?" Todd asked.

Again, I snapped, "Go away."

Chris knelt to eye level, "Mrs. Bailey, you are my teacher and friend, I am not going to leave you like this after a bad accident. Please co-operate."

"Just hand over some Tylenol," I growled. "I am fine."

"Over my dead body," Todd replied. Walking around the couch with his medical kits. "Chief, I can't help her without permission."

"No problem." The Chief picked up the handcuffs and began quoting. "You have the right to remain silent...."

"What are you doing?" I demanded.

"With you under arrest, I have the power to send you straight to the hospital," He walked closer while he spoke. "It might be the best way to keep you out of harm's way anyway. Anything you say or do, can and will be held against you in a court of law."

"You have nothing to charge me with. I would sue for false imprisonment. You would never do that to your reputation," I responded.

He sat on the coffee table in front of me, leaning in close. His voice dropped so low, I could barely hear him, his favorite technique for getting his message across. "You might be the queen of stubbornness, but I can be the king of stubbornness when I wish to be. Let the tongues wag, if it means you get the medical care you so obviously need. So, what will it be?"

Just then my phone rang inside my pants pocket. I pulled it out, but Chief Flint snagged and answered it before I could protest.

"Who is this? Yes, Skylar, this is Chief Flint and your mother is right here. We are discussing some car troubles she had on her way over here." He paused as Skylar replied. "Oh, yes, the groceries. I will have your Uncle Corbin deliver them soon. Oh, ah, no, she is not available, but I will tell her you called."

He snapped the phone off, and placing it behind him, just out of my reach. "Now, you are going to be examined by these capable young men to make sure nothing important was broken or punctured, because you can't take care of your lovely family if you die from complications. I am going to go out to the van and arrange for Officer Cross to deliver the groceries. He will then stay with your children until we straighten a few things up here." He paused for effect. "There will be no arguments. Got it?"

Knowing I was beat, both in energy and stubbornness, I nodded.

"Men, do your thing. Let me know when you are done. You can use the first bedroom for more privacy." He walked out the door, with my phone, and slammed the door shut.

"Think you can stand?" Todd asked.

"I could walk out that door if I wanted to," I glared at him.

With one young man on each side, I was hoisted to my feet as I bit back a curse. "Fudgesicle!"

"You can let them rip," Chris said, gently guiding down the hall, while Todd followed with the medical bags. "We've heard worse."

Ask, and you shall receive, as paraphrased from the Bible. Once the bedroom door had closed and Todd lowered the blinds, they set to work poking and prodding to find the extent of the damage. My replies were the very opposite of lady-like, especially as they helped remove my T-shirt to check for broken ribs.

Pink bruises from the seat belt had started to develop on my rib cage across my shoulder and one across my hip. They would get worse over the next few days, turning all shades of the rainbow from purple to yellow. I knew this from a lifetime of bruise experience.

"You really should go to the hospital for x-rays," said Chris, sweetly, handing me some packaged pain killers.

I admit I was not polite when I told him where he could stuff that idea. Then added, "Even if it was broken, Doc would treat them just the same. You know as well as I do, you can't cast broken ribs in place."

There was a knock on the door, announcing the Chief. "Will she live to terrorize another day?"

"Yes, sir. No *obvious* broken bones," Todd sighed. His meaning was clear. He highly recommended a trip to the hospital for x-rays. Without that test, hidden injuries could cause more trouble. In his opinion, it was better safe than sorry.

It is not that I don't trust doctors, or eschew their specialized years of education. I do respect their dedication to the care of all of God's children. They are, however, not infallible, as my family learned after the death of my mother. I learned much later, she wasn't comfortable with the cancer treatment prescribed by her doctor, but he offered no other alternative at the time, not trusting the newer, better radiation machines that were developed just a few years before. My father drove her to the hospital for her second, stronger round of chemotherapy. After the third dose, the hospital called us to visit for her last days.

Doctor McCarthy restored my faith in the profession when he declared curing people was half science and half art. The unique genetic physique of each person demands co-operation between both patient and doctor to choose the right course of treatment for all ailments. He acknowledges my emotional fear of hospitals, and does his best to accommodate, while also trusting me to know my limits. Since then I have rushed to the hospital just twice, both times for injured family members.

"I agree with Todd on this one, Mrs. Bailey, so please consider it. This is one of the times you really should get x-rayed." Chris knew my feelings on the topic and respected them. Todd just thought I should just get over my fears.

Trying to break the tension, while helping replace my shirt, Chris added with a sad smile, "This will make baking day even harder."

"Thank you so much for reminding me," I sneered, exasperatedly rolling my eyes at him.

Chris laughed, "At least you have a good crew of helpers, because it would be shame not to have everyone fighting over your cookies."

Todd and Chris packed up their bags, and left the house. I took a moment to gather my wits before leaving the relative comfort of the quiet bedroom to face the bear named Chief. I could hear him wearing down the squeaking floor in the living room.

Chapter Twenty-Two

SENSING MY ENTRY, Chief Flint turned from surveying the scene out the front windows.

"What happens now?" I asked, boldly walking to his side. Might as well face the Pied Piper.

His living room portrayed a lovely view of the carnage of run-down plants in the field. Most of the gawkers had driven off, back to their lives. Mr. Wilson was finishing hitching up the tow truck, with Josiah watching on.

His eyes softened slightly, "That is exactly what I was going to ask you. Or maybe 'who now?"

"What do you mean?"

He indicated I sit down in the living room, where somehow the sugarless, caffeine free soda can, in my absence, had morphed into my favorite fountain drink.

"A gift from Mr. Wilson," Chief explained, "when he came personally to look at the van."

Gulping half in one breath, I swallowed all the generic pain pills the EMT boys left for me, and then, choosing firm support over comfort, I eased gingerly into his turn-of-the-century ornate wooden rocking chair.

Taking a seat across from me on the couch, Chief Flint waited patiently as I settled into a less painful position, before he raised one finger, "This morning, I sent Officer Engebrecht to follow up on that lead you gave us. You were right. Samantha Stone had copied the recipe. Harvey showed it to her eight or nine months back and bribed her into making the treats for him every month."

Second finger raised, to continue, "Meanwhile, Nancy Pickler walked in with her story, ID'ing the ring from the picture as the ring she once owned, but claimed Harvey never asked her for anything."

Third finger came up, "And finally, Officer Engebrecht sees that Tammy Connor is back in town. When he goes to get her statement about Monday night, she confesses to the candy bars. And, at your suggestion, I am told."

Wrapping up his speech, he stated, "That is three people for three of Harvey's items. So, who else did you talk to that hasn't confessed, yet? That might be the person who sliced your brake line in half."

"So, it was deliberate," I replied, sucking more sugar to fight the stress.

"Mr. Wilson just confirmed it," he confirmed. "Someone, most likely at your last stop, sliced the brake fluid line almost clean through. What store and where did you park for that?"

"I stopped for your dry-cleaning. Kristi's on Dinglewood Street," I answered distractedly, trying to take it all in. "Uh, I parked in the back under the trees to keep the van cooler."

"Secluded, you mean. In the center of town, the purple van attracts attention, which, in a way, makes it safer. But parking it out of sight presented an opportunity," he sighed, "Now do you see how dangerous it is to be snooping around a killer? You have more curiosity than a cat, but they at least have nine lives."

His attempt at humor did not amuse me, "Me-ow" I replied.

Chief slammed his palm on the table. "You were damn lucky you weren't killed today, Rainbow, or killed someone else."

"I know that!" I screamed at him, choking on the last word as the ribs screamed back, a rack of pain shook my whole body. Stifling a yelp as pain wrapped around my side, I breathed slowly in and out, until the black cloud cleared out of my vision. I replied softly, "You really think I wanted to get a killer mad at me for the fun of it?"

Calmly, he offered, "You said it yourself, you encourage curiosity."

"For learning and scientific discovery, not for chasing criminals," I said.

Knock, knock.

"Evidently, whomever killed Harvey thinks otherwise." Chief let that hang in the air while he sauntered to the door to confer with his officer.

To distract myself from the throbbing pain, I eased out of the rocking chair to walk around the room. While Chief Flint's office was a modern conglomerate of stainless steel, his house was surprisingly warm. The rocking chair wasn't the only antique in the room. A beautiful Queen Anne-style highboy curio cabinet sat in the corner. The stain shone fresh, evenly laid through the fluid curves, but the tongue and groove connections reveal its true age of over three hundred years old. It was a beautiful restoration, as was his buffet. I would never declare myself to be an expert on antiques but I had studied antiques in art school. The smooth maple buffet with carved scalloped edged designs was a true classic Chippendale style block front chest. I appreciated the time and love that poured into the restoration of the two-hundred-year-old beauty.

The half-unpacked boxes haphazardly placed on top and around it hid the true beauty from first glance. The mess of boxes was totally understandable considering he had only been there a week, and a very busy week at that. I walked over to a box to see what was inside. It had some dishes from the kitchen, and a few knick-knacks still wrapped in newspaper. Well, he hadn't had time to unpack much, not with chasing down a murderer.

Wait just one minute! That was our local newspaper wrapped around his dishes. That meant he was either packing up again, or putting these things in storage. I unwrapped the top item. It was a framed picture of a young girl swinging on a tire hung from a maple tree. A water tower and windmill in the distance were the clues I needed.

Realizing I didn't hear the Chief speaking at the door anymore, I turned to find him right behind me, holding out his hand for the frame.

"Your wife, Laura, on the Pennington farm, I believe." I placed the frame carefully in his hand. He looked surprised, as I explained, "She lived here for four, maybe five summers with her grandparents, if I recall. I didn't know her much because those summers I spent on my father's farm up north. That is why her picture in your office seemed familiar but I couldn't place her then."

"Yes," He said, staring at the photo. "Her favorite memories came from this farm and the community around it."

"That would be the village of Edgewood, which had little more than a feed-store, hardware store, post office and three bars. But they attended St. Matthew's Lutheran Church, which is why I heard of her. If I recall, her grandparents died in a car accident that next winter and her mother sold the farm to family members. Laura never returned." History lesson ended, I caught his eye, "But now you came to honor her memory? Or be close to her again?"

I thought, at first, he wasn't going to reply. When he did answer, his voice was a mile away. "Laura was vibrant, in her own quiet way. Most days, I knew I made a difference on the force, but sometimes, well, then I had Laura. I would come home, worn out from seeing the worst in people, she was like a breath of fresh air."

Gingerly he returned the photo to the buffet, "Laura had a gift for storytelling, honed in her many years as a kindergarten teacher. When she spoke of those summers, she made them come alive with warmth and love, the ideal place to raise the family we were never blessed with. When she died, a part of me died, too."

Looking at me, "So, to appease your curiosity, when I saw the job opening, I just applied."

"Then why are you leaving?"

"How did you...?" He questioned.

"Yesterday's newspaper wrapped around a precious photograph," I pointed to the date. "I thought you might be wrapping it for storage, but not this photo."

He sighed, "Blindsiding unsuspecting people with observations to get confessions? You should be a police officer."

I ignored his commentary, "I happily prefer a career as mother, and don't change the subject. You are thinking about leaving, are you not?"

"Thinking about it, yes," he admitted.

"Why, if I may ask?"

"If you may ask?" He mocked my curiosity. "Well, let me tell you what I have discovered about Laura's 'caring little town who always gives a helping hand and a smile'. To the people here, I am the outsider and the enemy, not the murderer - who is probably also their cousin twice removed or something. No one is willing to talk about the actual crime to me. Yet, they would love to hook me up with their granddaughter, or stuff me with three-day old chocolate cake. The only person who seems to give a damn about catching the killer of Harvey Henson is you."

He scoffed, threw his hands in the air, and stalked off to the kitchen. "Why am I even talking to you about this? You wonder why the killer would be after you? Just look around. Everyone you talk to spills their guts."

I followed him and found him cleaning up his TV dinner dishes. "I just listen. And sometime that is all they need."

He continued running water, mixing soapy water for the dishes, his back to me. After the silence dragged on, I tried a different tract. "How long has she been gone?"

The Chief paused amid washing his blue with yellow daisies coffee mug, "Thirteen months and twenty-three days."

"Long enough for mourning without making rash decisions," I agreed. "Which means you chose to come here for a reason."

"You think you have me all figured out." He said, placing the mug in the sink to dry.

"Just the opposite, really. I have no idea why a strong, determined and decorated officer would give up after a week."

"I am not giving up. I just don't belong here," He said, slamming his fist on the counter, followed by a whispered swear word. Regaining his composure, he sighed as he sat down at the kitchen table. "The city council should have hired Corbin to be the chief, with your ear to the ground the two of you would be unstoppable."

"There is where you are wrong. I do hear things at times. Who wouldn't around here with all the jabber-boxes? But I do my best to stay out of the gossip mills. Just this week I heard many negative things about Harvey's past that I didn't want or need to know," I shuddered. "I prefer to look for the positive in all things. Life is too short and hard to focus on anything else."

I sat down across from him, "Other things I have just observed and put them together. Very much like a detective, but I don't want your job. Being a wife and mother is the only full-time job for me. And Corbin doesn't have the experience of age. I saw all those achievements on the wall. You didn't get them riding on someone's shirt tails. You have so much to teach him."

Electronic musical notes playing Weird Al Yankovic's "Just Eat it", the boy's ringtone for their father's number interrupted my admonition.

Chief retrieved my phone from his pocket. "Mr. Bailey. He called earlier. I said you were resting."

I accepted the phone before turning away for privacy, "Martin, honey, I am fine."

"Rainbow, you are not fine!" Martin hissed, his hushed tones barely disguising his panic. I could hear the rush of customers ordering in the background. "Where are you right now? I am coming to get you!"

"Martin, sweetie, calm down. I am a bit bruised, but I am fine."

"Rainbow, you could have broken your neck with that whiplash. I am taking you to the hospital!"

I cut him off. "Martin Fitzgerald Bailey, I think I would know if I had broken something. Don't you dare start listening to the town rumors. I was strong enough to give birth to five children at home, I am strong enough to survive a bumpy ride."

"You are telling me you didn't crash into the Chief's rental house with Wilson's van and cut your head?"

"No, honey, I didn't. I only plowed through a corn field. I am fine." I said. Well, sort of fine. I knew I couldn't hide the bruises from him forever, but he didn't need to worry about it. "Now, you are going to stay at work. I will be heading home soon to bake cookies for the rest of the day. I will call when I get home, and you can check on me there, Okay? I love you."

"Love you, too," said Martin, almost giving in, but not quite yet. "Is the Chief still there?"

"Yes," I admitted, wondering where this was going.

"Let me talk to him," he said.

"Why, Martin?" I was tired, exasperated, and getting hungry. Breakfast had been earlier than normal and I still had a long day ahead of me.

"Please, for me?" He replied, with no explanation.

I sighed. Martin, my beloved, knew he married a strong, independent woman. Well, maybe, that was probably an understatement. Martin had only known me for two years, and half that time I was still in college.

We fell in love over common ground- small town life, creative spirit, and independence- but we quickly learned our styles were total opposites. Martin was meticulous in his creative endeavor, by recording his recipes for future replication, much like a scientist. My artistry was more emotional, free flowing, just like the way I lived my life. While he planned methodically, I tended to jump in with both feet which meant more for him to handle.

Since our vows, he has had to worked with my focused best, and my stubborn crazy worst, which usually hit at the same time. Falling over a dead body was probably the worst in the last sixteen years. Martin put up with my crazy life, the least I could do is honor a simple request. Perhaps the Chief would relieve his mind.

"Only for you," Handing over the phone I explained to Chief Flint. "My knight in shining armor wants a word with you."

I left the kitchen while Martin conferred with the Chief. The strain in Martin's voice left no doubt the topic of conversation. Poor Martin was on the sidelines of this situation, while I was in the thick of it. He was worried about the safety of his wife and the mother of his children. In the end, it didn't matter what Martin said to the Chief of Police. Chief Flint admitted, just moments ago, I was no longer on the suspect list, so he couldn't lock me up for safety. And I refused to be intimidated into hiding.

The situation had to change soon. The attacks were escalating and next time could injure my family. Why? Was it something I saw? Or something I did? This morning I spoke with the Chief, ran errands and talk to a few friends. Had someone been watching me? That would be extremely difficult, since I knew everyone in town. Surely, I would have noticed someone following me through town. Especially through the streets to the dry-cleaner's house. On the other hand, I hadn't been watching either, just going about my business in my normally quiet hometown.

Closing my eyes, I focused on my steps around the dry cleaner's house from parking under the tree in the back to front door. I remember waving to Mrs. Olson as she fed the birds between batches of dough. Her oven had a knack for burning the two cookies on the end. The birds loved her for it. Otherwise, the street had been as quiet as it should be in the middle of a work and school day in early May.

This wasn't working. I couldn't name the killer. I could not even imagine any of the people I spoke with earlier as someone who would harm me, or Harvey. Yet, someone knew the town so well, it couldn't be someone just passing by. Our only hope would be to keep Chief Flint here working for the city. We needed Chief's impartiality along with his experience. If the Chief quit and the job was handed to Corbin, old feuds could surface fast.

With no useful details coming to mind, I gave up. There was something more important at the moment. After all that soda, I needed to find the bathroom. Heading down the hallway, past the Chief's bedroom, my feet continued past the bathroom to explore to the second bedroom. The door was half open revealing a pile of tarps, wood stain, and rags all piled against a beautiful, but weathered, eighteenth century secretary, a desk-bookcase combination with dovetailed corners and drawers. Peering in for a better view, I could see the original varnish had been stripped, awaiting a new protection layer of stain.

"Snooping again?" Chief Flint remarked, arms crossed, leaning his bulk against the door frame.

"I was looking for the bathroom until this beauty caught my eye. The scroll work is divine." I ran my hand over the intricate designs carved lovingly in the oak standing tall before me. "Restoring a family heirloom?"

"No," Chief hesitated, sighing softly before continuing. "Laura's hobby. She was the expert. She would find the dirtiest junk from the dump or estate sales, strip and stain them, and make a hefty profit. I simply helped with repairs."

With just barely a touch, the fall-front opened to reveal three small drawers. Each fit snug in their slots, sliding out and in with ease. "It feels smooth. Almost brand new. As if I am back in the year it was made."

"The three original drawers were missing," he admitted. "By using an old oak picture frame for the sides, and bottom from a broken oak drawer, both about the right age, I built replacements. I also replaced the lopper supports that were chipped and off track."

"Tight tongue and groove corners. That takes talent." I admitted.

Chief shrugged, "It was nice working with my hands. Laura replicated an old English recipe for gluing the arches in."

"How much longer until it is finished?" I asked.

"Probably never," Chief said, closing the desk and nodding toward the door. "Like I said, Laura's hobby."

I frowned, "Yet you moved it all the way out here."

"It was the last one we worked on together," he admitted.

I nodded, "Good reason."

"I have Rainbow Bailey's approval. My life is now complete," he snarked. "Now, bathroom is back this way."

Childish it was, but I couldn't help it: I stuck out my tongue and crossed my eyes as I walked past him into the bathroom.

Chapter Twenty-three

WHILE I FRESHENED UP, I took some time to regroup my thoughts. Small communities were a shy and cautious lot. They were not used to meeting new people, compared to larger cities where people moved in and out all the time. Johnathan Flint was at cross-roads, obviously struggling with his decision to take the job. If only he had more time to get to know the community, and they know him before the tragedy struck, then events would play out differently.

I couldn't change the time frame, that was water under the bridge. But maybe, just maybe, I could help bridge the communication gap.

"Ready to go?" Chief Flint handed over my purse substitute, rescued by someone from the Purple People Eater van.

Digging inside I found a pencil and my photocopied planner. I ripped off the top page, now out of date, and followed him out to his car.

"Remember something?" he asked.

"This all reminds me of a story, and I want to 'paint' it down."

"Paint? With a pencil?" he snorted.

"A picture is worth a thousand words; a thousand words makes a story. So, yes, I paint stories." Once I was buckled in, I began to let the thoughts in my head escape onto the page. "Would you care to hear the story of Tops and Bottoms?"

"By all means, enlighten me," I could hear Chief Flint rolled his eyes, as he put the car in gear.

"This story begins with a young man disillusioned with the big city, where the sun was hidden by the tall buildings. It was all he had ever known but needed a change. His friend from outside the city spoke of the sun so bright in the countryside. It intrigued him. His grandfather had farmed, so he thought he would try it. He bought some land in the country."

"Laura's grandfather was the farmer," he interjected. "and my grandfather owned a cobbler shop."

"Stop interrupting," I continued. "Now being a city boy, he did things differently. He analyzed the soil for the right kind of crops, and brought new-fangled machines to help do the work. The farmers and townspeople around him looked at him weirdly. They were shy of the new-fangled ideas."

He looked sideways at me, "Hmmmph."

"The farmers were of two types: the families that grew *tops* and the families that grew *bottoms*. Lettuce, broccoli, and celery, food that is found on top of the soil, were found on the tops' farms. Bottoms' grew carrots, radishes and beets, where the food is the root of the plants. The young man, believing those markets were saturated and not wanting to encroach or offend his new neighbors, decided to grow a middle plant: corn.

"Making this up on the fly, are you?" he asked.

"Based on the real book Tops and Bottoms by Janet Stevens." I countered, "Do you always interrupt people during interrogations?"

"By all means, continue," he said.

"It was a great idea actually. Things went well for a short time, and they all would have gotten along in a year or so. The young man would learn their customs, learn that slowing down for a long chat was a sign of respect for the others ideas and opinions. Meanwhile the community would learn new ways from the inventive young man, that it wasn't disrespect for them, but respect for the shortness of life that drove him to improve things now."

Chief parked his car near the police station, shutting off the engine, "I am sensing a 'but' in this story."

"You would be correct," I admitted, still sketching as I spoke. "A tragedy struck the community just after the tops, bottoms, and middle had been planted. Two children had fallen down a very deep well- a top and a bottom. Now time was of the essence, but the leader of the tops and the leader of the bottoms were fighting over how to get them out. The young man had an idea, and the machinery, to get the children out quickly, but the leaders and thus the community members were too busy fighting to even try to listen. And the ones who would stop and listen would rather feed him three-day old chocolate cake and chat for four hours instead of jumping to action."

"Sounds awfully familiar," he cracked a smile.

"Hush, let me finish. The young man was distraught. He had heard that these communities were loving and kind and welcoming. Here they were bickering like the little children they needed to save. It was so frustrating, he thought it would be much easier to just pack up, leaving the children and the community to their fate."

"How does it end?" he asked, as he grabbed for the door handle.

I finished the drawing just in time: The Chief as my mind's eye saw him, showing off his newly finished antique secretary desk. Only this one had various vegetables delicately carved in the wood, instead of the standard curves and curly-cues.

"I don't know," I said. "Not my story, but his to choose, and only his. He could return to all he knows, comforted in its traditions, stagnant in the familiar. But I would hope he would find a way to reach out to his new community, without compromising his own standards. Learn to bend in the breeze, if you will." I finished the drawing, placing it upside down on his hand.

I left the Chief standing outside the car, hesitantly viewing the drawing, while I reclaimed my property from Sheri. Besides my own white Astro van, the Chief had also given permission to reclaim my phone and purse. I guess one good thing came from plowing through the streets on a run-away van.

Stuffing the keys in my pocket, I rediscovered the drawing I made of the tattoo.

Chief Flint came up from behind me, offering my son's phone, accusing, "And you said you weren't hiding any clues from me."

I showed it to him. "You know what this means? Because I don't. I knew I had seen the tattoo somewhere before, so I drew a copy to see if it triggered memories later."

"Yes," he paused, sighed, before offering information. "That is the tattoo that Harvey had. Joe Carson, his partner had it also. It is a symbol meaning prosperity. Where did you find it?"

"Thomas at the paper had copies of a newspaper story in a file, as research into Harvey's life. There I saw a picture of Joe, with this on his arm. I probably also noticed it when I caught an unfortunate glimpse of the autopsy photos, though I tried to avoid looking at them." I frowned, "Are you say his 'gang' used it?"

"Yes, when Joe was arrested, his partners all had the same tattoo." Chief Flint jingled his keys, "Ready? I will follow you home."

"You don't have to do that," I protested.

He just stared at me, arms crossed. The classic 'I am going to get my way' stance he used when threatening to handcuff me. The same stance Martin and Corbin try to use on me from time to time. I let them get away with it, once in a while, when it suits my purpose.

"Fine. Thank you," I acquiesced, giving him a quick but painful hug, then bouncing back with a smile. "Sorry, I just got excited to drive my van again. Oh, did you get your clothes out of the Purple People Eater?"

"Yes. What do I owe you?"

"Nothing," I held my hand up to block his bossy stare again. "And that is not a bribe. That is me being responsible for my actions. Besides it really didn't cost me thing." I led the way to the garage. "Kristi has more guests than she can feed coming next week, while I currently have too much food, thanks to the community bakers. I love the barter system. It works to the advantage of everyone involved."

He just shook his head at me, with a stubborn slight smile on his face, and escorted me to the garage.

Once we were out of ear shot of the front desk, Chief asked, "That story you drew?"

"Yes?" I asked.

"Where do you fit in?"

"That is easy. I am a Bottom Clan who hates beets but loves broccoli and celery. So, I married a Top, unheard of at the time. In our blended family, we eat all colors of the rainbow, and raise milk cows for cheese."

"You would," This time the smile split wide open, a twinkle danced in his eyes.

As he shut the driver's door for me, he said through the open window, "You say you know everyone in this town and can't see any of them as a murderer. I am surprised you haven't suspected me. I had just arrived."

"That is easy," I ticked off my reasons, "You were riding with Corbin that night, the boys at Harvest House would never have let you in without letting Paula know you were there, and you were with me when the box of treasures were stolen. You can't be the killer. True, you might have an accomplice from town. But then I am back to the idea that someone I know is a killer. It has to be, I realize that, yet I don't want to believe it. I simply don't want to see it. That is why we need you, an outsider, to do your investigative best."

He nodded, seeming to agree with my analysis, "I will pull in behind you as you drive around front."

I drove out the police garage and around to the front. Chief pulled in behind me, as promised. Following me the six blocks home, he waited for me to go inside before he pulled away.

Chapter Twenty-Four

COOKIE BAKING WAS IN FULL SWING. Audrey had taken the reins and ordered everyone to a cookie station. Audrey and Emily were mixers, Travis was a scooper and wrapper, Skylar and Hunter were bakers and runners, while the taster, Corbin, was gleefully getting fatter.

Corbin stood up from the counter when I entered, "Everything is under control, Cousin. And I promise I haven't peeked at the recipe. Scouts' honor."

"Glad to hear, but you were in 4-H, never a scout."

"My, aren't you testy today."

"No, so far you have been the tester," I established. "I can see it on your shirt. Go get cleaned up before you leave."

"No can do, cousin. I have been ordered here for the remainder of the day by both Chief Flint and "Chief" Martin. He came by with lunch a little bit ago. Now give me those keys. You are officially grounded."

So tired of yet another well-meaning loved one in my life giving me orders, I was going to protest his uppity commanding attitude, but for two things. One, I had no plans to go anywhere else today, and, two, I had five sets of worried eyes looking at me. I handed over the keys and he put them in his pocket.

"What did you tell them?" I whispered to him.

"Just that you had an engine break down, but I think they suspect something else." Handing me the phone, he added, "I also promised Martin you would call as soon as you got in."

Calling Martin was one of the hardest phone calls I ever made. He wanted to rush home, but I finally convinced him that I would stay home today and that I was fine. It wasn't easy, but I played down the pain, both physical and emotional. Yes, my ribs and shoulder hurt from the seat belt and my left hip where it slammed into the door on a few of those curves, but the pain served a great reminder of the blessings in my life, which included all those currently baking in my house.

Martin gave up arguing after soliciting my promise that I would stay home to rest. That was fine by me. Emotionally and mentally, I was drained. The week leading up to auction weekend was hectic in its own rite. Having a murder investigation in the mix ruffled already strained feathers. The stress was taking its toll, but no rest for the weary, at least until after this weekend. If only the murderer were caught, then the town, and my family, could focus again.

The Chief had said the kickboxing group was at the top of his list for proximity reasons. I had helped eliminate some of the names, but how the treasures related to those ladies surprised me. I had no idea how, or even if, the other little treasures would fit into our group, or the community at large. Thinking about the possibilities this afternoon, however, was not going to finish my responsibilities for this weekend.

Thanks to pain medicine, my arms and shoulders let me slowly change into my favorite cooking shirt. Pushing the murder topic aside, I pondered the other revelations of the morning. The more I thought about it, the more I knew it was time to call my lawyer.

"Timberlake," Jake answered on the second ring.

"Jake, it's Rainbow. What is your going rate for a confidential conversation? Would a dozen of my secret recipe do?" I offered.

"Mrs. Bailey, if the Chief arrested you and you need bail, we will have to go through official channels to find a criminal attorney," Jake replied. "As mayor, I can't represent both you and the city in criminal proceedings."

"Oh, no, Jake. I am not the client, much to your chagrin, I know," Jake had never forgiven me for the year he pulled my pigtails in first grade. A harmless prank he thought. Then his eye connected to my right fist, and even with all his smooth talking, his day ended in suspension instead of mine.

"In that case, what do you need?" He asked. "Quickly as I am due to meet a judge any minute."

"Confidentiality." I said. "Lawyer client privilege."

"You know something I need to know but you don't want others to know who told me. Is that it?"

"Fresh hot cookies reserved just for you," I replied.

"Alright. My lips are sealed. Legally, if you wish. What do you have?"

"Well, you know that our new chief is a widower. Did you ever ask the name of his wife?" I asked.

"No. She is deceased, so it never came up," Jake replied.

"You might want to research a marriage certificate," I hinted.

"And why would she be important?" He asked. "She is deceased, right?"

"Oh, you know me," I said. "I don't spread rumors or personal information. But I will save you a dozen cookies." I hung up before joining my family in the kitchen.

Someone had reheated today's lunch for me. I didn't know I was hungry until my stomach growled a compliant at the sight of it. Martin's home-cooked specials, even cooked in a restaurant, still tasted better than any take-out. Hunger satisfied, I felt much better. Once I had put the dishes in the dishwasher, Corbin gave a nod to Emily. She came running over to hug me, sticky hands and all. It was a good thing I had my grungy shirt on.

Still, she hugged me so carefully, that I knew the cat was out of the bag so to speak. Someone had blabbed and told the kids. "Corbin?" I asked over Emily's head.

"They could tell something was wrong from the way you moved." He frowned.

Confession time, whether I liked it or not. Replaying the morning events, I downplayed the danger as much as possible.

Skylar spoke first, "Mom, if it wasn't for our calculator, you would never have been involved in this."

"And if it wasn't for you, I would never have known to down shift to slow the van," I retorted. "Life is learning something new every day. Today I learned the trick worked."

What else could I say to alleviate their fears? "Now, I refuse to let this person stop us from living our lives. We have cookies to bake! So, let's turned on some music and return to work."

I had no memory of my mother ever making that recipe before. I found it when the twins were little. When my dad was rewiring his old farm house kitchen, when he asked me to go through some of her old kitchen things. Her own handwriting declared them "Very Good", so I tried them. It was one of the first times Martin actually liked my cooking. Each double batch made ninety-six rolled and sugar pressed cookies, needing only five or six minutes in the oven. With the large numbers we baked for the sale, the quick bake time was a must.

While they danced, boogied and baked around the kitchen, the only job my children allowed me was bagging. I tried to give them a break mixing the dough or rolling the cookies, but all five children insisted they were fine. After each batch cooled, Corbin delivered the pile into my hands to be wrapped and priced. Audrey plopped three huge boxes of sandwich bags on the coffee table, along with the pile of zip-ties.

By the time Martin came home, we had around eighty-five dozen baked, cooled and wrapped cookies for the sale on Saturday and some extremely tired bodies. That is why I only bake these about once a year. After this marathon, no one wants to make more for a year.

Martin beelined straight for me and gave me a hug. "I would have come home, if you wanted me."

"I do want you," I reassured him, face buried in his shoulder. Aromas of honey ham, and sweet pickles filled the air. "I want and need you in my life. But you could do nothing at that moment, and I'm going to be okay now. I am glad you are home, though. This is the best time of day, to have the whole family together again."

Later, after our children headed to bed, he helped me undress and take a shower. The hot water felt so good on my shoulders, as the pounding spray found its way to every bruise I knew I had and then some.

Martin, my love, was there to help me re-dress and cradle in bed. I am not sure how much sleep he got, but I fell asleep instantly. When I woke in the morning, he was already in the shower, getting ready for the extra busy day.

Chapter Twenty-Five

SET UP DAY HAD ARRIVED. Starting early in the morning, every able-bodied community member began setting up tables, laid out auction items, or delivered food items. City workers installed barricades around town to help direct the swarm of traffic expected on Saturday. Our three hotels and five bed and breakfasts, booked since last year, wash all the bedding for their guests arriving tonight.

The Bailey family alarm clocks called us out of bed an hour after the sun came up. As a family, we headed to the Pit Stop to help Martin pre-cook for the event. This year it was an extra comfort to me, all to be working together after this long week.

The morning was spent cutting, slicing, and wrapping up all kinds of sub sandwiches to be sold for lunch today and tomorrow. It was a long, long day, so we limited the menu to a few easy items for the convenience of both us and the customers. Many of the town workers stop by our restaurant for quick lunch or dinner since they put in a full day of work. They don't all come just to our shop. The other restaurants are just as busy. But tonight, there were enough customers for all the restaurants, to be full and then some.

Just after lunch, my boys headed out with Uncle Arlis to set up booths and tables at the church. Once they returned, two hours later, my girls and I headed out early to set up the goods on those table.

I found myself working alongside JC Bancock. I had been too busy to think much all day, but now I couldn't help but wonder if she had a connection to Harvey in any way. I decided to stay away from the topic though, when I asked her about this weekend.

"It will be nice to see you around this weekend. I know you usually go see your sister. Where does she live again?"

JC stopped folding the clothes in her hand, but didn't look up, "She lives in Carlinville."

"Oh, that is right. I remember now. It is next to Shawnee tribal burial lands. We went there two years ago when the boys studied the burial practices of American Indians." I said, then paused, remembering the River's Luck Casino on the Mississippi River there. The coin in Harvey's box was from the River's Luck Casino. I knew that place had sounded familiar.

I put down the baby bibs I was stacking and looked at her face. Our eyes locked.

"You don't really have a sister in that area, do you?" I asked.

The normally brash JC sighed, "Actually I do, but she and I don't talk much since she joined GA."

"GA?" I asked.

"Gamblers Anonymous," she continued, "I tried to join with her, but I just can't break the habit. I don't know how she can do it, living so close. I have tried, you know. It is just that I am one of the lucky ones who usually break even, eventually. It is not like I am in debt up to my ears."

"I am sorry," I said. "I didn't know."

"And you probably wouldn't have if it wasn't for Harvey," JC said, disgusted. Not sure if it directed to Harvey or herself. "He helped me clean out my back yard after the big storm last August. I gave him a tip and accidentally gave him one of the coins. I guess he kept it in his treasures?"

"Yes, but we didn't know we would find anything, honest. We thought it was just a hide and seek game for his friends. Besides gambling isn't illegal," I offered.

"No, but it might affect my job running the company. Potential clients might not trust someone whose hobby is gambling. That is why I go to my sister's place instead of the casinos closer," she explained. "If anyone should figure it out, I am glad it was you, Rainbow. You know how to keep secrets."

"Thanks for the compliment," I smiled. "Did Harvey ever figure it out?"

"No. That I know of," JC replied. "He noticed that it was different and I just said it was my lucky charm coin, and that he did such a good job that he could keep it."

"I think you should tell the Chief of Police." I said. "He needs to know everything to do with Harvey, to narrow down the suspect list."

JC looked at me like I was crazy, "What are you thinking? The less anyone knows the better."

"Yes, I am sure. That is why the town council voted for him. Only highly decorated detectives know how to keep confidences in delicate situations. He had to handle many valued pieces of info discreetly before this."

“Alright,” she gave a big sigh. "You convinced me. But I don't want Sheri overhearing."

"I can help with that. Here is his cell phone number." I prattled it off. "He gave it to me yesterday after the van incident."

She smiled as she dialed, "Yeah, I heard about the People Eater going wild on a munching spree."

I playfully growled at her, then left her to her phone call.

"Rainbow," Esther Brumfield, this year's organizer of our church's garage sale, called my name. "I forgot to pick up a bundle of items donated at the Power Fitness. I called Janice about getting them, but the office is closed already. Would you be willing to pick it up? There is a lamp, some discontinued sweatshirts and a few other items, in a pile she said, at the office."

"Sure, I can do that," I said. “No time like the present.”

I told Audrey and Emily where I was going and left them at the church. Emily was busy playing with baby Henry so his mom could keep working and Audrey was knee deep in sorting toys by age group.

"Okay, Mom, but if you are not back in thirty minutes, I am calling the cops," Audrey said, checking her watch. Frowning worry lines were already etched in her forehead, just like her father.

It would be a short fifteen-minute trip. Five-minute drive, five minutes to load and five minutes to drive back. I agreed to the conditions, "Shouldn't be more than fifteen minutes. Twenty minutes if traffic holds me up."

I grabbed my keys and drove over to the Power Fitness. Parking in back, closer to the office door, for easier loading. No other cars were parked in the lot. Most of the regulars were getting their exercise by preparing for tomorrow's event.

I unlocked the back door of the office by the washing machine and turned on the lights to look for the items. I found them on the floor in the corner and put them into a laundry basket to carry them outside.

Gathering the lamp, the base dropped a screw and fell off. No problem. I could fix that with the screw driver Janice kept handy in the bottom drawer.

Fixing the lamp's base was quick, but putting the screw driver back was not. I tried to slide the drawer shut, but it wouldn't close. I took it out and reached in the hole for the obstruction, finding a small bundle of brown speckled papers.

I unrolled them to read them so I could file them correctly. On top was a newspaper article of the bank robbery three years ago in a small town fifty miles south of us. The report described the robber as a female of medium height, average looking. There was an accomplice who provided a distraction for the robbery to occur. Neither one was apprehended.

I put the pile on the desk and looked at the next article. It was of another bank robbery two years ago, same Modus Operandi. The third story was the same, only just eight months ago. All robberies were within ninety miles of Charlotteville and each M.O. sounded similar to the crime report of Joe Carson, with one exception: his were all in a year, but these were spread out.

I sat down on the chair to think, moving Janice's exercise t-shirt off the seat. The t-shirt itself was unusual: short waisted, but with 3/4 length sleeves. The exercise room was always warm, I never knew how she could stand to wear long sleeves. Could she be covering something up? A tattoo maybe?

Uh, oh, I might have stumbled over something again. I didn't know the connection yet, but it was time to put this all away and get out of there fast. As I put it behind the drawer and carefully closed the drawer, a shadow crossed the thresh-hold of the office door.

"Oh, Janice, you scared me. I was just fixing the lamp base for the fundraiser. A screw on the bottom was loose. Thank you for donating it. The church appreciates it." I babbled on. Time to shut up. "Well I better be going back. We still have to do a lot before tomorrow."

"Sure, no problem. I am happy to donate to a good cause." Her words were positive, yet she was frowning.

I started to walk around the desk toward the other parts of the pile, while she headed straight to the desk. Unfortunately, the drawer had not closed all the way, but I was hoping she didn't notice.

I quickly gathered items, both hands holding the laundry basket and was turning toward the hallway when I heard her call, "Stop right there."

Dang it! If every cell in my body hadn't been trained so well by each teacher and parent figure to respect an authoritative voice, I would have run away fast to freedom. Instead, my feet did a quick turn about.

"Did I forget something, Janice?" I asked as innocently as possible.

She held up the bundle of newspaper reports in one hand, "Yeah, these."

The other hand wrapped around sharp letter opener, poised to swing at me.

Chapter Twenty-Six

THERE I STOOD arms full of odds and ends for the rummage sale, the sharp tip of the envelop opener just a few feet away, and still too many steps to cross to the open office door and freedom.

"How could you kill Harmless Harvey?" burst from my lips in an attempt to stall.

Smirking, Janice exclaimed, "Harmless? What a joke. There was nothing harmless about Harvey. He walked all around town watching, listening, and digging up his little treasures. The snoop got what he deserved."

"You followed us Wednesday, looking for Harvey's treasure box?"

"I was already there. I had part of a map from Harvey's room, found it in the caboose of a toy train, but that was only half of a map. I looked all over for the other half, but never found it. Where did you find it?"

To keep her talking, I said, "There was an identical caboose in the living room. We didn't even know about the treasures then, or even where the map would lead."

"But now you know. It led to his box of things that belonged to other people. Things that should have stayed buried in the past. And here you come following in his footsteps, snooping into things that are none of your business."

"I don't snoop!" I shouted back.

What is she talking about? What did I find? What did I know? Think, Rainbow, Quick!

She laughed at me, "I've watched you. You are smart, much smarter than Harvey. One by one, you connected the items in the box to the former owners, and all you had were pictures to go by. I knew it was only a matter of time before you found my secret."

"Joe Carson." It suddenly all fell into place. I knew Joe's picture looked familiar. "He was your father. I can see the resemblance now. And the robberies in the area are just like he did. Just following in daddy's footstep, I suppose. Your shirt sleeves. They cover up a matching tattoo."

"See?" She rolled up a sleeve to reveal the same tattoo on Harvey and Joe. "I knew you would put it all together, the way you snoop into everyone's business."

I ignored that difference of opinion to keep her talking, "But Joe Carson didn't kill anyone. Why kill his former partner?"

"Late Monday afternoon, while I was working in the yard, Harvey came to me with these in hand." She waved the newspaper clippings. "He had noticed the similarities, connected the dots. He wanted me to stop. 'Robbing is wrong,' he said. 'It hurts other people.' He didn't want Joe's daughter to go to jail, like he had, but if I didn't stop, he was going to turn me in. I couldn't let him do that."

"So, you stabbed him."

"I ended that argument when he turned to walk away. One big thrust under the rib cage with the dandelion weeder I had in my hand. I just needed to get rid of the body. I wrapped him up, and called my partner. He rode with me here, and helped me tip Harvey in. He waited out the class in the mechanical room and drove home with me. It would have worked out perfectly if you hadn't found the body so fast."

"Now what to do with you?" She started walking around the desk. "I tried to warn you to stop snooping. Twice. The snake was beautiful, don't you think? I found him sun bathing on a large rock in the woods. Couldn't believe my luck. A great distraction and my first warning to back off. I loved the theatrics, by the way."

"Thank you, I think," I whispered, backing up, matching her steps.

"But you didn't learn," Janice's voice deepened. "Next came the car brakes. I thought that would stop you, one way or another. Yet here you are, still snooping."

The sharp letter opener glinting from the overhead lightbulbs, she added, "Too bad you didn't learn a lesson from Harvey's death."

Sounded like my cue to run. Aiming the lamp at her knife hand, I threw the entire basket of knickknacks into her face, and managed three out of the five steps needed to cross the office door threshold into the shop, before tripping over the cord to her personal coffee pot. Swoosh! POP! The letter opener blade landed just above my head in the door frame.

Gulp! Rolling sideways, I kicked free of the cord and half crawled out the office into the merchandise shop. There are two doorways out of the shop. I aimed for the exit to the outside, taking two steps before Janice body slammed me off course from behind. Together we fell into the air freshener oil display. The shelves collapsed, spilling the slippery oil everywhere. Whoosh! The force of her highly toned body knocked the air out of my lungs. Pain ricocheted through my already bruised ribs, I saw stars.

Try as I might to wiggle free, she tightened her grip and slammed my head to the floor. Mad as a hornet, she hauled me up and spun me around. Her hands found my throat, cutting off any returning airflow.

While I exercise once or twice a week, Janice was a professional fitness instructor with finely tuned muscles. I knew there was no way I could fight her off with my bare hands. Instead, I reached around the counter for something, anything to help.

My hand closed on a shape I recognized, chocolate sauce used for the smoothies we sold, just as the edges of my vision start to turn cloudy from lack of blood to my brain. Popping the lid was no problem for these practiced hands as I squeezed the brown stream right at her eyes.

"You bitch!" She screamed, momentarily blinded, her hands released. I kicked her to the side and rolled up, grabbing the counter for support. I followed through with a quick kick before her vision cleared, knocking her into the vitamin display. Unfortunately, Janice and the slippery mess blocked my easy exit path to the outside.

New destination was the opposite door leading into the rest of Power Fitness. Taking a few deep breaths, I scrambled as fast as I could. She came scrambling up behind, so I knocked over any loose display in my path: the towels, clothes rack, and hand grip display, as I ran the ten feet to the door.

Slipping in behind me, I heard her trip and growl, slapping her hand on the counter to catch herself, knocking the butcher block of knives to the floor. I grabbed the door handle and released the lock.

Thunk, Thunk. Two more blades we use for cutting fruit and vegetables for the smoothies hit the door frame, blocking the door from swinging completely open. Falling through the small crack, I gasped as a pair of new hands hoist me to a standing position.

"Whoa, Mrs. Bailey, What is going on here?"

"Run," I gasped to Craig Maurey.

Too late. The door behind me wrenched open. I pushed against Craig, but he just stood there.

"What happened to you?" he asked, loosening his grip slightly.

I rolled to the side as Janice grabbed my arm, twisting it high behind my back. As I spun in a complete circle, I caught a glimpse of the damage.

Chocolate sauce rimmed her eyes, creating the thieving raccoon look. Her cheek bled where a falling object had obviously taken a bite. None of the new cosmetics changed the strength of her grasp as she crushed my arm to her chest, and laid the cold steel of a paring knife next to my throat.

Tears clouded my vision, tears of pain and fear.

"Shut up!" Janice demanded. "Did you bring the bag?"

"Yes, but today? There is not enough time before I will be missed at work."

The overpowering smell of mixed perfumed oil soaked into Janice's clothes made my eyes water.

"Not a bank job. You're gonna help me take care of her," Janice said.

It finally dawned on Craig what she wanted him for. "What? No. I didn't sign up for this. I hid Harvey, I didn't kill him."

Tears of frustration ran down my face. One adversary was hard enough, two was too many.

"Too late to back out now. She knows all of it, the robberies, the tattoos, and now she knows who you are. We are going to finish this. If we do it right, there won't be any more problems."

"That is what you told me last time," Craig started routing in the bag.

"And this is where it ends. Only if you do what I tell you," demanded Janice. "Leave the bag on the table. Get some rope from the storage room, then get the surveillance tapes in the office."

"Isn't there any other way?" Craig asked, looking at me.

"Do it. Now." Janice growled. Craig dropped the open bag and retreated into the storage room.

Lowering her voice, she whispered to me. "So, what shall it be, Little Snoop? A robbery right here? And you walked right into it and got your throat cut? That would explain the fight and the bruises. Shall we do it here, or back in the shop?"

Weakly, I tried to pry her arm away from my neck, but her arms held like steel bands as she playfully scraped my bare skin.

"You don't have to do this." I put as much positive in my voice as I could, but even I could hear it squeak without confidence.

"Come now, Rainbow, there is no way the Chief of Police wouldn't hear about this from you. Thanks to the town grapevine, I have heard about every trip you made this week to visit your new boyfriend. This explains why you fought in the town council meetings for him over your own cousin."

"He was the best candidate for the job, that is all," I said, stalling the best I could.

"And you expect anyone to believe that? I couldn't believe my luck when you ended up crashing on your way to his house! Everyone knows he took the time to inspect your injuries personally before driving you home. After all your shenanigans this week, Martin will be glad to get rid of you.

"Martin would never believe that!"

Dropping the rope on his way to the security tapes in the back, Craig's face was grim as his eyes met mine. "I am sorry."

"Just hurry up," Janice called. To me, she continued, "You know, I was thinking of moving away after this, but now I think I will stick around to hold Martin's hand as he recovers from his grief."

I exploded, "He would never hook up with a smelly rotten bitch like you!"

She removed the knife to twist my back arm up higher. I squealed in pain and bent forward, as she smacked the back of my head with the butt of the knife and pushed me into the wall.

Floating stars signified the exploding headache coming from every angle. Just as quickly, she hauled me back up, one arm around my waist, the knife back at my throat.

Smiling, she added. "Such language for someone in your condition. Is that what you teach your children by keeping them at home? Soon I will know all your secrets from them. I will discover everything your annoying children know.

And if I must, I will kill them too. It gets easier, the more you do it. Harvey was a surprise, but I am really going to enjoy this one."

Hearing a sound to her right, she twisted slightly. "Welcome to the party. We were just talking about you."

"Police! Drop your weapon and put your hands up!" demanded Chief Flint, service revolver in hand, pointed at Janice's head. Or mine, it was hard to tell since she was hiding behind me.

In a blink, the knife tip was repositioned, now denting my skin.

"Drop your weapon, Flint."

"Put down the knife," the Chief insisted.

"Go ahead and take the shot, Flint. But take good aim, because I plan on taking her with me." She shifted back and forth to thwart his aim, while keeping a steady pinpoint of pressure on my neck.

I felt a tiny trickle run down my collar. It hurt no more than a paper-cut, but I was so scared, I wanted to scream. Only the realization that opening my jaw could thrust the tip of the knife in deeper kept my muscles locked.

Chief Flint must have seen it, too. "You don't want to make things worse than it already is. Put the knife down and we can talk about it."

"You want to talk? Sure. Tell me what have I got to lose, Chief?" she laughed, then I felt the knife slide a little to the right. Her voice grew colder as she added, "But you might want to put the gun down first. You are the one killing her now."

He hesitated another second before he shrugged, removing his finger from the trigger, pointing the gun down a bit. "Now move the knife, so we can talk before back up gets here."

I felt the point slide out to rest on the outside of my skin, but not any farther. I took a slow deep breath, hoping the new oxygen would inspire a few positive thoughts.

"I said down!" Janice growled. "Gun on Floor!"

The knife moved down to my chest, as his gun lowered to the floor.

"Kick it to me."

"Drop your knife first."

She thought it over, then held the knife in front of my body, aimed for my heart. Red slime on the tip confirmed my earlier assessment, sending my pulse jumping. "Down on three. One, two, three."

As she dropped the knife, he kicked it sideways under the magazine rack. Before the knife clattered to the ground, a macabre dance began. The Chief took two steps forward, while Janice dragged me two steps backward to the open bag hidden out of his view to grab a gun of her own. He paused in mid-stride finding the tables turned and a loaded semi-automatic aimed at his heart.

"I don't believe you have any back-up coming, Chief. If you did, they would have been in here by now," Janice claimed, tightening her grip of the gun.

"More deaths will not help you, Janice. One death you could claim was an accident, then you panicked. Three make you a mass murderer. You don't want that," he said.

"Said the wannabe hero," She spat at him. "You think you know what I want? You don't. You think I am sorry about Harvey? Wrong. He got what he had coming. And so will you both, for getting in the way. The question is: Heart or head."

NO! My head screamed at me, now that there was fresh blood and oxygen hitting my brain. Janice now had only one arm around me. What did my children learn to do in a library book on Martial Arts a few years ago?

I made a fist, swinging it with all my might up into the wrist holding the gun. One shot went wild. Dropping my weight like a sack of potatoes while taking a bite out of the arm around my neck, her arm then swung down too far trying to over compensate firing three more shots, and two more as she flipped over my curled body, landing hard on her back.

Janice was resilient, and as agile as a cat. Her initial shock over my actions dimmed quickly, as she moved the gun out of easy reach of my final kick. She jumped to her feet, landing right in front of the shop door as I ran to the Chief's side, noticing the dark stains forming on his upper left arm and left thigh.

Janice re-aimed, and snarled, "End of the line for the lovers. Who is first?"

Chapter Twenty-Seven

LOOKING DOWN THE BARREL OF A GUN again was even worse with Janice on the other end. But the next booming sound wasn't for me or the Chief, as the shop door behind her exploded, knocking her wildly to the ground again.

A trail of fire followed seconds later. I didn't stop to wonder why, but grabbed at the Chief to boost him up and out of the path of flames. Like honey bees to a field of flowers, that trail of fire was following the trail of sweet-smelling oil. Janice, having landed nearer the door, was right in its sights, as it spread fast through the old dry carpet.

Trying to get off the carpet, I half dragged the Chief down the hall toward the locker rooms. It was the only area I knew that had tile, not carpet.

My shoes, having some residual oil from our earlier fight, slipped on the tile and we fell down, as another bullet hit the paneling over our head. I pushed off the one wall, and threw the Chief past the men's locker room door and into the storage room, slamming the door in Janice's face as she skidded around the corner.

No way to lock the door on the inside, the Chief threw his weight against a metal shelf opposite the door to wedge against the wall, spilling paints and cleaning bottles, then fell on top of me as Janice let loose a volley of bullets at the door.

As the chamber clicked empty, Janice howled in frustrations that soon morphed into screams as the fire caught up to her greasy body. Moments later her bellows faded, blending into the overhead fire alarms.

Pushing him off me, I yelled over the siren, "Is it bad?"

"Won't matter if we don't get out of here," he deflected my questions. "There is an exit, right?"

Grabbing washcloths, and a few rubber exercise bands, I pushed his hands away first from his thigh, and then his shoulder, tying quick tight pressure bandages.

"Ah, not really. We will have to make one. To do that, I might need your help. But letting you bleed to death on this floor is not part of the plan." I rambled as I tied, and tightened. I knew it was good and tight, when he winced. The direct pressure would have to do for now.

Smoke and heat soon joined the deadly threat. Now bandaged, Chief Flint used spare water bottles to wet down towels for relief from the smoke as I surveyed our supplies.

I knew the layout of this building very well. Down the tiled hallway, we had five rooms to pick from: Men's locker room, Women's locker room, Tanning room, Hot tub, and this store room. Behind and in back of all the rooms that had running water, was a mechanical access room with door to the outside. I picked the store room to hide because of possibilities to break into that access room.

With smoke beginning to float into the upper edges of the room, and sounds of the fire burning on the far wall, I quickly paced out the dimensions to find the area of wall that should meet the access hall. I found a hammer and a wrench, but three swings with a small hammer barely made a dent in the drywall, and there was plywood behind that. I needed something with more force.

Keeping Skylar and Hunter's physics lessons in mind, I dug through the dusty odds and ends that lined the room. I located two mostly filled tanks of helium left over from the winter carnival, plus a mop bucket on wheels.

Every sore muscle in my upper body complained when I rolled the tanks into position, tip ends to the back, but adrenaline kept me moving. As the smoky veil lowered from the ceiling, the sore and bruised ribs were the least of my problems.

"Throw me some more exercise bands," I coughed.

With Chief's help to balance, I strapped them down with more rubber exercise bands, sealing the deal with some duct tape. We would only get one shot at it, so I needed it secure.

In just the few moments I used to prepare our escape route, the smoke had half-filled the tiny room. Chief's water-logged rags helped to ease the sting of breathing the toxic smoke. But we could do nothing about the rising temperature of the room, nor the farthest wall as the fire began to burn its way through. I lined the cart up, and prayed for good aim, as I swung the wrench down on the tip ends of the canisters.

Swoosh! The cart gained momentum over the two feet of distance with enough force to smashed through the drywall and crack into the plywood walls. Pulling the cart back, I pulled the loose drywall and in desperation, as I knew time was running out. Finally, I just laid down and kicked the splinted wood to make the hole bigger.

Chief Flint stopped me with a hand on my shoulder. "Big enough for you. Go!"

"No!" I tried to respond, but coughed instead.

"Go!" He coughed, and pushed me toward the hole.

This time I listened. I climbed through the hole, but I didn't run outside. The air wasn't much better in the crawl space, but I took a deep breath while laying low, then stood up for better leverage. Remembering the very first kick my children learned in the Martial Arts book, I took a cross over back step and kicked with all my might. It worked. Two more kicks like that and the wood splintered to create a hole I thought he would fit.

Beckoning to the Chief, I assisted his crawl out. Good arm over my shoulder, we half walked, half ran through the dense smoke to the door I knew was just five feet away.

Bursting out into the daylight and fresh air, we collapsed in a heap, trying to catch our breath.

"Hey, over here," a voice called in the distance.

Looking up, I saw Craig Maurey running toward us, with two firemen right behind. Scooped into a fireman's carry, Craig and one fireman dashed the Chief down the alley to an awaiting ambulance. The other fireman put his mask on my face, swooped me away in his arms, to safety across the street.

By the time my fireman reached the ambulance, it was already loaded with Chief Flint. Since we only have one ambulance in town, they tossed me in the front seat and drove away. I didn't complain much, as I was too busy concentrating on proper breathing between coughing up black tar. Plus, I knew the Chief needed medical help fast. Once we reach the hospital, I would just call Martin to pick me up. I leaned my overheated body against the door frame and closed my eyes, letting the cool fresh air from the window wash over me, as my lungs convulsed spewing out the toxic fumes from the fire.

Chapter Twenty-Eight

SINCE I MOVED TO THIS TOWN, after my mother's death, the only Community Auction I missed in its entirety was in the Fourth grade thanks to Chicken Pox. At the time, I thought that was the worst possible outcome. This year I spent the day in my least favorite place ever: the hospital.

I was very young when my mother died, but I remember visiting in a sterile white room, as she wasted away from Cancer and the treatments. I never wanted my kids to see me in a place like that, so I always refused to go. I told Martin all about this fear before we were married, but it finally sunk in when I insisted on giving birth to the twins at home.

When I opened my eyes after the fire, I was already strapped down to a hospital bed, complete with oxygen tubes and IV drip, and staring at a white ceiling. A very white ceiling, being held up by very white walls.

My panicked, spastic lung attack brought a familiar face in view. Martin held me while I heaved to breath, then cooled my face with a washcloth when it settled down. That was when I noticed five other familiar faces crowding around. This was my nightmare come true.

Panic washed over me, again, and I tried to push my way out of the bed, but Martin held me down.

"Get me out of here," I tried to scream, as a nurse came into the room and stuck a needle in the IV.

"You need to be here," Martin called soothingly. "I will be right here with you. I won't let anything happen to you. But we need to get your blood chemicals balanced and your lungs cleared. I promise I will be right here."

"NO White Walls," I mouthed, "NO!". Thrashing, yelling, coughing, machines beeped warnings as my heart raced in a full-blown panic attack allowing the medicine to quickly entered my blood stream.

The room faded to black, nightmarish dreams, of smoke, heat, and gunshots. Time and again, as the room would brighten again, and I heard snatches of conversations, beeps and whirls of machines, coughs, my emotions dissolved into screams and hysteria.

"Honey, sweetie, don't worry. You will be fine if you just calm down," Martin soothed.

"Mom, its okay," I awoke to Audrey holding my hand. I heard Emily on the other side, "Mom, remember the Little Engine That Could story? I will read it to you."

The more conscious I became, the more I coughed and cried, until I hyperventilated my way to another blackout.

"Rainbow, this is your dad. I came as soon as I heard," My father, William Koontz added. I know he tried to help, but I didn't want him to see me there either.

"Sedating isn't helping. If I need to put her completely out, she risks even more complications." Doc McCarthy said. "Martin, I am open to suggestions."

"Hey, Dad, I think we have an idea," One of the twins offered, as the last thing I heard before I blacked out again from hyperventilating.

The bleeps, whooshes and pings softened and changed to birds chirping. Harsh lights turned into warm sunshine and a soft cool breeze. The nightmares faded in the fresh daylight.

This time my eyes opened to sunshine fighting through a canopy of trees, and a very haggard looking Martin holding my hand.

"Hello, sleepy head." He said. "Drink?" He placed a small cup filled with a dark bubbling liquid in my hand.

Eagerly I slurped it down, before really noticing I was in a bed. Outside. That didn't make sense.

"More?" He asked, refilling the cup.

"Where...?" I tried to croak.

"Take a deep breath. Now drink some more. Then I can answer your questions."

One gulp later, and my throat had cleared some. "Get me out of here."

"Where do you think you are?"

"I am in" coughing interrupted me, "a hospital."

"Does this look like you are in a hospital building?" My beloved said, handing me another small cupful and looking at the trees,

I pointed to the hospital bed, the brick walls surrounding us, and stared at him.

"Ah, yes. I can explain that, but not until you have eaten brunch out here in the fresh air. Hungry?" He presented me with a picnic basket of my favorite Pit Stop sandwiches and chips.

Suddenly I was starving. "I eat, you talk." I croaked, my voice still hoarse from the tubes.

It had been Travis' idea to take the machines away. He had noticed even when I was asleep I wiggled more the noisier the room was. Yet, I was still in the hospital confines, and those hated white walls. Audrey had suggested the courtyard as a reprieve from the hospital room and Uncle Arlis had picked up the food for the picnic.

Eventually, I would need to go back inside the building. After all, it was the only way to reach the parking lot. But for now, Martin was right. I was not truly in the hospital. Doc wanted me to stay for more tests to be sure my lungs were clear.

"Absolutely NOT!" I interrupted.

"We will talk about that after lunch," Martin shrugged.

Martin talked while I ate, filling in the time I missed. I learned that Chief Flint was just across the hall from my room. He had required surgery to clean the bullet wounds, but was doing well, considering how much blood he had lost and the same heat and smoke conditions I had faced.

"Doc said you saved the Chief's life, how you tied up the wounds."

"No. He saved my life. Then he was shot for it." Remembering, I took a few quick breaths, and shuddered. "All my fault. I fought to get loose and he was hit.

"Hey!" Martin squealed.

"What?" Startled, I looked around.

Martin leaned in for a kiss, "I love you. That is all that matters right here, right now."

And he was right. Time alone with Martin was precious. Yet, other very important people were missing.

"Martin, honey, where are the children?" I whispered sweetly.

"Safe, with your father," he smiled, with a twinkle in his eye. "You know they couldn't possibly get into trouble with their Grandpa."

"Mmmm." I tried to frown, but he kissed it away.

"They are safe. I promise," he said.

Chapter Twenty-Nine

WITH LUNCH COMPLETE, I had to face going back through the hospital hallways to the parking lot. Skyler and Hunter brought a wheelchair, as I was *not* going back inside on a bed. "There is something we want to show you, Mom."

"We think you will like it."

I closed my eyes for the trip through the hallway.

"You can open your eyes now, Rainbow." Martin stopped the ride in a hospital room. But this was no ordinary hospital room. In no stretch of the imagination could I call this a white room anymore.

"It was my idea, Mom, but everyone helped," explained Emily.

Posters of all kinds were plastered on the walls, outlined with balloons of all sizes, shapes and colors, bouncing on equally colorful strings. Horizontal surfaces were buried in flower pots and vases. Even the ceiling was covered in streamers and crepe paper. Any medical equipment not screwed into the wall was absent.

Instead, the room was filled with people. Besides Martin, Skylar, and Hunter, there was Audrey, Travis,

Emily, Aunt Irene, Uncle Arlis, and my dad, all looking hopefully at me.

"Grandpa stopped by the house to pick up a few sleeping bags, lanterns and board games. You can go home if you want, but you will be all alone, as we are camping out here," Travis announced with glee.

Speechless, I cried big happy tears.

Corbin came by later in the afternoon to get my statement. It was very hard to recall all the nasty details with my children right there. Knowing I would have to tell them eventually, I just blurted it all out.

"So that is how the flammable air fresheners spilled!" Corbin exclaimed. "The fire chief traced the beginnings of the fire to a box of those refillable packets the shop sold. They spilled on to the coffee cup warmer that flipped on when it also fell. Once the oil hit the right temp, a small fire started which heated a big batch fast, causing the explosion."

When I asked about Janice, he reluctantly gave the news that her body had been near the hot tub. That was just on the other side from where we broke through and climbed out. No autopsy needed as there were burns over eighty percent of her body.

Meanwhile Craig Maurey was being extremely helpful, Corbin reported. After I saw him last in Power Fitness, he slipped out another door and hid in his car. He couldn't stand to see what Janice would do to the Chief or me, but didn't know how to stop her. After the sudden explosion started a fire, the bullet volley, and no one ran out, he dialed 911, and hadn't stopped talking since. Thanks to his cooperation, they found Janice's hidey-holes filled with the masks they used and unspent cash from the bank robberies.

"How did the Chief end up there anyway?" I asked.

"Old fashioned police work," Corbin replied. "As suspects dropped from the list, and his background checks came back, he was suspicious of Janice. He sent Caleb to get a judge to sign a search warrant for her house, and meanwhile went to keep track of her. He saw her car in the parking lot, pulled in, and then saw yours farther back. His gut told him to get in there pronto."

Early evening brought many more visitors dropping by to tell stories of the day including the highest price item on the auction block, a quilt hand stitched by St. Matthew's quilting club. The Bailey family cookies sold-out in record time and the Pit Stop booth, with Millie Parker and her friends assisting in our family crisis, had record sales.

Jake Timberland stopped by with a huge bouquet of red roses. He hid behind them in a whispered conversation. "Does he know?"

"Don't believe so."

"Any ideas?"

"Possibly." I whispered a reply, before Martin muscled in.

"That is my wife you are smothering," Martin said, removing the curtain of roses.

Jake teased, "Better you than me, Martin. I am still wondering how you managed to tame her."

Visitors were barred as of nine every evening, much to the relief of the nurses and the few other patients. But a few stragglers were able to sneak in.

Todd and Chris sauntered in as the children were setting up the sleeping bags. "Now this is a sight!" Todd announced. "I just had to see my dream come true, since we were here."

"Very funny." I frowned.

Chris laughed, "I love what you have done with the place. Looks almost homey."

"That was their plan," I replied. "But I still don't intend to stay long."

That night, surrounded by color and my loving family, I closed my eyes in search of rest. Peaceful it was not, as memories came forth as nightmares and haunted dreams. After the first startled jerks, my beloved Martin held me soothingly the rest of the night in an effort to stave the memories of the burning, smoky inferno. The children slept in their sleeping bags around and at the foot of my bed. I had convinced my father to stay the night with Uncle Arlis and Aunt Irene to save his back from the hard floor.

It was on mutual agreement that I was approved for early release on Sunday. My blood-oxygen levels were back to normal, and the coughing had mostly stopped. The six extra unwashed bodies in that room added to the need to send me home.

Arms filled with gifts and plants, Martin wheeled me across the hall to visit Chief Flint while the children took down the decorations. I was happy to see the Chief's room, though not blanketed in color as mine, still had quite a few get-well decorations on the windowsill for someone who moved into town not two weeks before.

"Looks nice in here," I referenced all the caring gifts and cards, "but it could still use a bit more color." I handed Martin the box of bright colored balloons and blooming plants to place wherever he could find space.

"Yes. The community definitely reached out to me now. I heard that your decorating crew did even more," the Chief smirked.

"I don't like white walls." I shrugged, trying to hide my shudder. I tried to sound light-hearted, "You have seen my house, not a plain, bare, white wall anywhere. White has no feel, energy or desires. It is an empty canvas waiting, needing to be filled, but the painter has no time left to fulfill them."

These white walls were getting to me, no matter how much I tried not to think about them. I tried to talk over the edges of panic, "No inspiration. Nothing to encourage you to dream, desire, or want to get better. It just sucks the life right out of you."

"Rainbow," the Chief kindly cut into my chatter, waiting for my complete attention. "Go home."

"I'm sorry you got shot," I blurted out, my voice cracking, tears filling my eyes. "I saw her aim and did my best to deflect it."

"Not your fault," he coughed, dismissing my concerns. "My job. I just wish I had been faster, or worked harder."

Wincing, he reached for his water. Martin moved it closer for him.

"You did work hard! You figured it out before all of us. Especially me. I just realized it right before you arrived."

He put up his good hand like a stop sign, "Rainbow, if there is one thing I learned in my job, it is this: Do not take blame for other people's actions. You did not kill Harvey, nor pull the trigger on me. Those were her decisions, her actions, alone."

"Same for you. Your life, your actions." I nodded, somberly. "Any thoughts on that topic?"

"About that story?" he asked. "With all this extra downtime, yes, I have been thinking."

"And?"

"Did Laura know about the Tops and Bottoms, you think, and just glossed over it?"

Thinking back to her age when she was in town, I dismissed it. "Nah. She would have been too young and only here for the summer. She would have just known her family's friends. If she had attended school here, she would have figured it out eventually."

"School yard fights?"

"No," I laughed. "Nothing so drastic as that anymore. No, the family feuds now are more like wrong side of the tracks kind of thing. Each person is known by their family connection, and each side considers the other on the wrong side."

As the children came in behind us, Chief Flint nodded, "I see. Now Mr. Bailey, and children, why don't you take her home and away from these white walls. I have the feeling we will all sleep better."

As soon as all seven of us were in the van headed home, Martin whispered, "Tops and Bottoms? What was that all about?"

"The Chief was married to Laura Pennington, of the Jensen clan." I whispered back.

Martin whistled, "He is living in a Maurey rental, isn't he?"

"Yep."

"Let's hope no one else figures that out until he recovers." Martin replied.

I nodded, already plotting plan B options.

While Chief Flint might have slept better in the hospital without me there, I did not. Well, not quite true. I did sleep Sunday after Martin cooked my favorite fried chicken and mashed potatoes, served to me in bed, surrounded by my beloved family. After lunch, he shooed the kids into the rest of the house, leaving Audrey behind reading a book to keep me company. If I dreamt that afternoon, I don't remember specifics, but when I woke in the evening, I was ready to get busy.

"I have to go, Martin," I explained as I pulled on clean clothes. "I have to. It is the only way for me to finish it. To put it behind me."

"But why now? Can't it wait until morning? You just got out of the hospital." Martin firmly stood behind me wrapped his arms around me. "You need to rest."

I turned around and melted into his chest. "I love you dear. And I am so glad you are here for me. But you have been married to me for how long now?"

"Eighteen beautiful years," he murmured. "And I am looking forward to many many more."

"Well so am I. You knew when you married me that I had many quirks."

"Yes."

"Then you know I just have to do this," I insisted.

Martin gently tipped my head back to look me in the eyes. "Fine, but I won't let you go alone. While you get what you need pulled together, I will call your dad to come back from Irene's to stay with the kids."

An hour later I was intensely working in my studio above the Pit Stop. The space had been a small, two-bedroom apartment, but when the last tenant moved out and our own family grew to fill all corners of our house, I claimed it for myself. Years ago, I learned night was the best time for my painting passion, when the world all around me was quiet and no young distractions underfoot.

Martin slept on a cot we kept in the bedroom we used as an office. All night, I let my jumbled thoughts and feelings flow, palate in hand, on to the blank canvases set on easels before me. While the paint danced, the back of my mind focused on the new problems that the town faced, even if they didn't know it yet.

By morning I had a plan of sorts and left Martin to set it in motion while I took a nap. A few hours later I emerged from the bedroom. While I ate the Monday lunch special upstairs, my family presented a progress report.

The twins reported the mayor and school board president was willing to meet here for a quick lunch meeting on Wednesday. No official votes could happen, but a quick conference before that night's meeting was possible. That meant we had only forty-eight hours to finish crunching numbers, design presentations and finalize details. Lunch finished, I returned to my painting, leaving all else in the hands of Martin and the children.

Chapter Thirty

"TIME IS TICKING, RAINBOW," Jake Timberland, cornered me as I watched out the Pit Stop window. He stood like a brick wall in my way, a trick he learned as a football linebacker. "I have to be back in the office for a very important meeting in less than an hour."

Taking one last glance out the window, I sighed. He was right. I asked for just a bit of his time and I needed his support today. But maybe I could stall just for a few more minutes.

Putting on my best smile, I capitulated, "You are correct, as usual. Your lunch time is valuable, I would like to invite you to a free lunch, anything off the menu, as a thank you for taking the time to come. When you have your order, head upstairs to my studio for a proposition my family has been working on. Skyler will help you get situated upstairs."

I offered the other three invitees: Mrs. Claire Hempel, the School Board president, and Bob Baker, the city accountant, and Mrs. Granger, the School Board accountant, the same deal. Secretly, I was hoping for two more arrivals, but it was not guaranteed they would make it in time.

Once my guests had found a seat upstairs, I was forced to stall no longer, "Ladies and Gentlemen, two years ago at this time, there was a suggestion to create a more complete physical fitness center at the high school."

"The original plans were benched because of the price tag, if I recall," interrupted Bob Baker, the city accountant.

"Which is why fundraising has already begun by the students," I added. "They want it, and are willing to work for it."

"And we couldn't decide on what should be in it," said the Mayor, who was also the baseball coach.

"Or where and how to make it work with the high school," added Mrs. Hempel.

I continued, "So the school just paid the membership dues at Power Fitness for the students on sports teams as they had for years. I know. But now that is burned to the ground. We really need a new plan." I motioned to Skylar and Hunter, "Boys, would you show them the plans you drew up?"

Hunter stepped up next to Skyler as Trevor removed a cloth with flare, off the display they had worked on for the last three days. "We started with the various previous suggestions found in the city archives. You see here, we have weight lifting, locker rooms, a swimming pool, and indoor track laid out. All of the current teams accounted for. The outside wall is butting up against the current high school back wall by the...."

As he went on, I stepped back to the door, pleased to see a late arrival to the party being escorted up by Emily.

"Welcome, Chief, so glad you could make it." One step at a time, he leaned heavily on the banister.

"Mrs. Bailey, glad to see the color back in your cheeks." Chief Flint nodded, as he reached the top. "I'm not staying for the meeting. I just came by to see Sheri. I was told she was here."

"Sorry, she didn't stay. But she did drop something off for you." I turned back towards the center of the room. "Now where did I put that?"

"You put it in the doll house, Mom," Emily answered.

"Oh, yes I did." I lead the way across the room. "Did you have any lunch, yet?"

"Ah, no. Thank you anyway."

Just then Audrey arrived with a platter, as Emily laid out a TV tray we had in the corner. "One Roast beef special, with potato salad, not fries. Made especially for you Chief."

He looked at it longingly, but hesitantly.

"Just the facts, sir," I imitated his finger counting style. "You need to eat for your strength and hospital food stinks. You were just released from that hospital so the food in your house is five days old or more. Also, if you don't eat this food, it will just go to waste. Add that all together equals: You. Sit. Eat."

He held up his hands, surrendering. "If I eat, will you stop talking?"

I put a fake zipper across my lips before I walked away, leaving the Chief in Emily's capable hands.

Mrs. Granger was explaining to the boys, "But this project needs to come out of school funds, not city funds, and that would require raising taxes. We tried that two years ago. You know that was voted down at the last general election."

"Yes, Ma'am," Skylar answered. "At the time, the plans for a new gymnasium was presented as a school budget item. However, what we are proposing is not a new school only gymnasium, but a community athletic center attached to the high school. This would be voted on, and funded by the city and residents as such."

"Your new design adds fifty percent to the cost, and that is just an estimate. This is a pretty expensive homeschool project you are just throwing out to us, young man," stated Mr. Barker. "But knowing the Bailey clan, I suppose you also have a plan where those funds will come from?"

"First of all," I chimed in, "This is not a homeschool project. This is a community service project."

"Secondly, many high school groups have pledged their money earnings from this weekend toward just upgrading the gym, which is the last resort in their minds. This project involves not a renovation of a few barbells , but building on a new gym, an option that they started with anyway."

"Does anyone know how much was raised last year's auction weekend?" Mrs. Granger chimed in.

Hunter already had the figures ready, "Of the eleven clubs and sports groups that had booths specifically to raise money for the gymnasium, the combined total equals almost twelve thousand dollars."

"Which just proves my point," argued Mr. Barker. "It will take ten years or more to get the money together."

"Not if we have community support and donations," I responded, "which I think we can get now that the Power Fitness is gone. This community needs somewhere to go for fitness, exercise, and rehab, which the Power Fitness had provided to some degree. We took the original ideas of a large cool pool for the swim team, small warmer pool for rehab, weight lifting, etc. It will touch every life in this community. "

Hunter added, "We are asking just one question at this informal gathering. Can the city board and school board get behind this plan that the school board presented two years ago, together? Can we, as a community, think that this is a good idea and work towards its completion together?"

They looked at each other, and the design. Bob Barker added, "I have heard of this kind of idea in other cities: A community center added on to a school. Scheduling would be a challenge at times, but it would be used year-round that way."

Slowly heads nodded in a consensus.

"Yes, it would benefit both the community and the school. But that is an unofficial vote, since this is not an official meeting. And then we are still stuck trying to find the funds for this out of thin air," Mr. Barker insisted.

"Well, to get the financing started," I announced as the second late guest walked in, "I am willing to sell the paintings you see here, in this room. They are still a bit wet since I just painted them based on this weekend's events."

"Now, Rainbow, you know we all appreciate your art work, and generous donations to the city offices over the years. But we are back to the 'just a drop in the bucket' beginning here. I mean, how much can these be worth?"

"Twenty thousand, for opening bid," called the voice from the back, as Veronica Talman stepped up and announced her presence.

Thump! At the sight of her, Chief Flint had jumped to his feet, but his leg wouldn't hold him and he came crashing back down, kicking over the food table.

"Veronica, I thought you had returned to New York," exclaimed Mrs. Granger, her aunt, as everyone turned to see the newcomer.

"I had, but Rainbow insisted I return." Veronica answered her aunt, while reaching over to help Chief. She added, "I have not had a man fall at my feet in a while. Thank you for the compliment."

Travis had just arrived with the dessert platter. I grabbed it and sent him off. "Travis, run down stairs for paper towels, and tell Dad to replace Chief's lunch. Audrey, and Em, please serve dessert," I directed.

Chief Flint, just stared at Veronica, in disbelief. I made the proper introductions. "Chief Johnathan Flint, this is Veronica Talman. Veronica, this is our new Chief of Police, Johnathan Flint. He was married to Laura Pennington recently diseased."

Veronica held out her hand, "So sorry to hear that. No wonder you look like you saw a ghost! Laura and I could have passed for twins in our younger days. I guess we still look alike?"

He reached out and grabbed her offered hand for support as he stood.

"Ah, just a bit, yes," he stammered, with a half-smile as the color began creeping back into his cheeks.

"Hey, Chief," I asked, while wiping the floor dry, "Did you find that message in the doll house you were looking for?"

That really made the color come back to his cheeks, "Uh, yeah. It was on the 18th century credenza."

"A message in the doll house? Sounds mysterious. The credenza in the living room or playroom?" Veronica inquired.

"The parlor actually," he replied. Then he added to me, "That is one antique dollhouse. Such intricate replicas of items from back in the day."

"You know antiques?" Veronica asked.

"Some," he admitted. "Laura loved them and I would help with the odd repair. I learned along the way."

Veronica caught my eye, as she said to the Chief, "We will talk later, so don't go anywhere. I need to dig my favorite client out of this mess, first."

Martin arrived with the new food for the Chief, as I followed Veronica. She inspected the five paintings drying on the easels. "I am very glad I did return. Stunning work. Three Days, Boo? You did this in three days?"

"Well, the donation from the paintings would be a start," Mr. Barker, still with a bit of chocolate cookie around his mouth, choked a bit on that figure, "is still a long way from what we need."

"Did I say twenty? I meant thirty. This is way different than her usual style. It is hard. It is crisp. Yet it yearns with emotion."

"Well, that is a bigger drop, but the whole amount will still be a hard sell to the people."

Veronica walked up to Mr. Bob Barker, her old boyfriend in high school.

Nose to nose she added, "Each, old sweetheart. That should give you a bigger drop."

"You are kidding!" He retorted.

"I never kid, lie or joke about art and its value. My business is built on my reputation," Veronica replied.

"Plus," I dove into the middle of them. I wanted the discussion flowing, not fists. "The school did have a budget plan for the renovations. And our community has an active base of workers. If we contract locally, and they are willing to work at cost, the total bill will drop. And if the community assists, we could get the funding together for the rest of the bill. You see, it will be a *community* project."

Skylar added, "We also have thoughts on membership fees for the daily costs after it is open. Keeping them low enough for usage, but enough to pay for employees and water bills and such."

Hunter concluded, "It is all laid out in these portfolios. We are asking that you look them over and help to present them to your boards having meetings this week. We can answer any questions you have."

"I will let the boys answer any questions you have right now," I offered to the board members as I noticed some uninvited new arrivals lead by Audrey. "Veronica, may I borrow you for a moment?"

Veronica and I walked over to flank Chief Flint as Vernon Flandan and his attorney, and cousin, Jason Flandan arrived.

"Mayor, there you are. We have a *major* breach of contract here," Jason beelined straight to Jake Timberland.

"Now hold on," Mr. Timberland called, walking over. "May I assume you are talking about Vernon's rental to the city on Chief Flint's behalf?"

"Most assuredly yes. It is clear in the contract that Vernon's grandfather estate will allow the property to be rented, but only to people not in Jensen clan!"

"Yes, yes, I just learned about it myself recently. But with everything going on, plus the fact that it was rented to the city, I thought it would give us some time to come up with a suitable alternative." Jake tried to stall.

"Excuse me?" inserted the Chief. "Is there a problem?"

"Yes. There is a problem. You are living in my house, and I just learned your wife was a Jensen. You need to move out today!" announced Vernon.

"Now, Vernon," said Mayor Timberland. "This is just a misunderstanding, and the board plans on rectifying it as soon as we have a meeting tonight. It wasn't done on purpose. In fact, your cousin, when the contract was written, had access to the same info as the rest of us. Chief Flint listed his wife as deceased without including a name, and none of us asked for specifics. Now, Chief Flint has only just been released from the hospital. We haven't even had a chance to explain it yet."

"Explain what?" Chief asked.

Veronica took over from here, doing exactly what I had hoped she would do. "Laura Pennington was from the Jensen family, and thus you are also, by marriage, a Jensen. Vernon here is from the Maurey family. These two families had a feud for some unknown reason ages ago. The prejudices still continue today."

"We still remember what it was about!" Vernon announced. "Don't you, Jason?"

Jason nodded. "Of course!"

"Only you would!" Veronica answered.

"They are kidding, right?" Chief asked Veronica.

"Not in the slightest, unfortunately," answered Veronica. "But tell me Chief, how would you like to see the house that particular dollhouse is modeled after? Even full of the very same antiques you saw in the dollhouse."

Shocked at the change in topic, he replied, "That many preserved antiques would be extremely impressive."

"Antique, yes. Preserved, they are not. Come, look out this window to the pink Victorian house."

"Hey," interrupted Vernon, "The housing situation."

"Pipe down and let the big kids talk." Veronica commanded Vernon. "Let the lawyers do what you pay them for. We are just being friendly over here."

Turning to Chief Flint, Veronica walked the Chief over to the window, "You can just see it here through the trees. That doll house was made as a Christmas gift from my great grandfather to my grandmother. I inherited that jumbled monstrosity six years ago. I don't live in town, so I haven't been able to do much more than walk through it and arrange for someone to keep an eye on the place. However, that person quit a month ago, vacating the apartment he was using."

Pointing to the left, she added, "See that garage house next to it? When it was originally built, the upstairs was for the stable boys. It has been completely remodeled into two modern apartments. Each with two bedrooms and one and a half bathrooms. I use one when I come for an overnight. The other goes to whomever I hire to take care of the place. No paycheck, but cheap rent, plus utilities."

"What responsibilities are there?" asked the Chief, barely peeling his eyes away from the window.

"Just checking the property, inside and outside, daily, and coordinating with the police if there is a problem." Veronica smiled at him. "And, I will waive the rental fee for time spend cataloging the inventory."

"Sounds like a good deal for an expert."

"It is. The problem is finding an expert, and those I do find are usually only looking for wheelchair accessible apartments. The stairs going up to the apartment scares them off. Think you could do it, even with an injured leg?"

"Probably not right away," I piped up. "But let Martin handle Vernon."

I turned to look right at the Chief, "That is if you want to take the offer. Will you stay here, in our town?"

He thought about it for a moment, while the men in the background were arguing over Equal Housing Laws. "You mean to ask, will I stay and deal with family feuds, an interfering busy homeschooling mother of five, an ornery secretary who shredded my resignation letter and put it in a wrapped box I discovered in the doll house, and whatever other craziness I will find in this quaint small town?"

Veronica and I smiled and nodded.

"Now I know why Laura loved her memories but did not ever contemplate visiting," He sighed, disbelieving. "I have no other good plans. So, I might as well take the deal. At least for now."

They shook hands, while I caught Martin before he headed back downstairs.

Soon he was approaching the group of arguing men. "Vernon, if I remember correctly my cousin Jim Flandan, your father, proudly served in a few American conflicts overseas."

"Yes, Sir," Vernon stood a little straighter at the memory. "All the Flandan men have proudly served in uniform."

"And Grandfather Patrick was even the sheriff for a time in our fair town."

"True again."

"Then I have one question for you. Which would make Patrick more furious: Kicking a policeman, wounded on the job, out of a house, *or* letting an unknowing Jensen to continue to live in the house for another ninety days to let his leg heal?"

Vernon Flandan deflated for a second before rebounding with a counter offer. "Thirty days and then he is out."

"Sixty days maximum, and the house will be cleaned so you won't even know it had been rented in the first place," Martin counter offered.

"You pay for Cousin Anna to do the cleaning." Vernon added. "I only trust her."

"You got a deal. Now let's go get some coffee. I have a new vanilla roast I want you to try," Martin concluded the deal and the men followed him down.

Chief Flint turned to me. "You want to explain to me what just happened?"

"Well, we bought you more time to heal, and a new apartment that I think you will love. Martin negotiated the deal because he is a born Maurey."

"But Laura was a Jensen? How is it that I had never heard of these clans?" The Chief asked.

"Yes, her grandma specifically," Veronica explained, while I started cleaning up. "And most people in town have learned to work with all people, thanks to Rainbow and Martin, but some such as Vernon still hold a grudge."

"Oh, how so?"

"Well, Martin is a Maurey by birthright, but Rainbow is a Jensen. When they got married, it caused such a ruckus in town. But, that didn't stop them. Rainbow personally wrote on the invite that people could come and celebrate with them, or stay away from the fun. That it was their choice which side of the fence they sat, and it would only hurt themselves. Rainbow is my hero, and helped me get started in my career. Which reminds me, I need to get going or I will miss my plane."

She started walking downstairs all the while leaving instructions. "Well, it has been fun as always, Boo! Now, the minute the paint is dry, call me. I will arrange for shipping to New York. Meanwhile, I will start the phone calls."

"Is that where you live? New York?" The Chief did his best to keep up with her, limping along with his cane.

"New Jersey actually. But my art gallery is in New York."

"You come back often?" Chief asked as he finally reached the bottom.

"Well, usually once a year." She answered with a smile. "But I will be back for the paintings, and when you move in. Oh, Chief, when you feel up to it, take a tour of the place. Rainbow has keys. If for some reason you change your mind, just let me know. I know we kind of railroaded you. I am just glad I was able to help buy you some time."

Looking at her watch, "Oops, I have got to go. Love your concepts, Rainbow, as usual. Chief, looking forward to seeing you again."

She shook hands and raced out to her rented bright red convertible. Speeding off, she narrowly missed Corbin crossing the street.

"Chief Flint, I am ready to give you a ride home whenever you need it," Corbin announced.

"Just as soon as I settle my bill," Chief responded. Turning to Martin, he asked, "How much?"

"For saving my wife? Lunch on us. It's the least we can do," Martin said.

The Chief looked around at every one in the shop, then at the lunch menu prices, taking a moment to respond. Placing money on the counter, he announced to all in the shop, "I was a good cop in St Louis. I didn't take the free lunches or other favors. And I intend to be a good Chief of Police in this town. So here is my money for that delicious lunch. Now it is up to *you* to decide what to do with it. You can put it in the cash register, or drop it into the charity jar for the community gym. That is up to you."

Martin picked up the money and stuffed it in jar on the counter to raise money for the new high school gym, smiling. "Well played, Chief, well played."

Chief turned around and cornered me at the door. "You planned that whole thing upstairs, didn't you?"

"The paintings, the meeting, and introducing Veronica, yes. I had no idea what was in the box from Sheri. And Veronica's offer was all hers."

"But you were hoping, weren't you?"

"Yes," I just smiled brightly. "I knew about the housing issue the minute I saw the picture of your wife."

"And you didn't tell me?"

"I figured you had enough on your plate with a murder to solve, and the big fair weekend. And there was nothing you do could about it. It was the city who needed to fix the contract."

"Alright, trouble maker," he laughed. "Now I better follow doctor's orders and get this leg up. I need to be at the top of my game before you get into trouble again, because I have a feeling this isn't the first time, nor the last."

Behind us, my kids giggled.

"No worries about me, Chief, I am happily going back to being a boring housewife and mother."

"Boring?" Chief Flint rolled his eyes, as Martin joined in the laughter. "Yeah, that is what I thought."

"Welcome to the community, Chief!" I smiled, as the Chief limped out the door to Corbin's police cruiser. "And remember Chief, you have friends here to help you anytime you need it."

The Chief paused at the car before climbing in. He turned around to add, "Rainbow, when I am not in uniform, my friends call my Jack."

Made in the USA
Columbia, SC
25 March 2019